PETINA GAPPAH

———

OUT OF DARKNESS, SHINING LIGHT

A Novel

FABER & FABER

First published in the UK in 2020
by Faber & Faber Ltd
Bloomsbury House
74–77 Great Russell Street
London WC1B 3DA

First published in the US in 2019
by Scribner, an Imprint of Simon & Schuster, Inc.
1230 Avenue of the Americas
New York, NY 10020

Typeset by Faber & Faber Ltd
Printed and bound by CPI Group (UK) Ltd, Groydon, CR0 4YY

All rights reserved
© Petina Gappah, 2019

The right of Petina Gappah to be identified as author of this work
has been asserted in accordance with Section 77 of the Copyright,
Designs and Patents Act 1988

*This book is a work of fiction. Any references to historical events,
real people, or real places are used fictitiously. Other names, characters, places,
and events are products of the author's imagination, and any resemblance to
actual events or places or persons, living or dead, is entirely coincidental.*

A CIP record for this book
is available from the British Library

ISBN 978–0–571–34532–8

MIX
Paper from
responsible sources
FSC
www.fsc.org
FSC® C020471

2 4 6 8 10 9 7 5 3 1

OUT OF
DARKNESS,
SHINING
LIGHT

BY THE SAME AUTHOR

An Elegy for Easterly
The Book of Memory
Rotten Row

For my son, Kushinga,
who, among many other names,
is also called David.

Kärt barn har många namn.
Rakkaalla lapsella on monta nimeä.
Kjært barn har mange navn.

For the whole Earth is the tomb of famous men; not only are they commemorated by columns and inscriptions in their own country, but in foreign lands there dwells also an unwritten memorial of them, graven not on stone but in the hearts of men.

Pericles on the Athenian dead,
from Thucydides's *History of the Peloponnesian War*

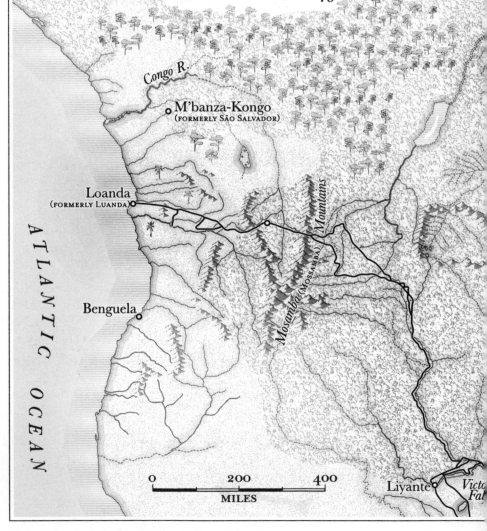

CENTRAL AFRICA

Showing the Journeys of David Livingstone,

*and his understanding of the geography of the area
based on his own travels and information
from traders and other travellers*

——————— 1852–1856
------------- 1858–1863
·················· 1866–1873

Congo R.

M'banza-Kongo
(FORMERLY SÃO SALVADOR)

Loanda
(FORMERLY LUANDA)

Mountains

Benguela

Mosamba (MOSSAMBA)

ATLANTIC OCEAN

0   200   400
MILES

Liyante

Victo
Fal

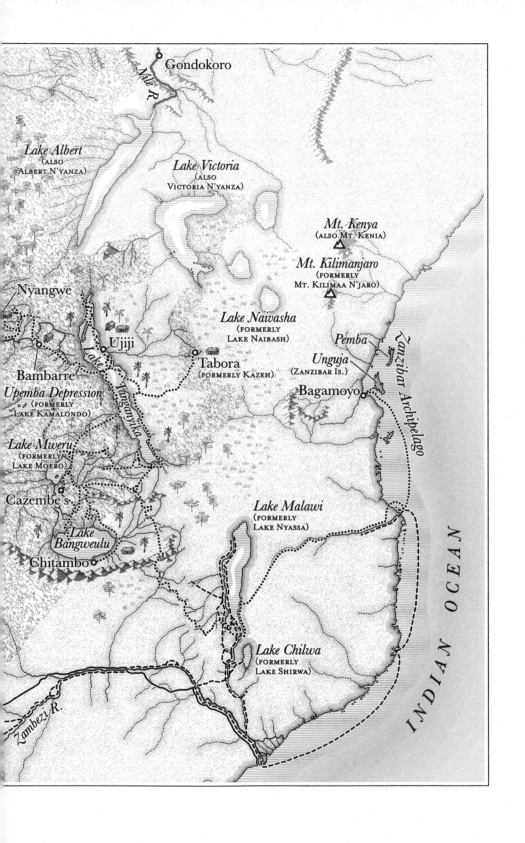

OUT OF DARKNESS, SHINING LIGHT

PROLOGUE

I trust in Providence still to help me. I know the four riv-
ers Zambesi, Kafué, Luapula, and Lomamé, their fountains
must exist in one region . . . I pray the good Lord of all to
favour me so as to allow me to discover the ancient fountains
of Herodotus, and if there is anything in the underground
excavations to confirm the precious old documents (τά
βιβλία), the Scriptures of truth, may He permit me to bring
it to light, and give me wisdom to make a proper use of it.

David Livingstone,
The Last Journals of David Livingstone

This is how we carried out of Africa the poor broken body of Bwana
Daudi, the Doctor, David Livingstone, so that he could be borne
across the sea and buried in his own land. For more than one thousand and five hundred miles, from the interior to the eastern coast,
we marched with his body; from Chitambo to Muanamuzungu,
from Chisalamala to Kumbakumba, from Lambalamfipa to Tabora,
until, two hundred and eighty-five days after we left Chitambo, we
reached Bagamoyo, that place of sorrow, whose very name means to
lay to rest the burden of your heart.

We set him down in the hushed peace of the church. And all
through that long night prayed and sang and keened the seven
hundred manumitted slaves from the Village of the Free. After the
tide came in the following day, they lined up on either side of the
path that led to the dhow of his final crossing. And we watched
until the white sail of that rickety wooden boat was a small dark

triangle on the far horizon, and all that we could see of him was the sky meeting the shimmering sea.

He gave up his life to the doomed, demented search for the last great secret of that heaven-descended spring, the world's longest river; he gave his all to uncover the secret that had preoccupied men of learning for more than two thousand years: the source of the Nile.

In the final two years of his life, both before and after he was relieved in Ujiji by the American, Bwana Stanley, he was as a man possessed. In every town and village and hamlet through which we passed, Bwana Daudi asked the same question. Had any person seen or heard of a place where four fountains rose, four great fountains that rose out of the ground, between two hills with conical tops? They were the fountains described in ancient times by a long-dead sage called Herodotus, he said, from the far-off land of Greece. To find these fountains, he believed, was to find the source of the Nile.

When they asked to know what this Nile was, he said it was the world's longest river, but more than a river, it was a miracle of Creation splendid beyond comprehension. 'For it flows for every day of the year, for more than one thousand miles through the most arid of deserts, all without being replenished, for there are no tributaries that flow to fill it,' he said.

Bwana Daudi was certain that these fountains linked to four great rivers that he knew already, those of Kafue, Lomame, Luapula, and Zambezi. Herodotus, he said, had written that water from these fountains flowed in two directions, with half going up to Egypt and the other half flowing south. And thus it was that we followed the southwards flow of the Luapula into the swamps of Bangweulu, but there, instead of finding the headwaters of the Nile, in the village of Chitambo, Bwana Daudi found his death.

He is as divided in death as he was in life. His bones lie now in his own land, entombed in the magnificence of ancient stone. In the grave we dug for him under the shade of a *mvula* tree, his heart, and all the essential parts of him, are at one with the soil of his travels. The grave of his bones proclaims that he was brought over land and sea by our faithful hands. The wise men of his age say he blazed into the darkness of our natal land to leave behind him a track of light where the white men who followed him could go in perfect safety.

This is all we sixty-nine have ever been in his world: the sixty -nine who carried his bones, the dark companions, *his* dark companions, the shadowy figures in the caravans in which he moved. We were only ever the *pagazi* on his journeys, the porters and bearers who carried his loads and built his huts and cooked his meals and washed his clothes and made his beds, the *askari* who fought his battles, his loyal and faithful retinue.

On the long and perilous journey to bring him home, ten of our party lost their lives. There are no stones to mark the places where they rest, no epitaphs to announce their deaths. And when we who remain follow where they led, no pilgrims will come to show their children where we lie. But out of that great and troubling darkness came shining light. Our sacrifice burnished the glory of his life.

This story has been told many times before, but always as the story of the Doctor. And sometimes, as appendages, as mere footnotes in his story, appear the names of Chuma and Susi. They were the first of his companions, the longest serving and the oldest, for the rest of us only joined them in the months just before Bwana Daudi's death.

In some incarnations, they are two friends. In yet others, they are two brothers. Always they are Bwana Daudi's most faithful servants, just the two of them carrying his bones; a testament to the strength of the bonds of servitude, confirming the piety of Christian faith, his faith, his piety, his sainthood. For who but a saint could inspire such service?

They are sometimes called Susi and Chuma, but more often, they are Chuma and Susi. Seldom do their full names appear: never are they James Chuma, whom Bwana Daudi rescued from the bondage of slavery, and Abdullah Susi, the Mohammedan shipbuilder from Shupanga who served a Christian master. They are remembered, if at all, as the lone bearers of Bwana Daudi's bones, as those who were there before.

What if we had known then what we know now?

When we bore his body out of Africa, we carried with us the maps of what the men of his world would come to call his last great discovery, the mighty river called the Lualaba. What if we had known then that our final act of loyalty to him would sow the seeds of our children's betrayal, their fate and their children's children's also; that the Lualaba of his drawings was the mouth of the great Congo of our downfall, the navigable river down which would come the white man, Winchester rifle aloft and Maxim gun charged?

In just eleven years, the England to which we gave back its glorious son would gather at a table with others and, in the casual act of drawing lines on a map, insert borders and boundaries where there had been none, tearing nations and families asunder. Down the Lualaba they came, down the great Congo, with steamships and guns, with rubber plantations and taxes and new names for all the burial places of our ancestors. And every one of the men, women, and children that we met on our journey, every friend and foe, slaver and enslaved, would, in a matter of years, be claimed as the newest subjects of Europe's kings and queen.

All that was to come, but first:

This is more than the story of two men, Susi and Chuma; it is also the story of the caravan leaders Chowpereh and Uledi Munyasere; of Amoda, son of Mahmud; and of Nathaniel Cumba, known as Mabruki. It is the story of the men from the Nassick Mission in India, manumitted slaves all, among them Carus Farrar and Farjallah Christie, who, as easily as though they were slicing a fish, opened up the Doctor in death, and of Jacob Wainwright, who inscribed the epitaph on the grave of his heart. It is the story of the women who travelled with us, Misozi and Ntaoéka, Khadijah and Laede, Binti Sumari and Kaniki.

It is the story of Halima, the Doctor's cook, who scolded long and hard until we said yes, yes, we would send him back whence he came, to his home across the water. It is the story of the boy Majwara, the youngest of the companions, who found the Doctor kneeling in death, and, with every beat of his drum, beat the life into our legs as we marched on that long and toilsome journey into the interior.

It is the story of Bwana Daudi, of his final years of suffering and his relief by Bwana Stanley and the sights that broke his spirit and wounded his heart even as he marched on, unto his death. It is the story of all these and many more, the story of the Doctor's and our own last journey: the march to his certain death, and on to Bagamoyo.

I

CHEMCHEMI YA HERODOTUS

I

Before embarking on this enterprise, Dr Livingstone had not definitely made up his mind which course he should take, as his position was truly deplorable. His servants consisted of Susi, Chuma, Hamoydah, Gardner, and Halimah, the female cook and wife of Hamoydah.

Henry Morton Stanley, *How I Found Livingstone*

It is strange, is it not, how the things you know will happen do not ever happen the way you think they will happen when they do happen? On the morning that we found him, I was woken by a dream of cloves. The familiar, sweetly cloying smell came so sharply to my nose that I might have been back at the spice market in Zanzibar, a slim-limbed girl again, supposedly learning how to pick out the best for the Liwali's kitchen, but really standing first on one leg, then the other, and my mother saying, but, Halima, you don't listen, which was true enough because I was paying more attention to the sounds of the day – the call of the *muezzin*, the cries of the auctioneers at the slave market, the donkeys braying in protest, the packs of dogs snarling over the corpses of slaves outside the customs house, and the screeching laughter of children.

I think of my mother often enough, but it is seldom that she comes to me in my dreams. She was the *suria* of the Liwali of Zanzibar, one of his favourite slaves, although she never bore him a child to become *umm al-walad*, and what a thing that would have been for her, to bear the Liwali's child; for he was the Sultan's representative back in the days when Said the Great, Seyyid Said bin Sultan that was, lived in Muscat, across the water in Oman, and not in Zanzibar.

My mother says I was born before the Sultan moved the capital from Muscat. In those days, the Sultan had the Liwali to act for him in Zanzibar, and yes, there was the great Lord of the Swahili in Zanzibar, the Mwinyi Mkuu, they called him, but the Sultan needed his own man, someone who was an Arab through and through, an Omani of the first rank.

Though to look at the Liwali, well, you could see at once there was an African slave or two in *his* blood, and that's no lie. He had his three official wives, the Liwali did, he had his three *horme*, they called them, and also his concubines, the ten *sariri* in his harem. That is plenty enough woman for any man, but it was not nearly as many concubines as Said the Great, for he had seventy-five wives and *sariri*, who gave him more than a hundred children.

My mother was the only dark-skinned *suria* among the Liwali's *sariri* concubines, for they were all Circassians and Turks and whatnot, and although they said a *suria* was the best kind of slave to be, and only the comely women were chosen to be *sariri*, for my mother, who was also a cook, being a *suria* only meant that she was doubly enslaved: at night, a slave in the Liwali's harem, and in the day, a slave in his kitchen.

The Liwali has been dead these many years. His house is now owned by Ludda Dhamji, a rich Indian merchant from Bombay. They say he is more powerful than the Liwali was, for he has lent Said Bhargash, the new Sultan, ever so much money. Ludda Dhamji controls the customs house too, and takes a share of every slave sold at the slave market and every single one that goes to Persia and Arabia, to India and up and down the whole coast of the Indian Ocean. That is wealth indeed.

I was roused from my dream, and all thoughts of my former life, by the sound of running feet and loud voices. I could tell at once that something was wrong. Ntaoéka and Laede had not yet made the fires, no surprise that, for it was between the morn and night.

For all that, I could make out their forms easily enough; the Moon was still bright. The watch was up, but so were others who need not have been. The porters and expedition leaders were in a flurry of movement. Even the most useless of the *pagazi*, like that thief Chirango, who normally needed Majwara's drum to beat some spirit into his lazy legs, moved as quickly as the others, going from one group to the next, and then from that group to the one after that.

Susi ran to the boy Majwara, Asmani ran to Uledi Munyasere, Saféné ran to Chowpereh. It was all confusion, like chickens before a rainstorm. Under the big *mvula* tree, the Nassick boys were conferring in a huddle.

There were seven of them, all freedmen who had been captured by slavers as boys and rescued by giant *jahazi* sent by the Queen from the land of Bwana Daudi. Ships, they called them, dhows that are as high as houses and almost as big as the Liwali's palace, Susi said. They had been taken in these *jahazi* ships to India, where they were taught to speak out of their own tongues, and instead learned all sorts of other *mzungu* tongues to speak. They were also given trades to learn and books to read, and paper to write on and clothes that made them look like *wazungu*.

In their midst was the tall figure of Jacob Wainwright, fully dressed even at this hour. It can rain the hail of a thousand storms, the sun can bake with the cruelty of Tippoo Tip's slave raids, and still Jacob will wear his suit.

It was given to him by the man he was named for, he says, and if you ask me, if the good man could only see how Jacob sweats in it every hour of every day, he might well have rethought his gift. I could see no sign of the other Wainwright, Jacob's brother John. Well, I say his brother, but Jacob himself claims that John is no brother of his, and it is no wonder that he will not claim such a brother. The man is lazier than a herd of sleeping hippos. He even lost our two best milking cows. You would think he had never tended a cow before. What they teach them at that school in India besides reading and talking English, I really don't know.

I had an inkling of what it might be that had raised the camp at such an hour. I made my way to the *mvula* tree and touched the shoulder of Matthew Wellington.

'Is it so?' I said.

He nodded but did not speak. I let out a cry that startled a nearby owl into flutter. Susi detached himself from the cluster of the most senior *pagazi* and came towards me. I flung myself into his arms. Susi has never needed an excuse to be near me, that he has not, not from the first time he saw me. If there is something I understand, it is the look that a man gives a woman when he wants her, and if I had a gold nugget for every one of those looks that Susi has given me, I would be the daughter of that rich Indian Ludda Dhamji, that I would.

Just as I was letting myself go in his arms, my man Amoda came up, and Susi hastily let me go, but not before I had felt the stiffness of him. With the Doctor lying just yards away, dead as anything! Filthy goat.

Before Amoda could remonstrate with me, Susi had pulled him to the side. My instinct was to find another woman. Heading to the hut where Ntaoéka had slept the night before, I let out a cry that split the heavens, thinking she would join me. No answer came. She had probably made a bed somewhere with that Mabruki, to whom she had so foolishly attached herself. Even in the perturbation of my spirits, I could not help remembering that just a week ago she had been saying he was no man at all, that he was nothing but a donkey, and a lazy one at that.

'Well,' I had said to her then, 'you could have had your pick when Bwana Daudi told you to choose. You could have had Gardner, you could have had Chuma, but you chose to be with Mabruki.'

Back when we were in Unyanyembe, and she had glued herself to our party without ever being invited, Bwana Daudi had said she was to choose one of his free men to be her husband. Right he was, because a good-looking thing like her had caused us no end of trouble from being untethered.

Within a week of being hired as washerwoman in Unyanyembe, she was making eyes at Amoda. There are many things you can say about that man of mine, but it is true that he has no trouble attracting women. He is almost as fine a specimen of a man as Susi, well grown and tall. But though he does not have Susi's hearty, merry laugh that you want to hear again and again, he has a way with him that would win any woman's heart. When I first saw him, back in Tabora when I was with my Arab merchant, he fairly drove me distracted. He was all I could think of until I had him. Of course, once I had him he soon showed himself for who he was, and I have the bruises to prove it, don't I. And I often wish that it had been Susi that I saw first instead.

But for as long as I was Halima, the daughter of Zafrene, the Liwali's favourite *suria*, I was not going to let Ntaoéka get away with simpering and smiling in my man's direction, even if that man was as hard a man to love as my Amoda. I had no problem using my fists on her, I most certainly did not. For that, I roused the anger of Bwana Daudi, who said it was all my fault. But after she started to make eyes at Susi, to the great anger of his woman Misozi he came to see things my way.

We had met Misozi in Ujiji, in the weeks before Bwana Stanley found us. She was especially helpful to me then, and no wonder; she had her eye on Susi. Her own man had gone on a trading mission to Tabora and not come back, she said. She would rather travel with us and be Susi's road woman than continue to wait for her own man in Ujiji. She has a most trying nature, Misozi, with the brains of a baby goat, but it was good to have another woman about, all the same.

After I made it clear to Ntaoéka that Amoda was not for her, she began to make eyes at Susi. When Misozi ran to complain to Bwana Daudi, it was then that he said she should pick someone else. 'I do not like to have such a fine-looking woman on the loose among us,' I heard him say to Amoda. 'I would rather that she choose any of my worthies.'

But look at her now; tethered though she is, she is still causing problems. She is like one of those pretty bowls in the Liwali's house: too shallow to drink tea from, but too small to eat dates from, so they sit on a high shelf, where they are only good to be looked at, and take up space for no reason.

Since the Nassickers arrived, six months after Bwana Stanley's departure, Ntaoéka has been giddy with excitement. I bet she would open her legs to any of them if they asked, and play the close buttock game too, particularly with that Jacob Wainwright. The way her eyes flutter about when she sees him, you would think she was trying to work up enough tears to get dust out of them.

I told Misozi that I supposed Ntaoéka regretted not waiting, because if she had chosen after the large group of men sent by Bwana

Stanley arrived, she could have had any of the fifty-five *pagazi* and the seven Nassickers that came with them. Bwana Daudi also called them the Nassick boys, and though they are young, with a little too much milk still to be squeezed out of their noses, they are far from being boys, particularly that Jacob Wainwright, a well-grown man who has seen at least one and twenty Ramadans. Proud as anything, he is, with all his English and his learning and his shoes and books and heavy *muzungu* suit.

But it was Misozi and not Ntaoéka who came out to me, wiping the sleep out of her eyes: 'What is it?'

'He is dead, he is gone, he is dead!' I wailed.

'Who?' Misozi said as she yawned.

Sometimes I think that the woman cannot possibly be as stupid as she looks. Who else could I possibly have meant, the donkey? With a woman like that, it is no wonder that Susi looks three times and then twice more at every woman he passes.

She went inside to get her wrapper cloth, and while she was in there, I saw Ntaoéka slinking her way from the direction of the hut where Carus Farrar had slept. So that was how that loaf was cooking. I wondered if Misozi knew. There would be time to tell all, not that I would say anything, of course, because, and this I can say straight, I have never been one to gossip.

'You also, Misozi,' Ntaoéka said. 'Who do you think Halima is talking about? Whose was the death we expected daily? Whose the frail body that was just hours from being a corpse? It can only be the Bwana.'

The two started arguing enough to make the head spin. I moved to the fire, where a group of men sat and talked. Among them were Susi, Amoda, Chuma, Carus Farrar, and the boy Majwara. They were waiting, Carus Farrar said, for the stiffness to leave his body so that they could lay him out. It would not be too long, he said, for Bwana Daudi had died sometime in the night, and the heat in the air would help the stiffness to leave his body.

More and more of the *pagazi* arrived and took up places around the fire. On every lip was the same question: how had it come to this? Susi and Majwara took it in turns to answer.

'Just before midnight,' Majwara said, 'I left the hut to tell Susi that he was to go to the Bwana, for his mind was quite delirious.'

Susi took up the tale. 'I went in at once. The Bwana was trying to rise from his bed. He was clearly not in his right mind as he said, "I have found the fountains, Susi. I have found the fountains. Is this the Luapula?"

'I told him we were in Bangweulu, at Chitambo's village,' Susi said, at which the Bwana started babbling in English, but the only words that Susi heard, and he is not sure he heard them properly, for they made no sense to him, were: 'Poor Mary lies on Shupanga brae, and beeks fornent the Sun.'

Mary, I knew, was the name of Mama Robert, Bwana Daudi's wife, and Shupanga, which is also where Susi comes from, is where she is buried. I interrupted to ask Susi what he thought those words meant, but he had no answer. We all turned as one to Jacob Wainwright, but he simply looked into the distance as though he had not heard the question. I have noticed before that if he does not know the answer to something, he pretends not to have heard the question.

'What happened after that?' I asked.

Susi continued his narration. 'I helped him back onto his bed, as the Bwana, now speaking in Swahili, asked how many days it was to the Luapula.

' "It will take three days' marching," I said.

"'Three days to go to the Luapula,' he said. "Oh dear, oh dear."'

After this, Susi said, he seemed to come to himself, and realise where he was. He then asked Susi to boil him some water.

'Had he eaten the dish I made him?' I asked. 'Groundnuts and grains it was, mashed together soft-soft so that he could swallow it all without chewing. I was that pleased when he asked for food.'

Susi shook his head and continued. He had gone outside to the fire and returned with the copper kettle full of water. Calling Susi close, the Bwana asked for his medicine chest and for a candle. He picked out a medicine, which he told Susi to place by his side.

'His stomach must have been upset,' Carus Farrar interrupted. 'I saw that bottle. It is a potion called calomel. It purges the contents of the stomach.'

'If his stomach was upset,' I said, 'it had nothing to do with my dish. Made it fresh I did, with the groundnuts that we got from Chitambo's women just yesterday.'

Susi went on. 'I am certain he did not eat your dish, Halima. It was still beside him when Bwana Daudi dismissed me. I then left, leaving Majwara in the hut.'

Majwara now took up the tale. A few hours after Susi had left the Bwana, he said, he roused Amoda, who had taken over the watch but had fallen asleep, with the words 'Come to Bwana, I am afraid; I don't know if he is alive.'

Amoda then roused Susi, Chuma, Carus Farrar, and Chowpe- reh. Passing inside the hut, they looked towards the bed. Bwana Daudi was not lying on it, but was kneeling next to it, seemingly engaged in prayer. They instinctively drew backwards. Pointing to him, Majwara said, 'When I lay down to sleep, he was just as he is now, and it is because I find that he does not move that I fear he is dead.'

Carus Farrar then said, 'The candle was stuck to the top of the box with its own wax and shed a light sufficient for us to see his form. Bwana Daudi had left his bed and was kneeling beside it, his body stretched forwards and his head buried in his hands upon the pillow. He did not stir. I advanced to him and placed my hands on his sunken cheeks. The Bwana felt cold and stiff to the touch. I turned to the others and nodded. I told them what we had all of us felt the instant we entered the hut. Bwana Daudi was no more.'

In the silence that followed Carus Farrar's narration, Majwara got up and moved off by himself. I left the men around the fire and followed him to an outcrop of rock a small distance away. He sat down. I sat next to him and waited as he wept into his hands. His face, when he lifted it, was a mask of grief.

When he was not acting as the *kirangozi* and beating the drum to which we marched, Majwara was the Bwana's own servant. He is no longer a child, but is not yet a man; he is the only one of his age among the six children, and is still most content alone with his drum. It is a great responsibility for one so young to have in his care the bathing and dressing of a grown man. Look at that, I keep forgetting that Bwana Daudi is no more. Amoda had often suggested to the Bwana that the boy was perhaps too young for the job, but Majwara, overhearing him, had insisted that this was the very job he wanted.

We had come upon him the year before. He was part of a cargo of the enslaved who were being herded to the coast. Whenever we came across such scenes, they caused the Bwana severe distress. He had been struck by Majwara's young looks, and, indeed, Chuma said later that he himself had been of such an age – just fifteen Ramadans, no more – when he too had been captured, and then rescued by Bwana Daudi.

Just as he had done with Chuma, Bwana Daudi persuaded Majwara's captors that the boy was too young and sick to travel all the way to the coast, and he would give them the price for a full man. Seeing a chance to make something quickly, they had handed the boy over to Bwana Daudi for five strings of beads, which the Doctor often joked was more than I had cost him, for he had bought me too; not for himself, but for Amoda.

Bwana Daudi's rescuing him, and his healing Majwara afterwards of the malaria fever, meant that the boy would have done anything the Bwana asked him. The only thing he had refused to do was change his name, even though Bwana Daudi had suggested several other names for him.

'Chuma is James, and you too shall be an apostle,' he said. 'You can be my Peter, and I will lean on you just as Jesus leaned on his rock.'

But Majwara had said he would keep his name. It was in memory of his mother, he said, for she had chosen that name for him above all others. 'I will never see her again,' he said, 'but she is with me in my name.'

'What a sentimental boy,' Bwana Daudi said, and clapped him on his back. 'Very well then, my young rock, you shall continue to be called Majwara.'

And now here we were, on this rock in Chitambo's village, and Bwana Daudi was dead in his hut.

Majwara and I sat together in silence. Then Majwara said, 'He asked for his medicine. I gave it to him, and he picked out what he needed. But what if it was the wrong one? What if, in the confusion of his illness, he picked the wrong one? And then I fell asleep. I was so weary. I should not have been so weary. What if he called out to me and I did not hear?'

'You did what you could, child,' I said, and patted him on his head. I had to raise my arm to do so, for though he is many moons younger than me, he towers over me like a sapling above the dug earth.

'He saved my life,' the boy wept, 'but I could not save his.'

I let him weep without talking. After his passion was spent, he said again, 'I will never see him again.'

'Yes, that is death,' I said to him. 'We will none of us see Bwana Daudi again in this life.'

Together, we walked back to the camp. By this time, the stiffness had left the Bwana's body, and the men had laid him out. We arrived to find them going into the hut in little groups to pay their respects. After all the men were done, I led the women in to see him.

They had laid him on his back on the mud bed. His hands were at his sides and his eyes closed. Against his scalp, his hair was grey and thin. It was strange to see him without his hat, for no day had ever gone by that he did not wear it. In the thin light that broke the darkness of the hut, it seemed as though he was asleep. A blue fly buzzed from the ceiling above. His medicine chest formed a table next to his bed.

As I looked at the uneaten dish of boiled grains and mashed groundnuts that rested on it, which he had asked for only the night before, it came to me that, truly, he was dead. And it came to me then that his death was everything to me.

2

[Tippoo Tib] describes him as quite an old man, and adds that his name was Livingstone but that in the interior he called himself David. Livingstone thus seems to have been obliged, for the sake of greater intimacy, to have himself called simply by his Christian name by his blacks.

Heinrich Brode, *Tippoo Tib,
the Story of His Career in Central Africa,
Narrated from His Own Accounts*

When Bwana Daudi first bought me for Amoda four years ago, Amoda told me that the Bwana was a learned man, that he was a *mganga* more skilled than all of the Sultan's men of medicine. I thought he was laughing at me because I do not know as much about the things of this world as he does. But in the time that I have been with Bwana Daudi, I have learned that all Amoda told me is true: from reading his large books in all sorts of tongues, Bwana Daudi knew well the diseases that strike both men and beasts.

He could heal almost anyone with potions and ointments. True, he had no joy in curing Chirango's eye after he lost it in that beating that Amoda gave him, and poor Chipangawazi did die after a week of the runs in Nyangwe, but he healed Majwara of the malaria fever and many others of aches of the flesh and joints.

He had no divining bones, horns, animal skins, or plant powders

25

like a real *mganga*, but he had other doctor things, potions and ointments that he said were used by the *mganga* of his own land. As well as his many ointments, powders, and potions, Bwana Daudi travelled with several instruments that he used to measure the height of the Earth and through which he looked at the stars. His reading of the stars aided us often in our travels, for this was a wisdom that was understood by many people, and indeed in some places, positions of honour were given to men who could read the stars. And he was forever writing. When he ran out of ink, he asked me to pound fresh, dark berries so that he could use their juice for ink.

It took some time for me to learn this about Bwana Daudi, which is why I did not immediately believe Amoda. For it seemed most peculiar to me that a man should leave the life he knows in his own land, should sail for months and months in a *jahazi* on an angry sea to come all this way just to wander about looking for the beginning of a river.

Why any man would leave his own land and his wife and children to tramp in these dreary swamps to enquire into the flowing of a river, and into that which does not concern him at all, is beyond my understanding, but Bwana Daudi had no wife, poor thing, he did not take another after his first wife, Mama Robert, died, more is the pity. Perhaps it was her death that made him abandon his children.

And though he tried enough to explain to me why he was looking for this Nile beginning, I never could quite understand it. I said to him, 'Go back to your children, because the Nile has been there since time began, and it will be there after you and I are in the soil, and what will you do then, because the Nile won't care about whether you know where it begins. It will flow on as it always has whether you find it or not. Look at that *bwana* of Mabruki's, Speke, I think he was called, yes, Bwana Speke, the very one whose grave Bwana Stanley's man Bombay wants to visit.

'Shot himself dead, didn't he, cleaning his gun. Bombay told me all about it when he was here with Bwana Stanley. A most stupid way to die if you ask me. Why did he clean his gun himself, as if he had no slaves to clean it for him? Well, he is in his grave now, and still the Nile flows.'

And I said to him, 'You are best off finding a young wife to warm your bed, and, yes, you are old and your teeth are bad, there is no getting away from that, but like my second master, the *qadi*, you are rich in cloth and gold and beads, and like the *qadi*, you could get yourself a pretty wife. Three wives he had, the *qadi* did, all pretty as sparkling jewels, but did he spend any money on them, mean as anything he was, and look where it got him. Dead, just like that, leaving it all behind, with his sons and bastards all fighting over every last thing.'

Laughing as he waved me away, he said, 'Come now, Halima, leave me to eat in silence.'

Now, Bwana Daudi may have been content to wander about for no reason, but if I had my way, I would be back in Zanzibar, far from this jungle and mud, snug in my own house, shut behind a door that would truly be a marvel to all. I told him often that I was not born to march in wildernesses, forests, and swamps looking for rivers, that I was not. Lived my very first years with my mother in one of the biggest palaces in Zanzibar, didn't I, at Beit el-Mtoni.

Before she became a bondswoman of the Liwali, my mother, Zafrene, was the cook for one of the Sultan's most petted and spoiled nieces. She was accused of theft, my mother, lucky for her it was at just about the time she caught the eye of the Liwali, and why not, for though she was a Nubian with skin like burnt coffee, she was tall and elegant, with teeth and eyes that were whiter than new milk. The Liwali bought both her and me from the Sultan's niece's husband, and that is how we became bonded to his household.

The women of the Liwali's harem said she had light fingers, my mother, Zafrene. I do not know about that, and to own the truth, there is nothing I hate more than a thief, as that lazy *pagazi* Chirango knows full well. Thought he could steal the cloth from a bolt that had not been opened, didn't he, and some beads along with it, and sell it all to me and have me blamed for it, but I soon showed him what was what.

After the Liwali's death, I passed on to the *qadi*, who was a judge in the *maẓālim* and sat as judge in that court pronouncing on who was not following the words of the Prophet, blessings be upon His name. Now, though I say blessings upon the Prophet's name, truth to tell, I am no Mohammedan, but when you live among Mohammedans you can't help but get into their ways of doing and saying things. I tried enough to get into it, had to pretend hard enough for the *qadi*, didn't I, but I must confess that though I did outwardly all that was wanted of me, and did it properly too, on the inside of me, I never could get along with it. It was too much to take in, all the *salat* and *zakāt* and *hadīth* and teachings and rulings and whatnots.

From the *qadi*'s household, I was sold off by his greedy sons to the Arab merchant who dragged me from Zanzibar to Tabora in the interior. What a life that was, living in a low mud house, and, in the whole of Tabora, not a single door you could call a door, nothing that you could stop to really look at.

If I was good to him and tended to him and cared and cooked well for him, my Arab merchant said, he would make me his main wife, would make me his *horme*, he said, and if I did not treat him well, it was off to Zanzibar with me, he said, to the slave market. To think of it. A bondswoman I may have been, but I have never once been sold in the market, where anyone could touch and prod me here and prod me there like I was some common *mjakazi* slave.

A greedier man you never saw, greedier even than the *qadi's* sons and bastards, and I had not thought that was possible, for they would have sold their wives and daughters in the market if they could get away with it, that they would. And if he was an Arab, well then, my father was an elephant and my mother a giraffe. Powerful ugly he was too. I do not know what I have ever done that I should be surrounded by ugly men. Well, there is Susi, but he has Misozi, hasn't he, and I was never one to cry over a tomato plant that is being tended in someone else's garden.

It was while I was with the Arab merchant that I caught Amoda's eye. So it came to be that Bwana Daudi bought me for him. He has two proper wives back in Zanzibar, Amoda does, with two sons almost grown and three small girls besides, but he had no wife for the road, and men, you know, they get itchy for a woman when they are on the road. He bargained hard, and what it came down to was that the Arab knew he had a good story to tell if he could say he sold his favourite slave to a white *mzungu*. The Arabs were keen to show it wasn't true, that the *wazungu* wanted slavery gone and done with.

Day in, day out, the whites pestered the Sultan with petitions, my Arab merchant said. They made all sorts of promises if only the Sultan would close down the slave market at Zanzibar. And where will we sell our slaves, if the market is closed, my merchant and his friends said in indignation, as they tore their teeth into my good food. They have had enough slaves, said my merchant, they have sent shiploads of the *shenzi* all over their islands in the Carib and in America and where have you, but now that they have enough of their own slaves, they will stop others from doing what they did. Sheer spite, his friends agreed.

So when the chance came for my Arab merchant to sell me to Bwana Daudi, well, it was as though the end of Ramadan had come for him, along with all of his feast days at once. If he could say to the other Arabs and to anyone who cared to listen that he had sold his favourite slave to a white English, well then. He could say they were not so high and mighty then, these English, going to the Sultan to close the market in the day and buying slaves in the night.

I was pleased enough to go, I will tell you that. As I say, Bwana Daudi had bought me to please Amoda, and I liked the sight of him well enough. And there is nothing like being in the arms of a man who knows what is what. But just like green limes, men are sometimes well looking enough on the outside, but once you open them up it is something else. Bwana Daudi gave me my own wages too, when he found out I could cook as well as I can. Not that I have cooked him anything proper, apart from that time we spent at Manyuema, for we have simply not enough provisions.

And now he is dead. I know but little about the world, that is true, but there is nothing you can tell me about how slaves are passed on and how they are freed. I know that Bwana Daudi bought me for Amoda but did not deed me to him. With his son in his own country across the water, unable to claim me as his own, Bwana Daudi's death has dissolved the bond between us. For the first time since I was a small child in my mother Zafrene's arms, I am free.

3

I have found it difficult to come to a conclusion on their char-
acter. They sometimes perform actions remarkably good, and
sometimes as strangely the opposite. I have been unable to
ascertain the motive for the good, or account for the callous-
ness of conscience with which they perpetrate the bad. After long
observation, I came to the conclusion that they are just such a
strange mixture of good and evil as men are everywhere else.

David Livingstone, *Missionary Travels*
and Researches in South Africa

That things could come to this sorrowful pass had been my fear since the Manyuema women were massacred before our eyes at Nyangwe. This was in the middle of the month that Bwana Daudi called July, just four months before we met with Bwana Stanley's party in Ujiji. Bwana Daudi had collapsed in his sorrow. It took him more than a week to recover.

He had had much to endure up to then. I often said to Misozi that he had enough illness in one body for a dozen men. There were hundreds upon hundreds of small, invisible creatures in his body that were eating at his bones, he said. Quite how they got in, he never explained, though it seemed perfectly clear to me that only a powerful witchcraft could explain it. When I urged him most seriously to find a *mganga* to cure him of this terrible witchcraft, he laughed me away.

He also suffered a sickness that gave him the runs when he ate anything. On top of that, his teeth were falling from his mouth. Between the missing teeth and the runs, his frame became thin and skeletal.

All he could eat then were the damper cakes he liked. They are easy enough to make: they are just flour and water cooked in a little salt butter that I make myself from milk that has gone off. Those damper cakes were the only thing that his bad teeth could take, that and a little *ugali*, not cooked the usual way, with the maize powder stirred in water until it stiffens, but cooked soft-soft so that it was almost a porridge, like you would feed to a weaning suckling.

But more serious than the affliction of his body was the wound inflicted on his heart. For many days afterwards, he could talk of nothing but the massacre. He even stopped asking about the Nile, that is how shaken he was. He would write about Manyuema to the world, he said. He would write about it in words of fire.

It had happened on market day. We had been among the Manyuema for weeks of peaceful rest. In that time, a quarrel had arisen between Bwana Daudi and a man called Dugumbe bin Habib, who was the chief ivory trader and slaver in Manyuema country. The two men had met before. Though I asked both Amoda and Susi, I was never able to understand what the quarrel between them was about, but it was something about this Dugumbe and his war with a man called Mirambo, who was a sultan somewhere in the interior and had killed scores of people in his raiding parties. Whatever it was, there was bad blood between them, that was clear.

On this day, five of Dugumbe's men came to the market. A warm day it was, but not so hot as to burn the skin, for there was a cool breeze from the clear sky. We were all in the market. There is nothing more we enjoyed than looking at the pretty things the Manyuema women brought on market day. The men liked to look at the women too, especially Bwana Daudi, who said he would write in his book that the Manyuema are remarkably beautiful in appearance.

The air sang with the Manyuema tongue. I did not understand it, but it rang pleasantly in the ear when spoken in the high chattering voices of the women as they sold their coloured fruit and wares and things and tended their children and plaited their hair. Pretty things they sold, pearls that they got from the river oysters they call *makesi*, and wooden beads and bowls. Paw-paw fruits they had too, and pink-fleshed guavas and prickly cucumbers, all pleasingly arranged to entice the eye. From one corner came the pleasant smell of roasting meat.

We traded and ate our fill. It was as we were leaving, content with our trading, that we saw Dugumbe's men. They carried their guns with them and passed Bwana Daudi without a greeting. Amoda said he would ask them what they were doing, bringing arms to the market. Bwana Daudi laid his hand on Amoda's arm and said, 'This is not our quarrel. Leave it be, for I do not like their looks.'

As we moved away, we heard the loud sound of a man in quarrel. One of the men had seized a fowl from a market stall and was arguing over it with the woman who sold it. The creature squawked along with her protests. Then he threw the bird to the ground and hit her full in the face with the butt of his gun. Amoda and Susi cried out at the same time she did.

As they moved in her direction, they were stopped short by the sound of guns. From the opposite end of the market, Dugumbe's four other men were now firing, and soon this quarrelsome fellow joined them. They fired their guns, those five men, first this way, and then that way, ratatata ratatata, that was the sound that filled the air, that and the screams and wails of the running women and their children too, dropping their fruits and vegetables, their pretty wares covered in their blood.

Amoda, Susi, and Bwana Daudi shepherded our party to some nearby bushes from where we could only watch helplessly as those poor women were massacred. Their only escape was by the river behind the market, but the canoes were too few. In their desperation to avoid the bullets, they jumped in the river and headed for an island that was too far out of reach, for we soon saw them disappear under the water. Bwana Daudi cried out in his tongue, but I do not know what he said. The fear of death was on the air, the smell of death too, for still the guns thundered, as the poor women ran to the river only to be stopped by the merciless bullets.

It was over as quickly as it began. As soon as Dugumbe's men left, Amoda, Susi, and Chuma tried to help the women who had fallen into the river. In their confusion, not knowing if these were friends or foes, the women fought back and struck across the water, where they all drowned.

Afterwards, Bwana Daudi insisted that he, Amoda, and the men count the bodies. More than four hundred it was, slain in daylight, with the sun shining above without a mind to what had just been done under its sight. This was the work of just five men with ten guns, done, too, in less than the amount of time it takes to make a goat stew.

We did what we could for the poor people. We dug their graves, made fires and cooked, and fed their children. The many in the river could not be counted or buried until they washed up downstream, if at all.

Bwana Daudi was in a trance of shock, that he was. I thought then that his heart would give from the misery of his low spirits. I said to him he had to let go of the sorrow, for it was sure to finish him. That is how the slaves die at the end of their journey from the interior to the coast. Sometimes, whole groups will fall to the ground and never get up again. Dead. Just like that.

My mother, Zafrene, who made such a journey herself as a girl, from a land close to Nubia it was, told me that it is not the weariness of walking all that way that does them in. It is their hearts that collapse after they learn that after walking all the way from where they came to get to Bagamoyo, with heavy ivory tusks on their heads and scars from the whips on their backs and marks from the slave sticks on their necks, they will not be sent back after all but will be forced on yet another journey across the water, to the market in Zanzibar, where they will be sold.

When they lay down their loads and realise there is no return, their hearts die within them. Their hearts just give out and crack. The *moyo* inside them goes *baga*, just like that, and stops beating. It is why all the slaves call it Bagamoyo, for it is the place of breaking hearts.

Bwana Daudi became consumed by a searing anger. Dugumbe began to put it about that it was Bwana Daudi's men, that it was Amoda and Chuma and Susi, who had caused the fight that started the shooting. I have never seen the Bwana more angry. To think that Dugumbe could kill all those people and then try to cover his deed by taking away the good name of Bwana Daudi and his men gave him a helpless sort of anger, for there was nothing at all he could do. Dugumbe had far too many men, and our provisions were almost depleted.

That was the beginning of the end for him. The heart within him simply went *baga* and broke inside him. Though it took him many more months to finally die, I believe it all started in Manyuema. For truly, he never recovered from the horrors of that day.

35

4

Public punishment to Chirango for stealing beads, fifteen cuts; diminished his load to 40 lbs, giving him blue and white beads to be strung . . . It was Halima who informed on Chirango, as he offered her beads for a cloth of a kind which she knew had not hitherto been taken out of the baggage. This was so far faithful in her, but she has an outrageous tongue.

David Livingstone, *The Last Journals of David Livingstone*

After the massacre of the poor Manyuema women at Nyangwe, Bwana Daudi became desperate to get to Ujiji, where his stores and provisions awaited him. It was from Zanzibar, through Bagamoyo, that Bwana Daudi's stores had come. They were supposed to wait for him in Ujiji, and after all that he had seen at Nyangwe, he needed them sorely. He had run out of paper and had to make do with writing over old books using the juice of berries.

It was the paper he missed the most. So you can only imagine the crushing disappointment that was to come. When we got there, we found that his provisions had all been plundered by that dishonest Arab man Sherif, who had been put in charge of them until Bwana Daudi came to claim them. He stole everything like the common thief that he is, even the paper, for which he had no use. Bwana Daudi kept saying, 'Even the paper, and not even the ink has been spared.'

To add salt to Bwana Daudi's wound, every day that we were there, stuck and unable to move, waiting for nothing, he had to look at that Sherif parading himself in the Bwana's cloth and smiling and salaaming his deceit at him. Salaaming and bowing all day long when he had stolen from Bwana Daudi. He had all the spite of a snake, that bastard bandit, because a snake will bite even what it does not eat. His concubine sashayed and swayed before us, clad in the Americano cloth that belonged to the Bwana, and it was all I could do not to tear it off her, the thieving slut.

I said to Bwana Daudi, 'We should send a party to beat up that Sherif and his concubine too. Amoda will want it, that is sure, and I am willing to be of their number and lead them too if it comes to that. I will pound them both like they are two cassava roots in my grinding mill.' But Bwana Daudi said only, 'I must have forbearance, Halima, as a Kristuman, I must do what Jesus would have done.'

But if you ask me there was more to it than that, for Bwana Daudi is not above having a man beaten if it is what has to be done. Just the other month, he ordered Chirango beaten for stealing the blue beads from the package that had not yet been opened. He received fifteen lashes with the whip, Chirango did, and afterwards the Doctor prayed that he would mend his ways, though if that whip did not mend him, no prayer will, because Amoda wields it with a hard hand, I will say that for him.

If there is something that man of mine can do as quickly as he can build a hut or ford a river, it is to beat a man, and a woman too, as I know all too well when he finds himself in liquor, although he is a Mohammedan. But I have the good fortune that my scars are all under my clothes where no one can see them, not like poor Chirango, who was beaten more badly than I ever was.

37

So it was not softness of heart that stopped Bwana Daudi from having Sherif beaten. It was that Bwana Daudi was afraid that Sherif would bring the slavers and they would turn on us, that I am certain, and Abdullah Susi said the same, and he should know, he has been with Bwana Daudi long enough. That is why Bwana Daudi did not go after Sherif.

Only when Bwana Stanley came to Ujiji, and the Bwana, and all of us, were saved, did we stop feeling bitter about Sherif's betrayal. I am certain as certain can be that the same fears that prevented him from dealing with Sherif also led Bwana to flee Dugumbe without sorting him out for his lies.

But as I say, Bwana Daudi does not hesitate to have men beaten when they deserve it. Chirango blames me for his beating, and I suppose he is right. He tried to sell me the blue beads from the package that had not been opened, Chirango did, and cloth from a new bolt. Now, I like a pretty thing or two to adorn myself, about that, I won't lie, but I won't take what is not mine. So, I told Bwana Daudi about it, and he said Chirango should be given fifteen lashes of the whip by Amoda.

Lost his eye too, Chirango did, when he turned the wrong way as Amoda beat him, and the whip caught him full in the face. His eye bled and swelled up something terrible. The Bwana offered to heal the eye, and when Chirango refused, he ordered the men to hold him down while he forced an ointment into it. Held back by Amoda and Susi he was, fought them something awful while Chuma and John Wainwright forced his head down. Then Bwana Daudi smeared something in his eye, and still Chirango fought the men.

A whole week it continued like that, with the men holding him down while Chirango cried in agony, held back first by Chuma and Mabruki, then Susi and Munyasere, then Carus Farrar and Toufiki

Ali, one of the strongest of the *pagazi*. Bulging muscles he has, with not an ounce of fat about him. The men held him down so that Bwana Daudi could treat his eye but it did not open again after that. There is a scar there now, and it is not a pretty sight; his eye bulges out like there is a small lime under it. For days and days, it wept a mix of blood and unpleasant-smelling pus, which made the men seek to avoid him more than they had before.

For days after the whipping, he had gone about with his leaking eye, muttering that between them, Amoda and Bwana Daudi had blinded him and his men had assisted him. But then he changed and knelt first before the Bwana, and then before Amoda, and cried out his penitence, but if you ask me, he meant not a word of it. There was something a little too cowed, a little too humble in his new manner. Not even the lowest slave in the Liwali's household held himself in this way. 'Chirango of the One Eye', he began to call himself, and laugh too when he said it, but it was a sound that carried no mirth.

Though he made efforts to ingratiate himself, the men remained unchanged towards him. They spoke roughly to him, in short sentences and barking orders, as one would to a dog. And no wonder. His face was sorrowful but his eyes were hard and he spoke trembling penitence in a voice that was like a knife.

He puts me in mind of a plucked chicken that has sat too long without being cooked, so that when you see the white flesh, you think all is well within, but when you slice it open, it is all green and crawling with maggots, and the smell hits you like a stone to your head. A maggoty fellow if I ever saw one is that Chirango.

He was not in the original group of men; that was just Susi, Chuma, and Amoda. Nor was he in the large group that followed with the Nassickers after Bwana Stanley left. Along with Ntaoéka's man Mabruki, he was one of the men who were left behind by Bwana Stanley, and if you ask me, Bwana Stanley was pleased enough that Chirango chose to stay instead of going back to the coast with him.

Even before the beating, I often caught him looking at Bwana Daudi with an unfriendly face. Mark my words, I said to Misozi, that Chirango is certainly up to no good. Though they won't believe me, that they won't, for they say, oh, Halima, you talk too much. Well, I may talk too much, but I have more than a tongue in my head. I have eyes too and what they tell me is that Chirango is up to no good at all.

5

The Doctor also reminded me . . . that . . . he had a stock of jel-lies and crackers, soups, fish, and potted ham, besides cheese, awaiting him in Unyanyembe, and that he would be delighted to share his good things; my imagination loved to dwell upon the luxuries at Unyanyembe. I pictured myself devouring the hams and crackers and jellies like a madman. I lived on my raving fancies. My poor vexed brain rioted on such homely things as wheaten bread and butter, hams, bacon, caviare, and I would have thought no price too high to pay for them . . . I thought that if a wheaten loaf with a nice pat of fresh butter were presented to me, I would be able, though dying, to spring up and dance a wild fandango.

Henry Morton Stanley, *How I Found Livingstone*

Bwana Stanley arrived just at the moment that I had begun to despair that we would ever leave Ujiji, for we had no provisions at all for the journey. As soon as he discovered Sherif's deceit, Bwana Daudi wanted to send messengers to Bagamoyo, to post word to Zanzibar of where he was, but we had nothing with which to pay them.

Nor could he spare Amoda, Susi, or Chuma, for it was just them and me who were with him then. By that time, we had not been joined by the Nassickers, Mabruki, Chirango, or the rest of the *pagazi*, and so it was just us, along with Misozi, who decided she liked the looks of Susi. There was no one else to send.

In desperation, Bwana Daudi thought our small group should strike out for Unyanyembe, where he had other provisions waiting. But though Amoda and Susi pressed him to this route, still he would not go, for it would have meant not looking for his precious fountains.

The Ujiji people were kind enough, I will give them that. They knew Bwana Daudi from his journey before, and knew that if he said that more things would come, they would come. In the meantime, they fed us even though we had nothing to trade with, and we helped in the small ways we could.

Then, one morning, after Bwana Daudi had finally decided to strike for Unyanyembe and Misozi had said she would come with us, we could scarcely believe it when Susi came running at top speed to where we were all gathered at the morning meal and gasped out, 'An English-man! I see him!'

He rushed back again before we could make sense of his words. Within a short time, he was back, leading a large party. And what a party it was. Behind Susi came a short *mzungu* man with so much hair about his face you could barely see his skin. I could not stop looking at his eyes. Unlike Bwana Daudi's, they had no colour in them and put one in mind of a ghost, and though the thought was frightening it was hard to look away.

Behind him came *pagazi* after *pagazi*, and more than twenty *askari* carrying shining guns and muskets, with not a single bit of rust on them. 'This is a wealthy traveller,' said Bwana Daudi.

Oh, the things he had with him. Piles and piles of goods, bales and bales of cloth, endless strings of beads, and I don't know what, along with two baths of tin, huge kettles, cooking pots, and tents. He walked up to Bwana Daudi and shook his hand and said a greeting. By this time, all of Ujiji had come to witness this meeting. Susi translated his words for us all and said he was a *mzungu* called Bwana Stanley who had come all this way to find his friend.

Susi told us that he said to Bwana Daudi: 'It can only be that you are Bwana Daudi.'

Well, if that is not the most stupid thing I have ever heard, I said to Susi, of course it could only be Bwana Daudi. He was the only *mzungu* among a great crowd of people who were not *wazungu*, wasn't he, so who else could he possibly have been if not himself?

Bwana Daudi greeted him warmly, and truly, he rejoiced like a chicken that had been spared the pot, that he did, though it was a quiet sort of rejoicing, as was usual with him. He kept calling Bwana Stanley an Americano, which I had thought to be a type of cloth, but what he meant was that the flag of Bwana Stanley was from America, just like the Americano cloth is from the same place. Very good cloth it is too, if a little stiff.

Bwana Stanley had strange things with him, like champagne, a sort of water that sparkled and bubbled as he and Bwana Daudi drank it out of great silver goblets. Farjallah Christie, who was Bwana Stanley's cook, kept some aside for me to try. It bubbled up my nose and made me sneeze. It was then that he told me that it was a *hongoro* and I had taken an intoxicating drink, the filthy goat. Best not to tell Amoda, I said, and drank it up.

Bwana Stanley liked his things proper, I can tell you that, it was just as though he was in his own house. Once a week, he washed in hot water out of one of the great big tin baths. When he and Bwana Daudi ate, he made Farjallah Christie, and his other manservant, Carus Farrar, lay out a table with cloth and silver on it. They were best at it because, like Jacob Wainwright and the others, they had also been to this Nassick school in India where freed slaves are taught the speech, manner, and ways of the English, but had left some years before.

After Bwana Stanley left us, Majwara took to doing this for Bwana Daudi too, for he admired the Nassick boys greatly and wanted very much to be like them. Bwana Daudi said to him, 'I shall tell the small *bwana*, in my next letter, that you continue to keep everything shipshape. Just like an English butler.'

A butler, Amoda said to me, is a person who brings things to table. As if I did not know such a thing. I could tell him all about men who bring food to table, didn't we have thousands of those, eunuchs and butlers and all the rest, at the Liwali's house, and at the *qadi*'s house too after that, ah, but he was a mean man, the *qadi*, it was all 'the Prophet says this' and 'the Prophet says that', and 'peace be upon His name and bounties on His blessings', but with no kindness to him. He would not allow even a crumb of stale bread for the blind beggars in Forodhani, and it is as well that he died and his son sold me on and I was there for only seven months.

In the Liwali's house in Zanzibar, people sat down to eat from silver and gold plates, they sat and feasted from dishes they picked out from the long *sefra* that ran almost the length of the room and was so covered with dishes of food that you could not see the wood it was made of. There were bowls and bowls of lamb cooked in ginger and rice boiled in chicken broth, rice boiled in tomato juice, rice cooked with beef and with fish, and with vegetables and chicken too, and for very special festivities rice boiled in cloves and coriander and cardamom and cinnamon and raisins.

There were syrups made of dates, syrups made from honey and tamarind, and the coffee, oh, it was spiced and scented, you could smell it miles away, the best coffee too, from Arabia and Abyssinia. And the spices, from everywhere they were; cassia and cloves, nutmeg and cinnamon, cardamom and saffron, and peppers of all colours. Though there were only ever two meals, one in the morning and another towards sunset, in between the meals there was coffee and tea and lemonade and sugared water, and cakes and fruit. And there were breads and sweetmeats too, and pastries so sweet that they hurt the teeth, and pomegranate seeds.

My teeth grind something terrible when I remember those pomegranate seeds. From Mesopotamia they were, pink and juicy and crunchy, just the thing to eat on a hot day, in between sips of water cold enough to quench the throat, for it was always kept in the shade of the coolest place in the kitchen.

I was meant to help my mother, Zafrene, take them round to all the women of the Liwali's harem, but I could never stop myself from slipping some into my mouth as I made my quick way to leave them in the bedrooms. And though my mother, Zafrene, scolded me, she always made sure there was enough in the bowls that I would not eat them all before they got to where they were destined to be.

I was getting powerful hungry just thinking of all this food. 'And what is more,' I snapped at Amoda, 'in the Liwali's house we did not have ants running in and out of the food while people ate, I will tell you that for nothing.'

I added, 'Nor did we have flies that hovered and buzzed around people's mouths so that you feared you would swallow them with your food.'

He said, 'Watch that I don't slap the Liwali's house out of you until you talk from the other side of your face.'

I made off, quick as anything, before he could strike me.

6

_____

Halimah, the female cook of the Doctor's establishment, was
. . . afraid the Doctor did not properly appreciate her culinary
abilities; but now she was amazed at the extraordinary quan-
tity of food eaten, and she was in a state of delightful excite-
ment . . . Poor, faithful soul! While we listened to the noise of
her furious gossip, the Doctor related her faithful services. 'You
have given me an appetite,' he said. 'Halimah is my cook, but
she never can tell the difference between tea and coffee.'

Henry Morton Stanley, *How I Found Livingstone*

I will be the first to say that when Bwana Stanley said he preferred
the food of his own cook, Farjallah Christie, I was not offended.
And that is the truth, no matter what Ntaoéka and Misozi may say
on the matter.

Just as Bwana Daudi had Amoda as his expedition leader, Bwana
Stanley had a hulking giant of a man, black as soot, with teeth that
protruded beyond his lips, who called himself Bombay, though his
real name was Sidi Mubarak. It appeared that Bwana Daudi was
not the only wandering *mzungu* in the world. There were many of
them, all looking for the beginning of this Nile River, and Bombay
had known them all. He had been everywhere, he said, travelling
with one *mzungu* after the other, with Bwana Burton and Bwana
Grant and Bwana Speke, who was his favourite. All he wanted

before he died, he said, was to visit the grave of Bwana Speke.

This Bombay said to me one day that Bwana Daudi had told Bwana Stanley all about me and how I could not tell the difference between coffee and tea, and though Bombay did not laugh, Farjallah Christie gave a smirk. Susi gave me a smiling wink, bless his good heart, but Amoda laughed fit to burst. That is what that man of mine is like, willing to join in the sport of any man who mocks me, and start it too if he has to.

I went to Bwana Daudi at once, though it was the hour of his ablutions and he was preparing to go to the river, and I would not let him leave his hut, and indeed, I said to him, I said, you forget that I was a daughter of the cook in the Liwali's kitchen who was also a *suria* in his harem, and we had all sorts of tea there, I can tell you that for nothing, tea served with mint and cinnamon, and coffee too, like you have never smelled, from Arabia it was, from Abyssinia too.

He was an Omani of the first rank, wasn't he, I said to Bwana Daudi, ugly though he was, the Liwali, he was an important man with a house in Shangani Point, bursting full with silks and spices and slaves and all sorts of tea and coffee we had in the stores and much more besides. It is all anyone can do to tell what is what when it is all jumbled together any which way in all these old tins, I said, this is not a proper kitchen this, this jungle and forest, these three-stone fires.

And yes, I said to him, my mother, who was the *suria* of the Sultan's Liwali as well as his cook, told me that there are people in Oman, wild people who live in the mountains, who can cook chickens or even a whole goat like nothing you have ever seen on hot rocks with nothing added but salt, but I am no mountain person from Oman, I am not. I am just Halima and it is more than I can do to produce a feast out of rocks and salt and nothing.

And he laughed and said, 'Halima,' he said, 'but you have an outrageous tongue,' and continued laughing as he walked down the river to his ablutions.

I shouted after him, you can say what you will about my tongue, and you will not be the first either, nor the last if it comes to that, it is what it is, my tongue is, but I will not have my character taken away from me, that I will not, Bwana or no Bwana, or else I am not the daughter of Zafrene. Not know the difference between tea and coffee indeed.

Still, though he joined Amoda in mocking me, he knew how to cook, Farjallah Christie, and I will not begrudge the skills of someone when they are clear, and what is more, he shared what he knew, which is not what most would do, and men for that matter. He knew what he was about, and could do things with a fish that were as good as any cook from Oman itself, which is as well because that Bwana Stanley of his was obsessed with food, I tell you.

Bwana Daudi made the mistake of telling him that there was plenty of food awaiting him with the stores that he had left in Unyanyembe. After that, Bwana Stanley could do nothing but talk of the good things in Unyanyembe. He talked more about this food and that food than Bwana Daudi talked about this Nile. That is all he did, eat and talk and talk and eat. He ate and he talked, and he talked and he ate and he ate and he talked. I have heard it said, from the time I was a girl, that I could talk enough for anyone, but that Bwana Stanley had nothing on him but a tongue, and when he was not lashing his *pagazi* with it, he talked on and on with the Doctor, long into the night.

'There is a lot to talk about,' his man Bombay told us. 'Your *bwana* has been out of the world six years and a great many things have happened in that time.'

As we sat over the fire on the nights when the two *bwana* talked to each other, Bombay told us about some of the things that had happened in those far-off lands. They barely made sense to me. They had dug into the earth in the land of Egypt to make a passage in the sea that led from England, where the Bwana came from, to India, where Bwana's lazy *askari* – sepoys, he called them – and the Nassickers come from.

Chuma, who likes to draw lines and squiggles on pieces of paper that he calls maps, wanted to know the exact location of it to see if he could draw it. 'This is great news indeed,' he said, beaming at me. 'This is the most marvellous of news. It means that we no longer have to round the Cape to get to India.'

'We' indeed. As if I have ever rounded the Cape in my life, or would even want to do any such thing. Round the Cape indeed. I am not likely to be rounding any Cape. If the Nassickers and those sepoy people are anything to go by, they don't know what it is to work in India, I will tell you that for nothing. India is no place for me. When the Bwana came from India, he had a great number of these sepoy people, they were to march with him, and get paid double the wages too, but did they march? Did they march.

They abandoned him when they got to the nearest settlement, didn't they, and marched themselves back to the coast. Back to India too, no doubt of that, rounding the Cape and whatnot, and they had better stay there if they know what is good for them, and they can stay there all their lives and round the Cape to their hearts' delight.

There was more news, Bombay said. There was a new president in America, a man called Grant. I asked if this was the same Bwana Grant with whom Ntaoéka's man Mabruki had travelled. Great friends they were, this Bwana Grant and Bwana Speke, until Bwana Speke blew his own head off after coming here to look for this Nile beginning. It was not the same Grant, Bombay said, and when I asked what a president was, he said it was someone chosen by the people, who said to him, 'Here, we want you to be our sultan.'

In this America where Bwana Stanley came from, and where there was a sultan called Grant, there had been a great war that lasted years and years, and it was all about slaves. I wanted to know more about this war and who had won the most slaves, and what they planned to do with those slaves now that they had them, but on they went talking about this passage of water in Egypt. Suez, Suez, they kept calling it, for that was the name of it, a supremely silly name if you ask me. If you are going to name something, why give it a name that means nothing at all? Then again, none of these *mzungu* names mean anything at all.

It made my head ache, I tell you, to hear of these new places. Apart from India, where the Nassickers say they are from, though they look like any of us; Abyssinia and Arabia, where the Liwali's coffee came from; Oman and Muscat, where the other sultan lived; Mecca, where the Mohammedans go to pray; Circassia, where most of the *sariri* of the Sultan's harem came from; and all the places where we got food and spices, like Malay and Mesopotamia, Asia and this England where Bwana Daudi is from, I had not heard of any other land.

For those four months that Bwana Stanley was with us, listening to Bombay telling us his stories night after night, I got a strange feeling, I tell you, to think that there were simply thousands upon thousands of people like the Bwana, and women too, far away in England, and in America too, doing what they did, and not knowing at all about the things that we did.

Then there were people in India, all Hindi like those lazy sepoys of the Bwana's, or stiff and proper like Jacob Wainwright; then there were people in Egypt and people in this land America, where Bwana

Stanley came from, all doing what they did, not knowing anything at all about us. It made me feel small and shrivelled, I tell you, like a raisin on the Liwali's drying roof, to hear about all these people in all those lands not knowing we were there.

And I simply could not understand how it was possible for any people to choose their sultan. That was nothing, said Bombay, the people living in the land next to Bwana Daudi's had even cut off the sultan's head, and his wife's too, and all their children. When I imagined someone cutting off Bhargash bin Sultan's head, or even the heads of his wives and the women of his harem, it made my head simply stiff with thinking, I tell you, as though it were my head that was for the chop.

'Why is the Sultan the Sultan?' I had asked my mother once.

'Stop your talking now,' she said. 'The Sultan just is.'

I even thought to ask the Liwali himself once. Some people said he was my father, my mother being his *suria* and me born in bondage, but that was not likely, and it is no loss not to know my father, I will tell you that for nothing, especially if the Liwali is a possibility. Imagine me with a father like that. He may have been an Omani of the first rank but he was as ugly as the underside of an underground oven and always he smelled of hot spices, old sweat, and burnt offal.

He was kind enough, the Liwali, I will give him that. Whenever he met me, moving from one task to another, and I stopped to ask him questions, he would chuck me under my chin and tell me to run off to my next job and not bother him. That is what I miss most about Bwana Daudi. If I asked him such a question, he answered me straight, even if I did not always understand him. I may not have understood everything, but he would answer anyway. But he can answer no questions where he is now, poor man, wherever it is that he is now.

7

A man who accompanied us to the Falls was a great admirer
of the ladies. Every pretty girl he saw filled his heart with rap-
ture. 'Oh, what a beauty I never saw her like before; I wonder
if she is married?' and earnestly and lovingly did he gaze after
the charming one till she had passed out of sight. He had four
wives at home, and hoped to have a number more before long.

David Livingstone, *Narrative of an Expedition*
to the Zambezi and Its Tributaries

I was as certain as I could be that the arrival of Bwana Stanley would surely mean the end of Bwana Daudi's Nile madness. It pleased me to think that when Bwana Daudi had recovered his strength, we would all go back to the coast with Bwana Stanley, and what a merry party we would be, for Bwana Stanley had brought new faces to us, and new faces bring new stories and new stories bring new knowledge.

For my own part, I was pleased to think of what awaited me in Zanzibar. Bwana Daudi had promised to free me and buy me my own little house, though I wondered how it would be with Amoda. I was just his road woman; he had his own women in Zanzibar, two of them even. Then again, I thought, he might wish to be on the road again. I would not have regretted his departure, nor his going back to his wives, for he could beat them instead of me. Perhaps they found him easier to love than I did, or perhaps with them he was lighter with his hand. I would not have regretted never seeing him again, but only if Bwana Daudi freed me like he said he would, and bought me my own house.

I would much rather have had Susi call on me in my house, but, well, he had Misozi. But perhaps Bwana Daudi would take me and Majwara and our little foundling Losi to England with him, he had bought us after all, and the two of us would go with him and all that he owned.

I call Losi my little daughter, though she is not mine *mine*, for I never could make them stay inside me long enough to grow. They just slid out of me, my children did, before they could breathe on their own, which may be just as well, poor things, for who wants to be born in bondage?

We found her abandoned by the side of the road just before we reached Ujiji, poor mite. All skin and bones she was, she had been left for dead, perhaps by a slaving party. 'You should be a mother, Halima,' Bwana Daudi said, 'and here is one to practise on until you have your very own *mtoto*.'

A piteous thing she was, and it took a lot of feeding to make her well again. Not a single soul begrudged her their food, indeed. I tried to explain to the Bwana that it was bad luck to take into your household a child you do not share blood with, for who knows what spirits and other things the child may bring.

'If we were at the coast,' he said, 'I would have sent her to the Nassick school in India, or even to England to my little Nannie, to my daughter Agnes, but what am I to do with her if you do not care for her?'

He waved away my doubts, and I am glad of it. She has been a blessing and a boon, Losi has. That was his soft heart all over. I often heard him lament over his poor lost Chitane, who died before I joined them. That must have been a child, I thought, or perhaps one of his *pagazi*, but no. This much-lamented Chitane was nothing but a small dog remarkable for having so much hair that those who saw it could not tell which end was which.

Drowned in a lake, this hairy little dog did. They were crossing a place with deep water and one of the *pagazi* had forgotten to cross with the creature. The dog had swum after the Bwana, only to drown before reaching him, for so wide was the crossing place that it had tired itself out from swimming. Bwana Daudi had named that lake forever after as Chitane's Water. To think he would lament over a mere dog, over one of those creatures behind whose eyes *djinns* like to lurk and hide.

Now, here was his soft heart again. And this was a child, not a dog. How could I say no to that? He had a way of getting to you, the Bwana did, and to get you to do the things you would not have done. I wanted to call her Zafrene, for my mother, but when she became strong enough to talk, all we could understand of her tongue was the word 'Losi', and that is what we called her.

So there we were, the three of us, Majwara, Losi, and me, the Bwana's foundlings. I was that excited to imagine that Bwana Stanley would force Bwana Daudi to give up all the Nile madness and go back to Zanzibar, then on to this famous England, but, no, Bwana Daudi would press on and not turn back. They argued about it, but Bwana Daudi stood firm. He would journey on until he dropped dead, if need be.

All that Bwana Stanley could do was to leave some of his men behind. And though I had never quite taken to Bwana Stanley and his boiled-groundnut eyes, it was certainly a gloomy day when he left us, for he took Bombay and his many companions with him. He left us severely diminished. Among the nine *pagazi* who chose to stay were Mabruki and Chirango. Bwana Stanley promised to send more men to meet us as soon as he got back, a bigger party of men, he said, to come with more supplies. We were to meet them in Unyanyembe.

8

Halima ran away in a quarrel with Ntaoéka: I went over to
Sultan bin Ali and sent a note after her, but she came back
of her own accord, and only wanted me to come outside and
tell her to enter. I did so, and added, 'You must not quarrel
again.' . . . She has been extremely good ever since I got her
from Katombo or Moene-mokaia: I never had to reprove her
once . . . I shall free her, and buy her a house and garden at
Zanzibar, when we get there.

David Livingstone, *The Last Journals of David Livingstone*

We reached Unyanyembe some months after Bwana Stanley had left. If you ask me, the hardest part of his travel since I joined his party was not the lack of food, or even the massacre at Manyuema, or not finding his provisions waiting, but the period we spent in Unyanyembe, waiting for Bwana Stanley's men to come. The weary waiting, Bwana Daudi called it, or the wearisome waiting.

He talked of nothing else but the waiting and how weary he was of waiting. It was enough to make me weary myself. He drove himself to distraction as he counted over and over again how many days it would take for the men to march from Bagamoyo.

When he was not counting the days, he would sit in the shade of his hut, writing about anything he thought of, a group of ants one day, children's games the next. One time he came to stand where I was shelling groundnuts while Losi, with her chattering voice, tried to help me. 'Have you not seen,' he said, 'that the children do not play like they are children, for they have no playthings?'

I did not know what he meant by playthings and said so. 'I mean the children play at being adults,' he said. 'There they are, building pretend huts, and going to pretend wars to catch pretend slaves. Look at Losi there, playing with those groundnuts, pretending to be you.'

'There is a lot of work,' I said, 'and I cannot stand here chatting, so if you do not mind, could you move off to bother someone else?'

He gave that laugh of his, shook his head, and moved off. Another time, I was pounding rice into flour as Losi again played beside me when he came and started talking to me about elephants, of all things. The man stood there prattling about elephants. Elephants indeed.

'Do you know, Halima,' he said, 'your ancestors in Africa used elephants as domestic animals at least as soon as the Asians?'

'Why would the ancestors have wanted to use elephants as domestic animals?' I asked. 'They must be hard to keep, elephants, for they eat everything in sight. Why, the other day, at the Liwali's—'

'Never mind that, but tell me what you think of this,' Bwana Daudi said. 'It is written that some Africans refused to sell their elephants to a commander from Greece, who was in Egypt.'

'Is this the same Egypt where this Nile is?' The minute I asked the question, I regretted it, for I knew that once started on the subject, he would go on and on about Herodotus this and Herodotus that, so I added quickly, 'What did he offer for these elephants?'

'A few brass pots,' Bwana Daudi said.

'Then they were quite right to refuse,' I said.

'They were indeed,' Bwana Daudi laughed. 'You see the matter quite right. For it took them months of hard labour to catch and tame elephants but their wives could make any number of cooking pots for nothing.'

There were many such moments with Bwana Daudi, and though they were mightily irritating at the time, for he simply would not let me get on with my work, I must confess that I soon came to miss his idle chatter. He began to sicken again. It was a sickness that made him refuse food, and his bones began to stick out like anything.

It was then, in Unyanyembe, that Amoda engaged Ntaoéka as a washerwoman. As soon as Bwana Daudi recovered, he said she was to choose one of his men. She then attached herself to Mabruki.

After this waiting, we were all relieved when the Nassick boys joined us. And what a parade they were. Their party were almost as big as the one Bwana Stanley had arrived with. The leading *askari* marched up smartly and stopped before the Bwana. They put their guns first on one side, then the other before firing into the air and saluting him.

Behind the *askari*, all dressed in European clothes, came the seven Nassick boys. I could see Ntaoéka simper and smile as she moved her eyes from one to the other. After the Nassick boys were some fifty-strong *pagazi*, and to hear them talk afterwards, the three months it took to march from Bagamoyo down to meet us in Ujiji was no pleasant experience, at least for the *pagazi*, for we soon came to learn that the Nassickers were too gentlemanly for any real work.

What was most cheering was that there were three more women to join our party, and they brought with them their children. Khadi-jah, the wife of Chowpereh, had two children with her, as did Laede, the wife of Munyasere. Binti Sumari, the wife of a *pagazi* called Adhiamberi, had one child. This made ten women, with Bahati, who was Chirango's woman before she died; Ntaoéka; and Susi's woman, Misozi.

I was that pleased to see the children, for they would make play-fellows for my own little Losi. And I was pleased to see more women, though to own the truth, with women you never know because where there are women, there is always talk.

And there was soon talk enough, that there was. Ever since they heard of Bwana Daudi's promise to me, Misozi and Ntaoéka were try-ing to argue me out of it. 'When we get there, Halima,' the Bwana said to me, he said, 'I will free you from my service and buy you a house in Zanzibar with a pretty little garden, far from the slave market.'

'Wherever have you heard,' Misozi said, 'of a bondswoman who owns a house? I do not know of any *mjakazi* who owns a house.'

'Where have you heard of such a thing?' echoed Ntaoéka. 'It is true that bondsmen can buy their own freedom and become *wahad-imu*, and then as freed *hadimu* can buy the freedom of their wives and children, but there is no such thing as a bondswoman owning a house.'

So I might never have had that house, but I know that he would have freed me in Zanzibar. He said he hated slavers, almost as much as Ntaoéka hates stinging ants. They talked on and on, he and Bwana Stanley, about how to stop the work of the slavers. But sometimes, I do not know what the difference is. The two Bwana talked like they both thought slavery must end, but Bombay told us that Bwana Stanley sometimes threatened his men with a slave stick.

And for all he talked against slavers and wept for the women of Manyuema, Bwana Daudi himself got a lot of help from the slave traders. He ate once with Tippoo Tip himself, Susi said, and with his brother Kumbakumba too, and accepted gifts of powder and guns. They were his dearest friends when he was friendless, he said.

And he bought me, yes, he did, the Bwana bought me with his own money, he bought me for Amoda after he lost his heart to me, but afterwards Amoda bothered and mithered me enough that I once ran off. After that Ntaoéka got it into her head to tell tales of me and Susi.

When I came back, the Bwana gave me a big warm cloth, this very one around my shoulders, and it is just the thing for the cold nights in these horrible swamps. But a cloth is not the same as a house, and Ntaoéka and Misozi may well have been right, for no one has ever heard of a bondswoman who owned a house. In any event, as my mother always said, you only know how many seeds a pomegranate contains when you break it open.

So there will be no house for Halima, and no garden either, pretty or otherwise, only this mad Amoda bin Mahmud, who looks at me like an angry jackal, particularly when Susi is near.

9

It is rather a minute thing to mention, and it will only be under-stood by those who have children of their own, but the cries of the little ones, in their infant sorrows, are the same in tone, at different ages, here as all over the world. We have been per-petually reminded of home and family by the wailings, which were once familiar to parental ears and heart, and felt thankful that to the sorrows of childhood our children would never have superadded the heart-rending woes of the slave trade.

David Livingstone, *The Last Journals of David Livingstone*

Not even the shadow that spread over the camp on the morning of Bwana Daudi's death could stop the children's laughter. By the time the sun rose, they were all up. Their voices were loud as they chased each other and the chickens. They were a small band of six, always together unless they were working or had been separated by some of their sudden quarrels.

My little Losi has come on very well. She chatters cheerfully as she plays, first in one tongue, then in another. No one picks up tongues faster than children do, it is a real gift, that. The only grown people I have seen with the same gift are Susi, Bombay, and Binti Sumari's man Adhiamberi, for the three of them know more tongues than I have fingers and toes to count with. Jacob Wainwright too is gifted in that way, for he picked up all sorts of tongues at his school in India.

They were pleased enough to rest these last days, the poor mites, because marching is hard on short legs. We normally would have been up long before dawn. 'We march at four a.m.,' the Bwana would have said, by which he meant that we were to wake the cockerels.

It is hot work, marching is, best done when the ground is cool and there is still dew on the leaves and grass. Marching days began with what the Bwana called the reveille, which meant Majwara beat the drum from tent to tent or hut to hut to rouse the men, then Ntaoéka, Misozi, Binti Sumari, Laede, and the other women would have joined me in lighting the fires, then we would have broken the night's fast with a meal, then on the road we would have gone, until: 'It is eight a.m.,' cried the Bwana, by which he meant we would break to eat before going again and resting when the sun was high in the sky.

As we travelled, the children skipped ahead to walk with Majwara, they were that fond of him. They would have run ahead, too, were it not for the constant rebukes from the caravan leaders. Amoda has now frightened them into behaving: if you go ahead of the *kiran-gozi*, he has told them, the slavers will get you and take you to the coast and you will walk a long time unless you drop stone dead and you will never be seen again.

It is a powerful admonition. Indeed, they like to play a game they call Kumbakumba, where they pretend to be Kumbakumba and Tippoo Tip, the slavers that we all fear the most. They divide themselves into two groups, one made up of the raiders, the other the raided. The raiders come upon the raided and mimic the sound of the guns as they say, 'Tippoo Tip, Tippoo Tip, Tippoo Tip.' Then they yell, 'Kumbakumba!' and make to grab one of the raided. The captured are then marched off and the whole thing ends with a shout of 'Kumbakumba!' and much shrieking laughter. Their quarrels are mainly over who is to be the raiders. No one ever wants to play the captured, they only grudgingly accept it so that they can be the captors in their turn.

That must be what Bwana Daudi meant when he said to me in Unyanyembe that the children do not act like children, but play at being grown. Tippoo Tip and Kumbakumba were born slaves, they were. Brothers too, they say, born to the same mother. And now look at them. Just like the children, they would rather capture than be captured.

I was about to call to Laede to help me with the water when Chirango came up to me. He gave an effusive greeting. I looked at him without saying a word.

Even before the whipping by Amoda for which he blames me, he was a troublesome one, always up to something. After his first woman, Bahati, died, he showed not the slightest care, and instead he got another woman, Kaniki, she is called. He also bought a young girl and boy for three strings of beads when we stopped at Nyamwezi. The girl was to be his concubine when she had sprouted breasts, he said, and the boy his servant. His woman Kaniki made sure that they did not join the other children in play.

It was not like it had been with Bwana Stanley's man Bombay and his boy Nasibu. When he arrived with Bwana Stanley, Bombay had Nasibu carry his gun for him. He was no higher than Losi. I thought he was Bombay's son at first, for the poor mite would not be separated from him, and often fell asleep with his head on Bombay's knee. 'Son,' he said, 'well I have sons enough, but they are with their mothers. Nasibu is my slave.'

Jacob Wainwright, who had been listening, frowned and said, 'Slave? Why do you need a slave?'

'I don't need him at all,' Bombay laughed. 'If he was not my slave he would have been with another of Bwana Stanley's men, and a bad master he would have had in him too. His mother sold him for a piece of cloth and some yams. She wanted him saved, she said, for the village was starving and another of her children was already dead, but the man she sold him to was hard on the boy and so Bwana Stanley said I could buy him. Got him dearly too, three long strings of red beads I paid for him.'

He saw Jacob's face and said, 'Look, what can I do with him, he has to come with me until we get back to the coast. Then I will put him with one of my women and she can be his mother while he grows.'

Chirango had not taken the children as Bombay had taken Nasibu. He had taken them for himself. And he had had the luck of an uncaught thief, at first, for Bwana Daudi had been ill again then, and did not see what was up. As soon as he recovered his health and discovered what Chirango had done, his anger was something terrible.

He was in a proper rage, the Bwana was, especially when Chirango made things worse by saying Bwana Daudi had a slave of his own, and pointed to Majwara.

'I pay the boy,' the Bwana said, 'I pay him for his services, but what you wish to do is to enslave children.' Chirango tried to argue that the children would be paid in food because they would have starved, but Bwana Daudi stopped the caravan for five days so that Gardner and Chowpereh could take the children back to their village in Nyamwezi.

He only has his eye on what benefits him, Chirango does. So when I saw him coming to me, I was immediately on my guard. He was licking his lips as usual. I have never in my life seen a more restless, twitchy person. His lips twitch, his fingers twitch, even his one eye twitches, darting here and there.

64

He is one of those disgusting chewers of that foul *miraa* leaf that some of the *pagazi* also call *quat*. There are more than a few chewers among the *pagazi*. I can count them with three hands, but he is the worst among them. It is a filthy habit, this chewing and chewing, because it means they must always be spitting out what they chew. It is spit, spit, spit all day long.

There is no *miraa* to be bought this far inland, and for that I thank the Prophet, upon His names be blessings, and so Chirango licks and licks his lips like a hungry man salivating over a feast. And when his lips are not twitching for *miraa*, his fingers are constantly moving, as though he is plucking at that instrument of his, even when he is not holding it.

A *njari* he calls it. I saw many instruments at the Liwali's house, but I never saw anything the likes of what Chirango plays. It is a big round calabash, painted with black and white patterns on the outside. On the inside is the instrument itself, a small bit of wood with long metal fingers attached to one end, sticking out like Bwana Daudi's poor teeth. It is these metal teeth that he plays, and they make the most melancholy sounds when he plucks at them. The sounds make the heart ache and make one think of long-ago, far-off things.

And to add to the licking of the lips and twitching of the fingers, Chirango's one eye flickers here and there and everywhere, as though it wants to see all that the other eye cannot see.

Since what happened with his eye, I have found it hard to look him squarely in the face. Whenever I have had to talk to him, which is not often, and for that I count my mercies, I look at a place just over his shoulder. He too seems to find it hard to look at me, and speaks as though to someone behind me. A right pair of legless crabs we must look.

'Chirango hears that they will bury the Bwana here,' he said.

'Then you hear more than I do,' I said, over his shoulder.

'Chirango is sure there will be a reward for his body,' he said, over mine.

'What do you mean?' I said.

'If we carry him back to the coast, there will be a reward. He was an important man in his kingdom. Look at how all the men of his kingdom wrote to another kingdom to have Bwana Stanley sent to look for him. He was a big man, a very big man, where he was from. Chirango is sure that there will be a fat purse for those who bring him back to the coast.'

'Is that so,' I said.

I glanced at him. He did not meet my eye but licked his lips.

'Indeed,' he said. 'Though Chirango does not have all his rights, he has communed with the men with white skin and knows that they would think greatly of all those who aid the Bwana on his way home.'

That is how he always talked, as though he were another person entirely, as though he were someone as grand as a *vizir* or maybe even the Liwali himself, and not the lip-licking Chirango before me, the bandit thief.

And I had almost forgotten about his claims.

Since he chose to stay behind when Bwana Stanley returned to the coast, Chirango has told anyone who will listen that he is the sultan of a land down in the south, of a land between two large rivers. His true name is the Chirango Kirango Mutapa Something-or-Other, only he cannot claim his rights fully because some people from a kingdom close to that of the Bwana, a race of people called the Portuguese, the same people who they say lived in Zanzibar before the Shirazi, drove his family out of their land near the Zambezi, near Shupanga, where Susi is from.

The same thing that happened to the Mwinyi Mkuu, the great

66

Lord of the Swahili in Zanzibar, he said, had happened to his family. They had been driven out of their own land. Their Sultan, this Mutapa, had been shrunk into a small chief, smaller even than the Mwinyi Mkuu, who was the great Lord of the Swahili, and had been left with no land at all to govern.

Well, I know the Mwinyi Mkuu, of course I do, all of Zanzibar does. My mother cooked for him, didn't she, a laughing man with pot-black skin who sometimes had business with the Liwali. On that much, Chirango is right. He is supposed to be the real sultan in Zanzibar, they say, but first the Shirazi, then these Portuguese people, then the Omanis came and his sultanate got smaller and smaller, or so they say. Well, his sultanate may be small but his appetite is as big as any I have seen, I will tell you that for nothing. Demolished a whole chicken by himself, he did, the night my mother cooked for him when he dined with the Liwali. Had room for my mother's best lamb too, which she cooked in its own juices ever so slowly and served with limes, raisins, and cardamom, and washed it all down with gallons and gallons of tamarind juice.

Susi and Amoda laughed when Chirango told them about his claims. Susi said to me later that there was indeed talk in his homeland that there had been such a kingdom as Chirango described, it was called the Mwenemutapa, or some such, and its people had built a great city that was now in ruins, though no one in his homeland had ever seen it, but he did not believe that anyone as wretched as Chirango could be part of it.

When Chirango had heard that the Bwana's wife had been buried on the river called Zambezi, he had muttered that she had no right to be buried on his land without his permission. From that moment, the others called him Mwinyi Mdogo, or the Pagazi Prince.

'And how many loads will the Mwinyi Mdogo carry today?'

'Could the Pagazi Prince pass the firewood?'

'Make way for Mwinyi Mdogo.'

'If the Pagazi Prince would be so kind as to make way for us lesser mortals.'

As Chirango stood before me, I said nothing further, and he likewise remained silent before moving off. As soon as Amoda broke off from the others, I rushed to find out what had been decided.

'We are going to ask for permission from Chitambo,' he said, 'so that we can bury him today. Susi and I and those of our faith all agree that it is fitting in the eyes of Allah that we should bury him before the sunset, in the normal way.'

'What?' I said. 'And you will bury him with his head towards Mecca too, will you?'

'What do you know about these things?' Amoda said.

'He was no Mohammedan, which you know as well as I, Amoda,' I said. 'Why must he be buried according to a faith that was not his? I may be a slave but I know as well as you that the Bwana was no Mohammedan. You know as well as I that he was a Kristuman.'

'And what do you know about Kristumen?'

'Nothing at all, but I know that they have a different god, just as those lazy sepoys who used to march with the Bwana have their Hindu gods. Bombay told me all about it. The gods all have lots of legs and arms everywhere and heads like those of elephants and monkeys, and it is not right to bury a man in the manner of a faith that is not his. You may as well be done with it and burn him until he is all ash, like a Hinduman.'

Amoda clenched his fists. 'You heard this from Bombay, did you? I knew it. All this time I knew it. I will Bombay you if you are not careful. I will Bombay you until you have no mouth left to talk about Hindu gods and Hindumen. Did you lie with him? Did you lie with him like you want to do with Susi? Or have you already lain with him? Bombay indeed.'

'Like I would lie with Bombay,' I said. 'All those teeth. All I say is, how do you bury a man out of his own land and out of his faith? And why would Chitambo agree to the burial of a man who is a stranger to him, not just a stranger, but a white stranger too, a *mzungu* who will bring who knows what sorts of spirits from across the waters?'

'This is where he died,' said Amoda.

I could tell from the stubborn set of his mouth that he did not wish to discuss it anymore. And sure enough, he added, 'You are just a bondswoman, anyway, what do you know of burials? This is not a *mjakazi* matter. This free men's business.'

When Amoda says to me that I am only a woman and a slave, it is a sure sign that he is on ground that is shaky. I can be stubborn myself if I put my mind to it, oh, yes, I can. Amoda is just lucky that I am a gentle, placid type, and not at all the quarrelsome sort who likes to talk and talk until your head aches, because I could make his life hard if I put my mind to it, that I could.

'His soul will not rest easy, I can tell you that,' I said.

Amoda turned to walk away.

'And then there is the money,' I said.

That stopped him.

'What money?' he said.

I had him. If there is any man who loves money more than Amoda, he is yet to be born. I repeated what Chirango had said. 'If he can be brought to the coast, there is sure to be a large purse waiting for the whole party. Only the other day, I said to Misozi, perhaps he has been wandering around because he burned his home and could not go back, but no, he is a great man in his own land after all, he is a *mganga* more skilled than most doctors. Just look at Bwana Stanley, coming all this way from another land with his bathtub and champagne and strange food and whatnot to fetch him. And all those letters he brought, from the important men of his own land. If he can be brought to the coast, with all his papers, there will be a large reward.

'And this beginning of the river that he wants to find, this Nile beginning, there will surely be others who want to find it too. Munyasere has talked of other men of his land who also seek the same place. They will want to know what knowledge he wrote down in his papers.'

I was about to mention Bwana Stanley, and the other Bwana that Bombay had worked for, not the bad-tempered one whose name I cannot recall, but the Bwana Speke that Bombay talked about all the time. 'Before I die,' he said more than once, 'I want to go to England to see Bwana Speke's grave.'

But I knew that further mention of Bombay would only enrage Amoda, so I only said, 'As you say, I am only a slave and what do I know of these things. This is the business of free men.'

I looked down and pretended not to see Amoda looking closely at me before he moved off without a word. I went to find Ntaoéka, Misozi, Laede, and the other women, who were gathering firewood. On the way, I met Losi, who ran into my arms. I threw her up to the air and bounced her. Her shrieks and giggles accompanied me until I reached the women.

10

When Ntaoéka chose to follow us rather than go to the coast,
I did not like to have a fine-looking woman among us un-
attached, and proposed that she should marry one of my three
worthies . . . but she smiled at the idea. Chuma was evidently
too lazy ever to get a wife; the other two were contemptible in
appearance, and she has a good presence and is buxom . . .
Circumstances led to the other women wishing Ntaoéka mar-
ried, and on my speaking to her again she consented. I have
noticed her ever since working hard from morning to night:
the first up in the cold mornings, making fire and hot water,
pounding, carrying water, wood, sweeping, cooking.

David Livingstone, *The Last Journals of David Livingstone*

By the time I reached the women, the news that the Bwana was to
be buried that day had spread throughout the camp. As I joined
them, Ntaoéka and Misozi were already discussing the news with
the others.

'Is it not strange that they want him buried here?' Ntaoéka said.
'And his children never to see his grave?'

'He will not rest easy,' Misozi said, and launched into one of her
monstrous tales of *shetani* ghosts. 'Those who are buried away from
home walk abroad,' she said. 'They know no rest and shriek and whisper their discontent from trees and bushes, they cry out from the soil
itself. They plague travellers and beg them to take them home.

'That is why Zanzibar is full of *shetani* spirits,' she added. 'All those dead slaves, buried away from home. And when they die at sea they become *vembwigo* and *chunusi*, sea ghosts that haunt sailors and sail in ghostly dhows.'

Once Misozi gets on the subject of ghosts and spirits there is no stopping her. When we gathered at night to tell stories it was this kind of story she mostly enjoyed. I had to cut her off before she got too carried away.

'I have already talked to Amoda,' I said, 'I have told him they cannot bury him here. And you, Misozi, you must talk to Susi. You tackle Mabruki, Ntaoéka, and Laede will talk to Munyasere. Khadijah and Binti Sumari will talk to their men too. If we get the caravan leaders to agree, then the other men will follow.'

Misozi, as always, was slow to catch on, but Ntaoéka, Laede, and I looked at each other in perfect understanding. This is how we normally managed things when we wanted something. We talked it over among ourselves first, then with our men separately, until they believed that our thinking was their own.

I had lain with three men before Amoda, yes, I had, and all but him were my masters, for though the Bwana bought me, he did not buy me for himself. What I can tell you is that a man's mind is most open in those moments when his seed is spent. It does not always work, but when it does, they find themselves saying, I have decided that things are to be this way or that way, and though it was us who made them decide that way, we know better than to let on.

I was about to say that I had already talked to Amoda, but there was no time for the usual subtleties to work with him, when we were interrupted by the sound of Majwara's drum.

We looked at each other in surprise. Majwara normally sounded the drum to summon the men together to talk of what needed to be done for each day's excursion. Since we had arrived at Chitambo, there had been no meetings because the Bwana had been too ill to give instructions. Instead, the caravan leaders had simply approached the men they needed for a given task.

As soon as he finished beating his drum, Majwara said, 'We are all to gather under the *mpundu* tree.'

Without further talk, I moved with the other women to the clearing he had indicated, under the tree some of the men called the *mpundu* and others the *mvula*, depending on the tongues they spoke. The men were already arranging themselves in their usual groups. Nearest to the tree, protecting themselves under its shade, Susi, Chuma, and Amoda sat with Chowpereh and Munyasere, the other caravan leaders. Mabruki sat close to them.

Next to them were the Nassickers. Further away, keeping a space between them and the Nassickers, the lesser *pagazi* made the largest group. There were more than fifty men in all, sitting in the sun out of the shade of the tree. I could see Chirango right at the back. The women and I joined the men and took our place near the *pagazi*. I drew Losi next to me and, as I listened, concentrated on plaiting her hair.

Amoda stood and said, 'You know what befell us this morning. We are to decide what to do with his body.'

'But we have already decided,' said Susi. 'What is there to decide again? He must be buried as quickly as possible, and for that reason, we must not delay in sending word to Chitambo, that we may bury him on this ground.'

'We must be careful how we approach Chitambo,' said Chuma. 'He could be vengeful because we have brought death to his land.'

In the murmuring that followed, I moved my hands from Losi's head, rose to indicate that I wished to speak, and said, 'What

Chuma says is wise. Chitambo will not thank you for bringing a dead stranger to his land. What spirits will he bring here, he will ask. The only thing to do is to carry Bwana Daudi to the coast so that he can be put on a dhow that will carry him to his own land.'

The murmur that started at my words grew into a rumbling as the men talked among each other. Amoda gave me a look but as he made no move to restrain me, I took this as a sign to go on. I turned to the group of Nassickers and spoke directly to them. 'He must be buried in the way of his faith,' I said. 'You will none of you sleep easy at night, I can tell you, if you do not bury him in the ways of his people.'

'That is enough, Halima,' Amoda said.

And indeed, I could see I had said enough.

I sat back down.

The Nassickers were now murmuring among themselves. Jacob Wainwright was looking more and more thoughtful. Chowpereh was speaking in a low voice to Susi, while, amid the inferior *pagazi*, Ali and Wadi Saféné were speaking furiously and making agitated gestures. Chirango, I noticed, was the only person who appeared calm. He had a curious little smile on his face and was looking into the distance, as though the matter was of no concern to him.

Amoda called on Wadi Saféné, who said he must be buried at once. 'Jacob Wainwright speaks his tongue, he knows his religion. Why not bury him in accordance with his faith, right here in Chitambo's village?'

'I am no cleric,' Jacob said. 'But I long for the glorious day when I am called into His reverend service. Certainly, I hope to wear the collar one day, but for now it is not fit. As my brothers in Christ can confirm to all of you who are not of the faith, and as the Doctor himself could have explained, to be buried is what is called a sacra-

74

ment, and one that I cannot deliver, for I am not yet ordained. And, moreover, it will not be a proper burial, for he will not be buried on ground that is consecrated.'

'What does that mean?' asked Ntaoéka.

'And what is this collar that you talk of?' said Misozi. 'Surely you cannot want to be a slave again and wear the sign of servitude?'

In an impatient voice, Jacob said, 'I have explained already, Misozi, that clerics wear a cloth collar around their neck. It is not the same as the collar of enslavement.'

In a more gentle voice, he turned to Ntaoéka and said, 'To be buried on ground that is consecrated means that he must be buried within the grounds of a place that is blessed, like a church.'

'Then there is no question,' Ntaoéka said. 'Jacob is right. We cannot bury him here.'

She said his name in a simpering, coy manner that made me look at her sharply. Her eyes met Jacob's and she looked down with a flutter of her lashes. Jacob looked down, then up again at her. The lump on his throat moved as he swallowed. I may not know about maps and books and stars, but I know what it means when a man looks at a woman like that. I glanced at Mabruki to see what he would make of it, but he had seen nothing.

'But the Reverend Wainwright said to us that all ground is hallowed where a good man lies,' said Matthew Wellington. 'Think of all those poor souls who are buried at sea.'

'It is what he always said he wanted for himself,' Chuma said. 'He said he wanted to be buried in any place that he fell, he said. It was certain that Africa would claim him, as it had his wife. She lies in Shupanga at the mouth of the Zambezi.'

From the back of the group of the inferior *pagazi*, Chirango coughed and made a movement with his arm. Amoda ignored him.

Before he could call on anyone else, I said, 'He wanted to be buried in a swamp like this, did he? And you yourselves, you would want to be buried in a swamp like this, would you, with no burial rites? How long did it take for us to get this far from Unyanyembe? And what about his children?'

'Women always talk of children,' said Chowpereh.

'As Chuma said, his wife is buried in Shupanga,' Susi said. But his face was looking troubled, and I noticed that he and Chuma were eyeing each other. I pressed the advantage.

'That is even more reason why he should not be buried here,' I said. 'Ntaoéka is right. Think of his children. How will they be able to visit the grave of their own father?'

'It is too much,' Ntaoéka said. She was now breathing loudly, in shallow and quick gasps, and her voice was trembling. 'It is too much. They have never seen the ground over their mother's bones. And now they will never see where their father lies.'

She raised her voice in a wailing lament.

Ntaoéka can always be trusted to burst into tears over the smallest thing. Even a spilled pot of water or a fire that won't burn the right way is guaranteed to set her off. It is how she escapes censure even when she causes trouble. That day in Unyanyembe when the Bwana rebuked me, and I ran away, it was she who had been at fault. I beat her because she had been making eyes at Amoda, but she had immediately burst into tears and the Bwana had taken pity on her and turned his wrath on me instead. That is why I ran off; I could not bear that she should receive all the comfort when she was the cause of everything.

This time, her tears were most welcome. I raised my voice to join her, nudging Misozi as I did so. She looked at me blankly. Laede, Khadijah, and Binti Sumari were quicker and raised their voices too. Misozi finally caught on and added her voice. My poor little Losi was startled by my sudden weeping and held my face in her hands to comfort me. I held her close to me. All talk was suspended until we had spent ourselves. In the silence that followed, Chirango coughed again.

'Have you something to say?' Amoda barked out.

'Chirango has nothing at all to say,' he said. 'What can Chirango say to you; to you, the wise and enlightened, the ones who have swallowed the knowledge of the white man without being choked by it, and who wear his clothes and speak his tongue, for he is only Chirango of the One Eye, though others know him as the Chirango Kirango, the prince of Dzimbahwe, descendant of Nyatsimba the Salt Gatherer of the Great Houses of Stone and father of the great prophetess Nyamhita Nehanda.

'Though Chirango may have higher claims than most, he has only this one eye that you all see – and we all know how it is that Chirango only has the one eye, though the less said on that subject the better – and so all that he can say in his now-humble position is that Bwana Daudi was a great man in his own land, a great man in ours too, for he held the whip over those brought low like Chirango and blinded them too, and so, being a great man, this whip wielder, he must lie with other great men, though it be us humble ones who take him thither.

'And it is as well to take him thither, for who knows what blame will be assigned to us should we leave this country without him. Who knows what accusations, what foul talk of neglect, and, per-chance, even murder, will follow us always. For when men report a death in a far-off land there is always talk talk, much talk. And if you should all get a large reward for bringing him home, well, Chirango says it is no more than you deserve for such a loyal service.'

At the mention of a reward, the men began to talk excitedly.

'Reward?' said Chowpereh 'What does he mean by reward?' He looked to Amoda as he spoke, rather than to Chirango himself, for an explanation. Amoda made no reply but merely looked at Chirango, who licked his lips.

When Amoda made no objection, he said, 'Chirango means only that you may get something for your troubles, and why not, after all the work that you will have done in the service of a great man.'

'That should have nothing to do with it,' Jacob Wainwright said. 'That should be no reason at all. What we do if we do anything must be done because we are men of honour, because we are men of God, doing that which is pleasing in the sight of God.'

Chuma spoke up. It was not often that he and Jacob agreed, but now he said, 'Jacob is right. We served him to the end of his days, and to the end we serve him.'

Majwara stood up. He shook like a leaf in high wind, poor thing, and no wonder, for I do not ever recall his speaking at these meetings; as the *kirangozi*, his job was to beat the drum to call them, not speak at them. His voice, not yet a man's, but not quite a child's, was low, but every word was clear. 'I will take him to the coast myself if you will not,' he said. 'He ransomed me from slavery. He cured me when I lay ill. I will take him myself if you will not do it.'

In the silence that followed, Chuma put his arm on the boy's trembling shoulders.

'But how will we carry him?' Amoda said. 'He will begin to smell by the end of the day, it will be worse than carrying a fish.'

I knew then that I had won through.

But I also knew what Amoda meant. In a matter of hours, the doctor would be like those poor ones who fell dead at the slave market in Zanzibar. He would blow up and all the air and water inside him would burst and his skin crack, and the worms come out of him, and, oh, the smell. Had his been the body of a slave who had fallen at the market, I can tell you that the smell would have been so strong that only the dogs would have approached to tear his flesh.

It was the word 'fish' that gave me the idea. It is not for nothing that I am a cook, I can tell you that.

'We will smoke him,' I said.

'Smoke him?' said Jacob, horrified.

The men looked at me as though I was mad.

'That's right, smoke him,' I said with purpose. 'Just as you would a fish. We could have preserved him in oil, if we had oil, but he would be too heavy. We could also salt him, if we had enough salt. Or you could lay him in the sun and dry him that way. Yes, that's the best way. Split him open. Take everything out, and dry him in the sun. Like spices on the Liwali's drying roof. He would be light enough to carry then. I know all about preserving flesh, don't I, being that I am the daughter—'

'—of the cook in the Liwali's kitchen . . . ,' tittered Ntaoéka.

'. . . who was also the Liwali's *suria* . . . ,' added Misozi.

'. . . but did not bear him a child to become *umm al-walad* . .'

'. . . and was his favourite though she was dark as midnight.'

She and Ntaoéka clapped hands to each other and laughed. That is the problem with these two. Just when you think you are together, they do something like that. I was just making up my mind whether I should say something cutting to them both when Amoda said, 'Have you lost your minds, you women? Is this the time?'

Susi smiled in my direction and said, 'Halima is right. It would take a great deal of drying, but it could be done.'

Carus Farrar said, 'And what do we do with the viscera, with his heart and his inside parts? We can't dry it all, surely.'

'We bury his heart here,' said Susi. He was smiling now. 'That is the perfect solution. We prepare his body for transport but bury his heart and innards here. And if he should ever visit us and ask us why we carried him away, we will say, we left you where you died.'

'And if he should visit us and say why did you leave me there, we will say, we brought you home,' added Wadi Saféné.

Susi smiled. 'Yes. It is right that we bury his heart here and carry his bones to his own land. Halima has presented us the perfect solution.'

I smiled to hear his approval but quickly wiped the smile off my face when I saw Amoda give me the eye of thunder. I pretended to admire the pattern I had made of Losi's plaited hair. Amoda's dark looks aside, I must say that my mind was not at rest at the thought of leaving any part of Bwana Daudi's body in these horrible swamps, but I knew better than to go on after I had carried my way. And that is how the men decided to bear his body to Zanzibar.

II

Successive crowds of people came to gaze. My appearance and
acts often cause a burst of laughter; sudden standing up pro-
duces a flight of women and children. To prevent peeping into
the hut which I occupy, and making the place quite dark, I
do my writing in the verandah. Chitané, the poodle dog, the
buffalo-calf, and our only remaining donkey are greeted with
the same amount of curiosity and laughter-exciting comment
as myself.

David Livingstone, *The Last*
Journals of David Livingstone

Sure enough, it was that empty vessel of a Misozi who caused the
catastrophe that almost befell us. When she finally understood what
was to be done, she clucked and fussed that the whole thing was
impossible, that we were all mad to even think of it, and that we
would come to regret it.

'Whoever heard,' she said, 'of a group of people marching from
place to place with a dead body?'

The meeting broke up soon after the decision had been made. But
before it broke up, the caravan leaders gave us jobs in our groups.
Bwana Daudi could not be prepared where he lay, Chowpereh said,
and Amoda said we were to build him a new hut. Chitambo should
be kept in ignorance of Bwana Daudi's passing, they all agreed. 'For

if Chitambo finds out,' Susi said, 'he will inflict upon us a fine so heavy that our means will be crippled, and we will not be able to pay our way to the coast.'

Well, Susi should have told his own woman that. The caravan leaders went off to find the best place to build a hut in which to prepare Bwana Daudi's body while the lower *pagazi* were sent with axes to cut wood. Another group were sent off to collect boughs and saplings.

'As for you women, Halima,' Susi said, 'we have need for more salt.' Wadi Saféné had salt that he had bought from Kalunganjovu's land, he said, but it would not be enough. The women and I were to go to the village to trade cloth and beads for as much salt as we could get.

We were to be careful, Susi said, not to raise suspicions. That is why I asked Kaniki and Laede to stay behind with Losi and the other children in case they followed us. Kaniki is Chirango's woman, and seems to exist only to serve him, for she rarely mixes with the rest of the women, living in his shadow and carrying his load for him, much like the two slave children he had once that the Bwana made him send back.

The children wanted to come with us, as they usually did, but I was afraid that they might let something slip. Ha! The children, indeed!

I should have known that it was not the children but Misozi whom we needed to take care about, for though she was a grown woman, she seemed unable to keep secrets clutched within her heart.

The women and I went straight to the Chief's main wife to pay our respects. She was surrounded by her own women. They chatted and laughed as they plaited their hair and, oh, the beautiful patterns they made. I thought one or two would look fine on Losi and

82

resolved to try them out as soon as I had undone the pattern I had just plaited.

They spoke another tongue, Chitambo's people; we had a few words here and there that were the same, but we had met on first going there a young woman who had, in her former years as a girl, been taken captive by the Mazitu, who had sold her to Kumbakumba's men. She escaped from Tabora and returned after three years. She spoke our tongue well enough, and it was through her that our dealings with Chitambo's women were conducted.

'Your master,' said the Chief's wife through the young woman, 'how did he sleep?'

'He slept well enough,' I said.

The young woman explained what I had said.

I was about to say more when I saw in the near distance a figure that I recognised. It was Chirango. He was talking to Chitambo's medicine man. I knew it was he, for we had all seen him, hadn't we, on the day we arrived, he was hard not to notice, for he wore different types of animal skin and had a face like he had lived forever. I was wondering what Chirango was doing with him but I soon had to pay attention to Misozi, who said, 'Well, yes,' then gave a shrill giggle.

I gave her a look that was full of meaning but she continued to giggle nervously. The young woman looked at Misozi so sharply that it forced me to add, 'He sleeps well enough.'

'Well enough, well enough,' echoed Misozi.

Then she added, 'He sleeps so well that he will not get up today.'

'What do you mean, will not get up today? Is he so very unwell?'

'He is well, well,' I said. In my eagerness to cover up for Misozi, my words tumbled out before I could think them. 'I mean he is not well, but he sleeps well, he sleeps very well.'

Misozi's eyes were now darting all over the place, like black ants that had been disturbed by the lifting of the stone under which they rested. 'It is as Halima says. He sleeps the sleep of the dead. Oh!' As soon as she said the dread word out loud, she clapped her hand over her mouth.

'Is your master dead in our land?' the woman said. She spoke in a loud voice to Chitambo's wife. They talked quickly in their own tongue. Chitambo's wife said something to the young woman and before we could stop her, she had run in the direction of the Chief's hut, leaving the Chief's wife to stare at us as though we were ourselves the Bwana's corpse.

Ntaoéka and I mumbled our goodbyes as they tried to stop us. We beat a steady retreat to warn the others, Ntaoéka and I scolding Misozi all the way. She was now silent as anything, a state that, as I said to her, would have suited us all very well just moments ago, but oh, no, not Misozi, she is never one to say nothing when the wrong thing can be said. In our hurry, I clean forgot all about seeing Chirango talking with Chitambo's medicine man.

The Chief's party were hard on our heels, for no sooner had we dismayed the others with the terrible news of Chitambo's certain knowledge of Bwana Daudi's death than we heard the Chief's retinue. And, in a matter of moments, we were face-to-face with Chitambo.

12

The laugh of the women is brimful of mirth. It is no simpering smile, nor senseless loud guffaw; but a merry ringing laugh, the sound of which does one's heart good. One begins with ha, Héé, then comes the chorus in which all join, Haééé! and they end by slapping their hands together, giving the spectator the idea of great heartiness. When first introduced to a chief, if we have observed a joyous twinkle of the eye accompanying his laugh, we have always set him down as a good fellow, and we have never been disappointed in him afterwards.

David Livingstone, *Narrative of an Expedition to the Zambezi and Its Tributaries*

I must say that he surprised us all greatly, that fat Chitambo. The first thing he did when he reached our group was to throw back his great big head with a great bellow. His people echoed his weeping. Then he turned to Chuma and said, in his terrible manner of speaking our tongue, 'Why you not tell me truth? I know that your master, he die this night. Why you not let me know? Why you afraid of me? I am good friend, yes, good, good friend to your Bwana, and good friend to you.'

Susi and Chuma prostrated themselves before the Chief. All the men got down on one knee in the way that they had seen Chitambo receive his people and begged him for forgiveness. Chitambo made a sign to raise them and sighed. 'Do not fear no longer,' he said. 'I too, I travel. I travel and more than once I go to coast, before road destroy by Mazitu. I go to coast and I know that you have no bad thinking, because death, it is bad, yes, and many time it follow the travellers on the journeys.'

The men clapped in gratitude. They played it well, I will give them that. They told him of their intention to prepare the body and to take it with them. They would not trouble them with Bwana Daudi's corpse, they said, they respected him far too much to inflict on him and his people, and on the spirits of this place, the body of a stranger.

As Chitambo listened, his big face showed great surprise. He consulted his own men, and there followed a furious conversation between them in their own tongue.

After a tense few minutes, he turned to our group and said, 'We talk,' he said, 'we talk and we agree and we say that we want that you bury him here. You afraid that I no give yes, but you no worry, I no give no. I go to coast before Mazitu they destroy road. I see many men. I too, I travel. I know that not all men the same.'

I was dismayed to hear this. Had I not said, only that morning, that Chitambo would not permit the Doctor's burial on his land? And now here he was, about to agree! But I need not have worried. The men had made up their minds, and though Chitambo tried to persuade them, they were firm in their resolve.

That being so, he led the men to higher ground where they could prepare Bwana Daudi's body. Chitambo then went back to his village but said he would soon be back with all of his people. They needed to prepare themselves for the mourning rites.

Misozi was now all smiles. 'There is nothing to fear,' she said, 'you see how he is.' And to hear her talk, it was as though it was she and she alone who had secured for us all Chitambo's grace and favour.

But I will say that it was certainly much easier to work without fearing what the Chief might get to know and hear. We could be ourselves again, and talk as we worked and let the children run where they pleased.

In this spirit of freedom, it did not take long for the *pagazi* to build a new hut on the place Chitambo had suggested. I will say this for my man Amoda, he is not afraid of hard work. There are caravan leaders like Munyasere and Chowpereh who simply stand and give orders, but Amoda is in there with the men, doing and commanding at the same time. Under his direction, the men made a good job of the hut, though it was less a hut than it was a pen. It was open at the top to allow in the sun and air, but closed off and protected at the sides so that no wild animal could get in.

Later that morning, Susi, with Toufiki Ali, Adhiamberi, Wadi Saféné, and a few other *pagazi*, paid a visit to Chitambo to ask to cut trees. When they came back, it was to tell us that Chitambo had decreed that the rest of that day should be set aside for all his people to mourn Bwana Daudi. There would be no planting that day and no other work. Instead, as he had promised, all his people were to come back for the official mourning. They arrived soon after that. Chitambo was no Liwali but was very grand-looking, I will give him that. He wore a large cloth of red that covered him from shoulder to ankle and flowed in his wake as his people walked behind him.

And his men! They looked like they were going to war, with their bows, arrows, and spears. They had fearsome white markings on their faces and chests. Their women sent out loud piercing sounds that were between keening and ululating. They made my blood run cold, that they did. Then came the drummers, beating away, while the women keened, then the whole group broke out in wailing lamentation.

Not to be outdone, our *askari* fired their guns into the air. They would have fired more rounds but for the raised arm of Amoda; they were having such a time of it that without his warning, they may have fired all their powder.

After the guns were fired, the people sat down. From among the crowd rose a man who wore a skirt of skins and feathers, and anklets of rattles all down his legs. He was the official mourner. Turning to Susi, he asked where Bwana Daudi had been born, how many planting seasons Bwana Daudi had lived, how many were the children he had left, and what were the names of his ancestors. Susi answered how he could.

The man then kicked his legs about, gave a loud ululation as he turned on the spot, kicked his legs about again, and sang something that sounded like: '*Lélo kwa Engérésé, muana sisi oa konda. Tu tamb' tamb' Engérésé, muana sisi oa konda.*'

Our children were simply entranced. Susi said to our party that this meant, 'Today the Englishman is dead. He had different hair from ours. Come and mourn the Englishman. He had different hair from ours.'

The mourner danced a bit more, shook his rattles, repeated his chant, and asked for payment. Chuma gave him two strings of beads.

Well, really. Two strings, just for that! I have never seen the likes of it. And why was he asking about birthplaces and planting years and ancestors and children and such and such if all he could find to talk about was his hair! The Liwali had poets that could have done more than this. If that is how they mourn people in these swamps, I said to Misozi and Ntaoéka, then we can't leave them soon enough, I can tell you that for nothing.

The only good thing that came out of the proceedings is that it gave the children a new game. '*Tamb' tamb' Engérésé*', they sang out the rest of the day. '*Muana sisi oa konda*', they chanted as they shook imaginary rattles on their legs.

Jacob Wainwright said Bwana Daudi would not have liked being called an English because he was a Scottish, but I don't know what he meant by that because the two *bwana*, Stanley and Bwana Daudi, spoke this same English tongue. I said as much to him, but he said well, the other *bwana* was Americano and not English.

I was about to say that I knew he was Americano, like the cloth, and to ask what he meant by Scottish when Ntaoéka said, 'But how do we get out of the swamps then? Because what Misozi said is right. It will be hard to travel with a dead body. People will think we are witches who eat the dead. They will say we are witches. Imagine that, they will say we are witches.'

Her breath was shallow and her voice high. As I shook my head at her manner, I noticed that Jacob Wainwright was looking at her as though he was in great pain.

Susi said, 'That is just what some of the men are saying, that it will not do to be seen to be carrying a body through strange villages.'

Forgetting for a minute how Jacob Wainwright was looking at another man's woman, I said, 'There is nothing for it but to disguise his body. Consider how best to make him up like a package for travel.'

Susi looked up and down at me and said, 'With that head of yours it is a pity you are a slave and a woman.'

I smiled, but wiped the smile off when I saw Ntaoéka giving me a knowing look. I wanted to tell Susi that I would be a slave for not much time longer, with my master dead and no inheritor to claim me, but I held my tongue. For I knew not what he might, in an unguarded moment, say to Amoda.

13

The nightly custom of gathering around the camp fire, and entertaining one another with stories, began ... after Sabadu, a page of King Mtesa, had astonished his hearers with the legend of the 'Blameless Priest'. Our circle was free to all, and was frequently well attended; for when it was seen that the more accomplished narrators were suitably rewarded, and that there was a great deal of amusement to be derived, few could resist the temptation to approach and listen, unless fatigue or illness prevented them.

Henry Morton Stanley, *My Dark Companions
and Their Strange Stories*

And, if you will believe it, even after all that, they still would not listen. I told them, didn't I, that we were all best off just opening him up and letting the sun get on with it, but, no, the men had to talk and argue and talk and argue. At first, they said they had to soak him in the brandy left for him by Bwana Stanley. Brandy will treat and pickle him, Farjallah Christie said, and they were all set to do that until Susi said, no, they should not use too much of the good brandy because it might be needed later for medicine.

Medicine, what medicine. Don't make me laugh. If you ask me, he had his eye on it himself. Susi likes his *pombe*, that he does, it was the only thing that ever came between him and the Bwana, got him into more than one spot of bother, that it did.

'A Kristuman would not behave in that way,' Bwana Daudi said, to which Susi said, 'It is just as well then, because I am no Kristuman so there is no call for me to behave like one.'

That upset the Bwana no end. They had words in Unyanyembe, after which Susi took off, to be followed by Chuma.

Bwana worried himself sick. When they returned after four days, Bwana Daudi forgave them. And it was not all heart either, I will tell you that for nothing. He had to, didn't he, because if he had not, a miserable party we would have been otherwise, with just Amoda, Chirango, Mabruki, the seven other *pagazi* left by Bwana Stanley, Misozi, and me.

This was around the time that he had said Ntaoéka was to choose one of the men. Just as she was working up to choosing Chuma, off he went with Susi, leaving her to choose Mabruki. Very foolish she felt, when Chuma came back to find her with Mabruki. Wept buckets, Ntaoéka did, but if you ask me, that was not heartache, that was just temper. And now it is either Carus Farrar or Jacob Wainwright that she has her eye on, or maybe even both. I have seen the way both men look at her, like a hungry man salivating over a roasting piece of meat.

He got his way, didn't he, Susi, in the end. After splashing a few drops over the poor Bwana's corpse, he announced that there was not enough brandy to do the work, the crafty dog. Then Farjallah Christie remembered that Wadi Saféné had got some salt when we passed through Kalunganjovu's land, and the men were all for salting him. Drove a hard bargain for his salt too, Wadi Saféné did, sixteen strings of beads he wanted, and two bolts of cloth, Americano and calico, the greedy such and such. All for a jar of salt the size of my Losi's head. It would not have been enough to pickle seven large fish, that it would not.

Brandy and salt indeed. I told them and told them. All they needed to do was to open him up and put him high above the ground and let the sun do the rest. After they finally agreed that was the only thing to be done, they had to talk on and on, this time about his inside parts, his viscera and whatnot, as Farjallah Christie called his heart, lungs, and kidneys and things.

It was some hours before they finally agreed to cut them out and bury them there. I would like to see anyone try to dry out lungs and hearts and livers, that I would. It is why whenever an animal was slaughtered at the Liwali's, the offal, as we called it, was the first thing we cooked. Made all sorts of delicacies and sweetbreads, that it did.

After all the talking, finally, on the afternoon of Chitambo's mourning day, the men built the new hut in the place Chitambo had indicated, in which they made a small platform and laid the Bwana down so that his body was level with their chests.

They asked me for cloths to cover him, and I gave them some, making sure they used an old Americano piece because, for sure, he was our Bwana, but master or no master, it was no reason to waste good cloth.

Inside the hut, Farjallah Christie and Carus Farrar prepared to open up his body. They were extremely learned in the bodies of both man and beast, for they had both been servants to doctors: Farjallah Christie in Zanzibar, and Carus Farrar in Bombay.

Bwana Daudi's frame was little more than skin and bone. It was not the work of a moment to make an incision that went up from his navel. From that opening, Carus Farrar reached into the body and drew out the viscera. His insides came tumbling out all at once, and, oh, the smell. I had to back away for fear that I would retch all over myself, and Jacob Wainwright, who was reading holy words from his big black book, had to stop to step away for air. As for Asmani, he dropped the cloth he held and turned and ran, and we had to get two more men to hold up the cloth.

I was desperate to leave and I told the men that I would go to the main camp to fetch a container for Bwana Daudi's insides. The camp had been set up on the driest land we found in these swamps. There had been space to build only five simple but large huts that were shared by the women, the six children, the Nassickers, and a separate, smaller hut for Bwana Daudi. The rest of the men took it in turn to sleep out in the open and keep watch over the camp.

Now, I do not know what mischief maker told the children he was to be opened up that day but as I walked behind the fleeing Asmani, I saw them heading in a gaggle to the hut, all agog to see Bwana Daudi's insides, the horrible creatures. I marshalled them back to the main camp, and on the way, I had to break a few quarrels between the children as they argued over whether his insides were as white as his outside self.

Sufficiently recovered, I returned with an old tin of flour that I thought would be big enough for the purpose. Carus Farrar and Farjallah Christie placed the heart in the tin box together with the other inside parts. As flies hovered over the dark mess of flesh, Carus Farrar pointed us to a clot of blood, as large as Amoda's angry fist, that lay on the side of his right lung. He had clearly been very sick, Carus Farrar said, for his lungs were withered and covered with black and white patches.

While they had been opening him up, some of the *pagazi* were digging a grave for his insides. There was an argument about whether to bury as well the knife that had opened him up. I would wash the knife as long as it took, I said, for it was by far the best we had. The men looked horrified and agreed to bury it.

93

Majwara then sounded the drum to call the party. Jacob read the burial service, and in the presence of all, we laid his heart to rest. On the *mpundu* tree above the grave of his heart, Jacob Wainwright carved Bwana Daudi's name and the date of his death.

After that, there was nothing to do but to leave his body exposed to the sun. The men kept watch over him day and night to see that no harm came to him. Even as the smell that wafted from him overpowered them, and the flies hovered, still they kept watch, standing vigil over his flesh and bones in groups of four or five. Twice a day, they changed the position of his body, so that all of him could receive the sun in equal measure.

The men took time to talk over the parts of him that hung outside, with no bone to attach them to him. They did not think I heard them, but, oh, the trouble they took to decide what to do with those, the frowning consultations, the whispering back and forth. You would think that was the most important part of a man, to hear them talk. And, of course, they did not want the women to know what they were talking about.

I soon cut through the agonised whispering.

'Whether you cut those parts off now, or wait for them to dry and fall off or shrink into him, they have to come off him, as sure is sure,' I said. 'It is going to happen, any which way you look at it. You may as well slice them off now, bury them with the rest, and have done with it.'

They looked at me with barely disguised horror.

'If you give me Farjallah's knife,' I said, 'I will slice them off myself, yes, I will. I have dismembered a goat or two in my time, yes, I have, and quickly too. There was a he-goat once at the Liwali's—'

'Halima,' Amoda said.

I took one look at his face and hurried. I spent the rest of that afternoon working with the women far from the men. So, I do not know what they decided to do with those parts, but what I do know is that there was some more digging around the *mvula* tree, and this time at night. The women and I laughed like anything, to think of the men gathering solemnly in the night to bury the things that made Bwana Daudi a man. But we took trouble to ensure that the men did not know why we laughed.

14

Now that I am on the point of starting on another trip into Africa I feel quite exhilarated: when one travels with the specific object in view of ameliorating the condition of the natives every act becomes ennobled . . .

The mere animal pleasure of travelling in a wild unexplored country is very great. When on lands of a couple of thousand feet elevation, brisk exercise imparts elasticity to the muscles, fresh and healthy blood circulates through the brain, the mind works well, the eye is clear, the step is firm, and a day's exertion always makes the evening's repose thoroughly enjoyable.

David Livingstone, *The Last
Journals of David Livingstone*

I had put it in my mind that the drying would take no more than two weeks, and I was right. Whenever the men slaughtered goats, it took about ten days for them to dry, faster even, if we turned the meat into strips. We could not strip Bwana Daudi, poor thing, and though I had compared him to one, he was certainly no goat, that much is true, but still, all the fleshy parts of him had sunk in and he was just skin and bone, he was, so we knew that it would not take long.

It was not just waiting around for nothing for those two weeks; we traded as much as we could with Chitambo's people and prepared provisions for the road ahead. The days were filled with the bustle of trade, skinning goats for meat, pounding flour for bread, sorting the Bwana's doctor's things and deciding what could be traded.

Chirango surprised me, I must say. This same Chirango who had been so lazy that he had bought two bondschildren to carry his things now would not let anyone come close to his load. Whenever the children played near to his load, he shouted for them to go away.

It was after he yelled at Losi that I told him that I had seen him talking to the medicine man in Chitambo's village. His face transformed at once. 'Well, Halima,' he said, 'it is not for Chirango to say you have not seen what you have seen or you have seen what you think you saw, for Chirango has no knowledge as to how well you can see at a distance, but all Chirango will say is that if indeed you saw what you think you saw, Chirango can only say he seeks aid from all who can help him to see whether his fortunes will recover.'

Losi was now pulling on my hand, while Chirango went on and on about his claims to this and his claims to that. Once he starts going on about his claims, there is no stopping him. I moved away in the direction Losi was pulling me, leaving him to talk to the air.

For the next few nights, while we waited for Bwana Daudi's body to dry, and after the work was done, we gathered in the usual way we had done before he fell ill. While Bwana Daudi had been so ill, and in the two days after his death, we had none of us sat in the usual way. But now, with the days of rest before us, we resumed our old ways.

We gathered around the fire to tell stories. Those of us who remembered told stories about where we came from and stories we had heard as children in our own lands. There was a thrill in hearing these stories, in feeling the same shivering anticipation as the Veiled Lady beckoned an elegant and seductive finger, and in gasping when her ghastly nature was revealed. Many of us chose to sacrifice sleep just for this. Misozi liked the most frightening of those stories, all about *shetani* ghosts and spirits that lived on sea and land. But when we went away to sleep alone, it was to go with a little fear. The heart would beat a little faster, and we lingered by the fire a little longer, but somehow, we managed to convince ourselves that these were mere stories that, even if they were true, had happened to people in places far from where we were, and there was nothing at all to fear.

Oftentimes, the stories included songs, and it was not uncommon for the songs to excite even more than the story, and for Majwara to get his drum and for the children, and some of the men too, to dance.

When Chirango told his stories, he played his *njari* instrument. He has a beautiful singing voice, I will give him that. But his songs and stories always lay a little heavy on the heart because they were all about his lost kingdom, and the people who had been in it, like Nyatsimba the Salt Gatherer, who had left his home in the great city of stone and travelled north to found a new kingdom, and his son Nyanhewe Matope, who had been punished by their ancestors for tricking his sister Nyamhita Nehanda into lying with him, and of Chioko, who had been tricked out of his kingdom by the Portuguese. When he played his *njari* as he told of these far-off places, Majwara often joined him with his drum.

When Bwana Daudi was alive, he liked to listen to the stories and songs, but not as much as Bwana Stanley when he had been with us. Such a surprise it was when Bwana Stanley came all the way from his land, America, and marched down from the coast to Ujiji to rescue Bwana Daudi. He liked our stories, Bwana Stanley. His man Bombay said Bwana Stanley planned to write a book of all the stories that we tell each other, though who would want to read them, I don't know.

Each person had their own style of telling stories. Susi liked to talk of the stories his father told him, the stories that were spun out like the nets of the fishermen in Shupanga. I like to listen to his voice. No one knows better the moods of the sea or how it responds to the moon and sun above it, the liquid silver it forms when the sun is at its highest, and the shimmering gold when it is sinking. The movement of the tides is as familiar to him as that of his own limbs. It is a surprise that one so attuned to the moods and ways of the ocean should have spent his life so far from it, but he explains it by saying that he wants to make money to fit his own dhow that he will build himself from wood and rope.

We knew already the stories of how we each of us came to be with the Bwana. The Nassickers who had been sent by Bwana Stanley had all been rescued as children. Though he was not a Nassicker, Chuma had also been rescued; he had joined the Bwana at just fifteen Ramadans. He had been sold away from his father, who was a chief among the Yao, along with his mother and two sisters. Susi and Amoda were freemen. They had never been enslaved. They had joined Bwana Daudi in Shupanga, then travelled with him to India, then back again.

Then there were the travellers like Mabruki and Uledi Munyasere. And of course, there were the inferior *pagazi*, most of whom had either come with Nassickers or been hired on the way from Unyanyembe, and who had no history at all with the Bwana.

Instead of telling the usual stories as we waited for Bwana Daudi to dry out, and the stories about where we came from, or even the stories that the children loved, the men talked about how they remembered him.

These were merry evenings. The men were now drunk on *pombe* sent by Chitambo daily to send away Bwana Daudi's spirit. We had all picked up a few things here and there about him, and of course we talked of him when he was with us, but you cannot talk so freely about a man when you can hear him moving in a hut a few yards away. And Bwana Daudi knew our tongues so well that to talk about him in this way was all but impossible.

But now, he lay drying in a mud hut, unable to hear us, poor thing, and we could talk of him as freely as we wished. Susi and Chuma, who had been with him the longest, talked the most. Even Chuma, who normally prefers to listen, was willing to talk. They talked of all the responses that people gave when they saw Bwana Daudi, laughter, surprise, mockery, pointing. More than a few of the children they had encountered on their travels had burst into tears on seeing him and had to be consoled by their mothers.

None had been so surprised, said Susi, as a man in Susi's home of Shupanga, who had watched the Bwana bathe in a river. He reported that indeed, he was white everywhere, but his brains came out when he washed his hair, then went back in again.

It took some time for the Bwana to convince the village that this was no sorcery, and that it was only the soap he used that created white suds that looked like they had come from within him.

'And you can imagine what Bwana Daudi felt,' Susi said, 'when we entered some of the villages and he reached out to children who screamed in terror when they saw him.'

'Yes,' laughed Chuma, 'we even had some of the mothers use him to make their children behave. Be good, they said, or we will call the white man to come and eat you.'

They laughed even harder when they talked about his expedition to the Zambezi, as Chuma described the boat's failing to move.

'It is quite the most foolish thing I have ever heard. He may have been a learned *mganga* man of medicine and what have you, but who has ever heard of a boat going up the stream of a river, and not down it?'

'There was a section of the river with even faster water, the Kebra-bassa rapids, the locals called it, and Bwana Daudi thought his boat could simply sail up against those fast currents.'

Susi said Bwana Daudi had been poor as a child, and indeed to hear him talk, he was as good as a slave, working, working, working like a slave in the day, then learning, learning, learning his books at night so that he could become a *mganga*. It is no wonder he did not want to go back to his own land, because it sounded like no life at all, all that learning and working and working and learning. It was terribly dark and cold too, Susi said, and they saw hardly any sun. I exclaimed to think that he had left his children to that life.

'Don't feel sorry for them,' Amoda said, 'they are taken care of.'

'He wanted to make all of us follow his Kristu,' Susi said, 'but he failed with me, I can tell you that. I have no truck with all that. And even Chuma here, he was made a Kristuman in India, and there was no work for the Bwana to do. It was not the Bwana's doing.'

As Susi burst into laughter, Jacob Wainwright frowned.

'And I heard from Bwana Speke that he quarrelled all the time with the other whites,' said Munyasere, 'and that is why he travelled alone.'

'And Wekotani, do you remember Wekotani, Chuma?' Susi's voice was now loud with merriment and *pombe*. 'That was not his doing either. Wekotani was turned by someone else entirely. And when you wanted to go off with him, Bwana said he was going to sell you if you went with him.'

They were now talking over each other and it was hard to follow who all these people were.

'But there was Sechele,' said Mariko.

Their response was to laugh even more heartily.

'You have talked of this Sechele before,' I pressed on. 'Who is he, and why do you call Mabruki Sechele?'

The men laughed even harder.

Susi said, 'Sechele was a sultan in Makololo country, down in the south. He was made to follow Kristu by the Bwana. The Bwana healed his son of malaria. Sechele, in gratitude, agreed that he would become a Kristuman. Then, after he turned him to Kristu, the Bwana made him send away his wives.'

'His wives?' asked Ntaoéka. 'What on Earth had they done wrong?'

Chuma said, 'It was not that they did anything wrong, but Kristumen can only have one wife each. So the Bwana made him pick just one wife and sent the rest back to their homes.'

'They left their children behind too,' said Chuma. 'The Bwana said they were born in sin, but with Sechele's guidance, they would embrace the new faith.'

'They were all sent back!' I was aghast with horror.

'Don't worry about them too much, Halima,' said Susi. 'When Bwana Daudi went back to Sechele's land, he found the wives had all returned. And some of them were heavy with child.'

The men close to Mabruki clapped him on the back and laughed again as they called him Sechele.

'This was his weakness,' Jacob Wainwright said. His voice was solemn and sonorous. 'The Bwana's weakness was that he did not sow the seed in any quantities.'

'Sechele sowed the seed instead,' Susi said. 'Just like that Mabruki of yours, Ntaoéka. He will be sowing the seed in you next, if he hasn't already.'

'Susi, you have drunk too much,' said Jacob Wainwright. The vein on the side of his neck was throbbing. I saw that he looked at

Ntaoéka as he spoke, but she seemed lost in her own thoughts.

Susi said, 'This is nothing, because you know who drank too much? The Bwana's wife. She was a fish, that one.'

The Bwana's wife, he said, had drunk herself to her death, and racked up debt after debt to men who sold her *pombe*. The thought of those poor children in that far-off land, so cold, so dark, and so dreadfully poor, with a mother who died from *pombe* and a father who died looking for rivers, wandering and wandering like he had no home, made me sorry, and I asked Chuma to name all of them.

'The one child of his that I knew the most was his daughter Agnes, for he often talked about her. His little Nannie, he called her.' Susi counted with his fingers as he said their names. 'Robert, one. Agnes, two. Thomas, three. William, four. Oswell, five. Zouga, six. Anna, seven. Mary, eight.'

'And the baby, ten,' said Chuma.

'Are those the children of just Mai Robert?' Ntaoéka said as she counted with him. 'And no other wife?'

'No wonder she drank herself to death,' said Misozi. 'That is ten children to care for with no one to share the work.'

'But maybe,' I said, 'maybe the older cared for the younger, who is to say that is not what happened? The Liwali's second *horme* had a sister who left many children and her husband did not marry again, no matter how much they asked him to, so the older children raised the younger, that they did.'

'But, Susi, you count wrong,' said Chuma.

Susi raised his voice; it was always this way with him when he had drunk *pombe*, he raised his voice in quarrel, and though there was no malice to it, it was loud and long and he could argue with a tree.

Jacob Wainwright said, 'Did he not have six altogether and five living? Chuma is right. You have named them wrong.'

Chuma scowled. He did not like to be rescued even by Jacob Wainwright. He quickly added, 'Zouga is the name of the last son, he is the same person as William, who is the same person as Oswell.'

'So that last son is named thrice,' I said. 'Do you mean that he has three names, like a Mohammedan who has been to Mecca?'

'He has just two names,' said Jacob Wainwright, 'but he was called Zouga as his other name because he was born near a river of that name. It was his pet name. And Anna is the same child as Mary. It is not two but one, so where you have five children you have two, some with three names, and one with two.'

'Why does that particular child have two names? And why do the other children not have two names, or three names?' said Ntaoéka.

'Maybe it is only the children born by a river who have three names,' said Misozi. 'Isn't that so? It is only children born by rivers who are given three names.'

Jacob Wainwright ignored the question. He took up another log and leaned over to stoke the fire. In the flare of firelight, his impatience was clear on his face. He prides himself on knowing the ways of the *wazungu* better than Chuma and Susi even, but he can never stand to be questioned too closely. For many of us, the Bwana was the only *mzungu* we knew, but he has met others, and has read their books and speaks their tongue as well as though he were *mzungu* himself.

He has met more than one *mzungu* person, he is always telling us, there was the captain of the dhow that rescued him, and all the sailors on it who helped the captain, then the *wazungu* teachers in India who taught him in English, and the one who gave him his name and his suit and his books, then Bwana Stanley, who brought him here, then Bwana Daudi.

When he spoke with Bwana Daudi, the words between them

flowed thick and fast, faster even than when Bwana Daudi talked to Susi or Chuma. But for all that, he does not always answer the questions we ask, and to hear him talk, there is no order at all in the things that these *wazungu* do sometimes.

The Mohammedans make no sense either, but at least they do not try to make sense. They just tell you that this is how things are, and it is for you to take or not take, and if you don't take it, they will make you. But Jacob Wainwright wants to make us believe that this God has all the power but cannot stop the floods from killing or animals from attacking.

I knew from his sudden close attention to the fire that he did not know much about the meanings of these *wazungu* names. My own name, Halima, means 'one who is of mild and gentle nature'. It is as though my mother knew just what sort of person I would become when she named me, not like the Liwali's third *suria*, the one from Circassia, who named her son Naseem, which means 'the breeze that blows softly across the land', but, oh, the trouble that boy gave to his family. The wind that blows off the coast in the rainy season, he was, the wind that capsizes every dhow too and brings down the new-planted palms and nothing good to any person. When I asked Jacob Wainwright to explain the meaning of these *wazungu* names, the same impatience entered his voice that overcame him now. He can never abide close questioning.

Susi now came back from the tree where he had gone to relieve himself. 'Have you counted the baby in the desert?' he said as he took up his *pombe*. He drank deeply and said, 'She need not have died either.'

Chuma said now, 'Susi, you should not talk so.'

Ignoring him, Susi said, 'Well, it is what it is.'

I asked how was it, what baby was this one now, and in what

desert had she died. Susi said, 'The Doctor had gone far out of Mak-ololo country with Ma Robert, who gave birth right there in the desert, and the child died there, and it was like he did not even care.'

Majwara, upset, said, 'But he was a good man. He gave me this coat. He saved my life. He ransomed me. He cured my fever.'

Afterwards, I could tell that Majwara's heart was still unsettled so I took him aside. 'Now, you listen to me,' I said. 'People can do good and still be bad, and do bad and still be good. Choose only to remember him as it gives you comfort.'

But in my heart, I must say that I was troubled. I looked to the hut where the smoke rose above his body. What manner of man was he? The men found it funny, this Sechele business, but I thought of those poor women, being told to go back simply because their husband had found a new god. How would they explain that to their families, what could they say? Who was Bwana Daudi to disgrace these women like that, to shame them before their people, to meddle like that and just go off, then come back years later?

He had not seemed to be this meddlesome when I talked to him, he had not seemed to care that he was surrounded by Mohammedans and Nassickers, and those like me who did not care one way or the other.

He had asked me once what I believed. I had told him my mother's stories, the ones I tell around the fire. They are stories that other slaves told her, stories from every place. They were all about the creation of the universe and the first man, Kintu, and the first woman, Wambui. Those were just stories, he said, and what did I really believe, and I told him that I did not trouble myself with such questions when there was food to be made and could he hurry along if he needed anything because he was delaying me, he was in the way and there was work to be done.

It troubled me to think of his children. Bwana Stanley had tried to make him go back with him, but the Bwana had refused to be persuaded. I remember the set of his mouth as he talked to Bwana Stanley and said, no, he was not going back, weak though he was, and ill with it too, but he would still go on. Had his wife tried to get him to turn back, to save the child? Had he spoken to her in that way?

What manner of a man was this, who thought that small things like the flowing of a river were of greater matter than the life of a child? How could he cure Majwara, and give the coat off his own back to a stranger, and still deny food to his own children? He had given me my Losi to love, and seen her through her childhood fevers and other ailments, and yet could not save his own child.

I thought of his grief for that dog Chitane that had drowned while they crossed a river, even to the point of speaking of that place of drowning as Chitane's Water. All that grief, and all that remembrance, for a dog. How could a man who grieved this much for a dog leave his own child to die?

I looked for a single unkind word Bwana Daudi had said to me. Apart from that unfair scolding after I ran off with Ntaoéka, I could find none. Yes, he had had Chirango beaten, and a few other men when they deserved it. But he had forgiven Susi and Chuma when they ran away, and me too, come to that. But perhaps he had had to forgive because he needed us all.

I thought of his abundant goodness to me. He had bought me for Amoda and promised me a house in Zanzibar. And there was all that had happened with the Manyuema at Nyangwe, the way he had grieved for those poor women, and his vow that he would write in letters of fire to tell the world all that he had seen. It was all too much.

Was this worth all of this trouble? Was he worth it? What were we doing, taking a father to his children when he had let one of those children die? His poor small baby had spent so few years on this Earth, but perhaps it was as well because it sounded as though Bwana Daudi had been no better than a slave in his own country.

My mother, Zafrene, told me once that the good things that grow from the ground come from the good thoughts of people who are buried, and the evil things come from the evil thoughts. That is why there is a mix of good and evil things in the world. I do not know whether she believed that or if it was just a story to tell children. But as I passed the tree where his heart and inside things lay that evening, I felt glad that we were taking most of him away to be buried in his own land. Whatever evils were in him would flourish in the soil of his own place. I thought of all the unknown things that lay ahead of us, and for the first time since I had persuaded the men to take Bwana Daudi home, I felt afraid.

II

MWILI WA DAUDI

It was to the intelligence and superior education of Jacob Wainwright ... that we were indebted for the earliest account of the eventful eighteen months during which he was attached to the party.

Horace Waller, in *The Last
Journals of David Livingstone*

After that sad event, Jacob Wainwright commenced keeping a diary and continued it for nine weary months, during which they were working their way to the coast, carrying with them the mortal remains of their late master. It is a most interesting record of their journey.

Letter from Reverend William Price,
the *Times*, 18 April, 1874

The Rev. William Price – who at the Church Missionary Station at Nassick, near Bombay, trained the 'Nassick Boys' who so nobly brought home Livingstone's body – has lately transplanted to Mombasa a considerable colony of liberated slaves found in slave dhows, captured by our cruisers, and made over to his care for education at Nassick. These children have been carefully trained by him in various industrial arts as well as in the Christian religion.

*Authorised Report of the Church Congress
Held at Plymouth: 3, 4, 5, & 6 October, 1876*

1

4 May 1873

First Entry from the Journal of Jacob Wainwright, written at Chitambo's Village; in which he gives Further Particulars of the Doctor's Final Sufferings, Narrates the Woeful Discovery made by the Boy Majwara, and Prays for Grace to Live under a Due Sense of the Mercies of God.

Praise be to the God of Israel and the God of Moses, who made the world and gave Life and Breath to all things bright and beautiful, all creatures great and small; the God of Grace and Mercy who so loved the world that He gave in sacrifice His Only Begotten Son, that we might have Life Everlasting and not Perish. He has made a Covenant with His Chosen; He has given his Servant His Word.

After his bodily suffering, the Doctor's Perfect Rest has come. He has left for another shore, to join that great multitude which no man can number, and whose Eternal Hope is in the Word made Flesh. Fear not, sayeth the Lord, for I have called thee by name and thou art Mine. May the Lord in His Munificence grant us Grace, that we may live always with a Due Sense of the Divine Mercies of God. And the Righteous shall gather and be counted in the Days of Wrath.

It was the boy Majwara who found the Doctor, dead on his knees, his hands clasped together under his bowed head. When I eventually went in with the others, it was to find his journal at his side, his pen having fallen to the ground. He had clearly attempted to write in his journal, a touching message of farewell perhaps, or an encouragement to those he left behind to be ever steadfast, but instead of distinguishable words, I saw only indecipherable scrawls followed by a long line that trailed off. The last words he had written in his journal were those of 27 April, four days previously, the day after we arrived at Chitambo's, when he had written, 'Knocked up quite, and remain – recover – sent to buy milch goats. We are on the banks of the Molilamo.'

I was not among the first to see the Doctor. It was only after the expedition leaders had consulted together that they roused me along with the rest of the *pagazi*. This is how it is with them: Matthew Wellington and Carus Farrar are who they consider the leaders of the seven of us from the Nassick school. And all because they laugh and smile with them, all because they drink *pombe* and chew the *quat* leaf like they are mere *pagazi*. Yet it is I, ignored and overlooked, who is a natural leader of men, for I do not hesitate to speak my mind and tell them when they do wrong. I fear no man, nor did I hesitate to tell even the Doctor when *he* did wrong.

'Jacob the Zealot', he called me, for I was more earnest, he said, than John the Evangelist. This is how he mocked God's Messenger! But I forgave him. Yes, I forgave him. There is no doubt in my mind that he spoke thus because he was unable to repel the truth of my words; they were as a burning lance to a festering boil, for I pride myself on my gift to convince.

At the school at Nassick, when I wanted to discuss a point of theology, I often found that there was no one around me to raise it with because little clusters of both the teachers and the other students melted away upon my approach, unable to counter the force of my conviction.

But it is not for me to put my personal disappointments to the fore. Instead, my eyes are turned up to the Throne of Heaven. For I know without a doubt that it is due entirely to my efforts, and to my ceaseless prayers, that the Doctor had risen to pray. I know that it is entirely my doing that he may yet go to his Eternal Rest in a state of Perfect Grace.

Even though my heart was sorrowing, I could not help but rejoice. For months now, I had tried to turn the Doctor's thoughts to Ujiji, and from thence to the coast and then on a ship home to England.

In my mind, I was on that ship with him, enduring the endless tossing of the waves so that, at journey's end, I would be ordained a priest and finally become the missionary I always dreamed I would be. I have no greater desire in my life than that. It is a dream that occupies my every waking thought, and on which I lay my head at night. Nothing moves me as much as the thought of returning to my own land, to bring to salvation the very people who sold me into bondage. But no, not to be their Saviour, for Christ alone has the Power, Jesus alone has the Glory. To be an Instrument of Salvation merely, is what I wish to be, to bring my people to the Love and Fear of the Lord.

I could have talked of my dream of a mission with the Doctor, but all he wanted was to talk about his own dream. On and on he talked about the fountains of Herodotus. His hope was that by finding the fountains spoken of by this ancient Greek, he would find the source of the Nile.

'I will do better than Speke and Burton, they should have followed Herodotus,' he said often.

I had my own doubts about this and expressed them to him. For I did not see how he could place so much credence, not to mention faith, in the words of a centuries-dead man who knew of those fountains only by report.

I reminded him that he had told me that this Herodotus had not actually seen the fountains himself, but had merely written of what he had heard. 'I cannot claim to know of these places that this Herodotus writes about,' I said to him, 'for my learning is not as advanced as yours, but I fear that this man may mislead you.'

He looked at me with a mix of surprise and irritation.

'What can *you* possibly know of the matter?' he asked. He spoke with such astonishment that he may well have been receiving advice from the birds that were flying above us.

'You gave me this book to read,' I said, and held out the book that he called his Ptolemy, 'and see how he describes the hippopotamus. He says of it that it is an animal the size of an ox with four legs with cloven hoofs, a horse's mane and tail, and conspicuous tusks, with a hide so tough that when dried it can be made into spear shafts. But as we both know, for we have seen it, the creature itself is nothing like its description of it. Let us rather read the Bible together and pray upon the matter.'

'I have read the Bible through four times in the last three years,' he said snappishly. 'I will not find the source of the Nile there. It is on Herodotus that I must rely.'

It grieved me sorely to hear him discuss in such a cavalier manner the Book of Books, as though it could be compared with the writings of a Greek who no doubt lived a life of Sin. For the Greeks believed in many gods, in gods too, that acted like men and lusted after women and changed shape to possess them. They lived lives of fornication and jealous quarrels and sired children out of wedlock, as though they were mere mortals; worse than mortals actually, for no Christian would act like those heathen gods.

'Is it not akin,' I pressed him, 'to placing faith in those sages who held once that the Earth was flat?'

'You are no geographer, Jacob,' he said, 'and what do you know about flat Earths?'

I found I surprised him most when I let slip some of the knowledge that I had acquired at the Nassick school. On those occasions, he gave me a quizzical, half-amused look, the same he had given me when I mentioned Herodotus and the hippopotamus. It grieved me sorely that he seemed to be of the same mind as those of my old teachers who thought that those of the Black Race had no need for knowledge that we could not directly apply, that we should limit our learning only to the skills that we could use to assist the explorers and missionaries as they went into our natal land, that our knowledge should be limited to that which we could do with our hands.

Though I talked thus, I was unable to persuade him to turn his thoughts homewards. And so it was that I resigned myself to preparing his Soul for his Real Home. For we have no Abiding Home on Earth, we long for a Home that is Far away. Realising that his end was near, I prayed for his Soul every night for the past month. 'Our Life is but a Vapour,' I said to the Lord, 'and this night his Soul may be required of him. Keep him then, dear Lord, in a State of Preparation for His Last Hour.' And so it is that the Lamb who takes away all Sin has answered me.

As they talked over the fire, the men discussed what he had been doing on his knees. 'It looks like he was praying,' said Farjallah Christie.

'But you know Bwana Daudi,' Susi said. 'It could also have been that in his delirium, some thought or observation came to him that he wanted to write in his journal.'

But though I remained silent, I knew better. For it is due to the Grace of God, who chose me as the Divine Instrument to manifest His Power, that the Doctor died on his knees, Blessed in the Sight of God. In the hour before he died, feeling a great presentiment, I rose from my tent and went into his hut. The men outside were sleeping, as was, inside, Majwara. The Doctor lay on his back, with his eyes closed. His breathing was shallow and steady.

As I watched his chest rise and fall, I was seized with the conviction that I could be an agent for his healing. Casting my eyes to the heavens, I called on the power of the Holy Ghost. I placed my hands on his shoulders. His eyes opened. He was feeble under my arms as he fought against my power. Careful not to wake the boy, I said a final, fervent prayer for his immortal soul. I left the hut and returned to my own quarters.

I am certain that the Power of my Faith moved him to rise after I left him, and moved him to continue the prayer that I had begun for him. And now he sleeps unknowing, to wake only at the Sound of the Last Trumpet. Then shall he be weighed in the Scales and tried in the Final Judgement. And I know that his soul is safe. For had I not gone in to pray for the Doctor, he would not have risen to his knees, and thus ended his Mortal Life Blessed in the Eyes of the Lord.

2

6 May 1873

Second Entry from the Journal of Jacob Wainwright, written at Chitambo's Village; in which Wainwright gives a Thanksgiving for the Bountiful Gifts of Providence as he Reflects on how he came from the Dark into the Radical Light of God's Grace.

When this journal is published, which is my eventual hope, Readers of this account will, no doubt, already be aware of the Nassick school of the Church Missionary Society, which I have mentioned more than once. It is the only school of its kind, being a school established to educate boys who were captured as slaves and freed by British gunboats. Certainly, the fame of this school has grown beyond the borders of the Principality of Bombay in India, where it is located in Saharinpoor, the city of refuge.

For the edification of those who may not yet be aware of it, however, it may perhaps be well if I explain that it was established by the Reverend William Price, in the Year of Our Lord 1854, and now finds itself under the command of the Reverend Charles William Isenberg, who has distinguished himself through many publications, most prominent of which is a dictionary of the Amharic language that is spoken by the Abyssinian people of the Horn of Africa.

Even those Readers who may be well acquainted with the Nassick school may, nonetheless, wonder who this Jacob Wainwright is who addresses them as the author of these pages. What is his provenance; how came he to be the most accomplished, best learned, and

117

most illustrious offshoot of that excellent school; and how came it to pass that he was so closely associated with the final days of Doctor Livingstone that he saved his Soul from the perdition of eternal damnation?

I must confess that I am normally of a retiring nature, and am not one who is keen to push himself forwards. Indeed, my inclination is to avoid as far as possible all public notice, for attention of that kind is above all most repugnant to me. But to answer these most interesting questions requires me, in this entry, to do what I should perhaps have done in the first, which is to provide an account of myself, and explain to the Reader who this Jacob Wainwright is who addresses himself so familiarly to the Reader.

When I reflect on my early life, it is with Thanksgiving for having come out of the darkness of slavery. Like the Doctor's man Chuma, I too, was born among the Yao people, where I was called Thenga, the only son of Mapira, a fisherman, and Ngunda, his second wife. I had a sister, Njemile, as well as other sisters and brothers through my father's first two wives. Their names have now been lost to me, for it is an age since I was taken from my homeland.

A most fearsome race, the Yao gained great wealth from the trade in human flesh, for they were practised in the sale of slaves. It was, however, most unusual that they sold their own; my misfortune rose from the long-standing enmity between my father, Mapira, and his brother, a native chief who felt uneasy in his power and saw a threat in every blood relation. He accused his brothers of sorcery, a grievous charge in those parts, and had them and their wives put to death.

Then he sold off their sons and gave their wives and their daughters in marriage to strangers, including my own poor mother and my sister Njemile. My brothers and I were sold, with other blood relatives, to Arab traders, who walked us to the coast.

I was not eight years old then. My memories of that journey are of being with giant, fearsome men who seemed to me to be made up of nothing but hair. I remember only fear and marching, more fear and more marching, marching and marching for many miles until we reached the coast. There we were handed over to a group of men who, as I found out later, were Suaheli Arabs. The next memory I have is of water, so much water, water that stretched before me like an endless field. Then the sensation of being tossed about on a dhow in that endless water, and sailing with others – I later learned – to Zanzibar, where we were to be sold at the slave market.

We were at sea for what seemed like an eternity when came the shout, '*Mzungu, mzungu!*' Our Arab captors were driven into a state of high panic at the sound of this word. They turned to us, their captives, with the most frightening of the commands they had given us thus far: we were all to jump into the sea. If we did not, they said, the *mzungu* people who were coming would capture us and eat us all.

Many of the people in the dhow were, like me, from the country of the Yao. The word '*mzungu*' sounded to our ears like 'Mazitu', a group of Nguni marauders from the south who were the only other people the Yao considered to be more fearsome than they. Even my uncle, who held fearful sway over his people, would have trembled greatly at the thought of Mazitu invading his land. If these Muzunguzitu were that fierce, this would surely be the end of us all.

There followed chaos and much consternation as, all around me, people jumped headlong into the water. Fear rooted me to the spot, for as terrifying as whatever it was these Muzunguzitu were, the dark, unwelcoming waters of the sea below frightened me even more. I was caught up in a small group of captives who moved towards the prow of the dhow, and there, trembling with the others, I hid.

Before long came towards us an even bigger dhow, and one that seemed to be moving with terrifying speed. Even more captives jumped from the sides into the waters below. Caught between the terror of being eaten by the Muzunguzitu and drowning in the ocean, I remained frozen where I was. There were a dozen or more with me, all boys. We crouched low, trying to make ourselves unseen as we waited for we knew not what.

Soon came the heavy tread of footsteps in our dhow. In a matter of moments, our captors became themselves the captives. From the prow where I crouched, I saw the Mzungu, men with strange skin who wore white clothes and had as much hair about their faces as our Arab captors. There were others as well, men of our race, but they were as terrifying to behold as their companions, for they were dressed in the same manner as the men with the strange skin and hair.

Both groups of men spoke a language we did not understand, until one said in the Yao tongue that they had come to get us. One of the black men reached for me, and lifted me, stiff and unyielding, to his chest. The others did the same to other small boys. We were more frightened still and fought against this further capture, until we finally understood that he meant not to eat us, but to rescue us.

But to rescue us and take us where?

Home was not possible: we were surrounded by the ocean on every side. Even if we had been asked where home was, how could we have known? All we saw around us was the endless ocean. We could not have said where home was even if we wanted to.

It was only when I had been at the school for two years that I understood what had happened that day.

As my Readers will be aware, many years before we were captured, the British had abolished the trade in slaves along the Indian

Ocean. What some Readers may not know is that this odious trade was nonetheless flourishing along the coastline of the Indian Ocean. For this reason, the British Navy ran blockades along the coast, to stop slaves' reaching Zanzibar, and to prevent those who had already been sold from reaching Persia, Arabia, and India.

The ship that rescued me, the SS *Daphne*, was one among a small fleet that patrolled the waters to recapture slaves from the dhows headed east. Once rescued, the slaves were sent to begin new lives in India, with the youngest among them being taken to the Nassick school, a haven and a home for the poor boys who had been captured and could not return to their homes.

It was to this school, in Saharinpoor in the Protectorate of Bombay, that I was taken with the other captives. And it was at this school that I left the name Thenga behind me and became Jacob, an Heir to Salvation saved for Labour in the Kingdom of Christ.

Every day, on the thirtieth day of November, the birthday that I chose for myself, which is also the anniversary of the day of my baptism, I pray for a Shower of Blessings on the men who rescued me from God only knows what fate. I could have stayed in Zanzibar or in Oman, or even in India, where I ended up, but not as the free man and Child of Christ I am today. No; I would have been nothing better than a heathen slave, shut out from Salvation and mired in darkness.

I was grateful, deeply grateful to my rescuers, the sailors on the SS *Daphne*. I had them always before me, these men who rescued me. But it was not the whites among them who showed me my path, but the others, as black as I am, the 'Krumen', they called themselves, who first gave me a wondrous glimpse of the man I could be.

They were from Freetown in the land of Sierra Leone on the west coast of Africa. What a wondrous name it seemed to me when I finally understood that this Freetown was a town founded by freed Christian slaves returned from England, a town that had as its neighbour a country called Liberia, founded by freed Christian slaves from America! Two shining lands of freedom, living in neighbourly accord, governed by those who had known what it meant to be bonded to others as chattel, and what it meant to be free in the Name of Jesus!

The work of the Krumen of Freetown was truly the Work of Freedom, for their job was to move up and down the coast of the Indian Ocean on the Freedom Ships that sailed the high seas. They rowed their small boats on perilous waters and stuck out their oars to pull in the drowning. It was one of these men who had lifted me, trembling and frightened, from the prow in which I had hidden.

At the Nassick school, I was reborn with a new name. With the other rescued children, I received instruction in the English language, and learned skills such as carpentry, welding, shipbuilding, cartography, smithing, and agriculture. None of these called to me as strongly as did the possibility of service to Our Lord, the Saviour. I took the first opportunity I could to be instructed in the Christian faith so that I could be baptised.

A Bishop Wainwright in England had given money so that ten boys could be accommodated and educated at the school. He had also donated Bibles and missals as our baptism gifts. Reverend Price suggested – in fact, he ordered – that the ten of us for whom Reverend Wainwright had chosen to stand Benefactor should take his name as our own, though we were free, he said, to choose our own Christian names. These, the Reverend encouraged us to choose ourselves from the Bible.

I had thought at first to take the same Christian name as the Doctor. What a David I would have been, against the Goliath of Sin and Ignorance! But it was the name John that held for me a peculiar attraction. It was the name of both the Baptist John, and the Prophet John whom God had so blessed and favoured by opening his eyes to His Glorious Revelation. For though I do not always understand all that the Prophet saw, the Seventh Seal and the Pale Horse, the Beast that comes out of the Sea and the Beast that comes out of the Earth, to read the Revelation fills me with absolute conviction of the Glory of the Lord.

The name John also had the attraction for me that it was the Christian name of Mr Bunyan, the Great Dreamer, who was given the visions that he saw and set down so faithfully in *The Pilgrim's Progress from This World, to That Which Is to Come*. I have pored over those pages, indeed, I have wept over them, for always, within them, I find something new and true. Were the Lord only to bless me by giving me such visions, I would consider it a true calling to set it all down.

This much had I invested in the name John. But before I could indicate my preference, the others had already been to see the Reverend Price to tell him their chosen names. They wished to be baptised Matthew, Luke, Timothy, James, and John. So the name John was taken before I could claim it, and taken too by a boy that I knew to be most unworthy of it!

There could hardly, Reverend Price said, be two John Wain-wrights at the school, and as the unworthy boy had chosen first, I was to choose another.

It was a bitter, bitter blow. I prayed that the Lord would reveal to me a new name. I prayed on no other matter for two days, and at the end of that period, I opened my Bible only for it to fall on Genesis. My eyes immediately fell on the passage where the Angel of Peniel asks: WHAT IS YOUR NAME? And the answer JACOB jumped off the page like an affirmation.

It seemed to be the Lord's very answer. Nor could I help but think that Jacob was also called ISRAEL. What name could be more fitting than the name of the father of the Twelve Tribes, among them the tribe of Judah, to which also belonged King David, the ancestor of our Savior Jesus Christ?

In the full confidence of my new name, I read more closely than I had ever before the passage that followed: 'Do not be afraid. For I have bought you and made you free. When you pass through the waters, I will be with you. When you pass through the rivers, they will not flow over you. When you walk through the fire, you will not be burned. The fire will not destroy you. For I am the Lord your God, the Holy One of Israel, who saves you.'

And so I left behind my heathen name of Thenga, and came to the Light of Christ as His servant Jacob. At the Nassick school, I found my own ship, my boats and my oars. Just as the Krumen saved lives using these, I would use the Grace and Salvation of Our Lord Jesus Christ. I felt certain that I had the calling of a mission-ary. I was to be a Shepherd among His Flock, attending to the Sal-vation and Moral Elevation of my heathen brothers and sisters. When I told this to the Reverend Isenberg, he said only, 'Well, well. Let us not get ahead of ourselves because you do, of course, labour under the unfortunate disadvantage of being black.'

Indeed, I said, I did not presume to want to minister to the white sheep, but only to the black. My mission would be back in Africa, where so many were still mired in Ignorance and Want, yearning for the Salvation of the Life Everlasting. I would work to end the True Slavery of my continent, the Enslavement to Darkness and heathen ways, of which this noxious trade in humans was but one sorrowful example.

Like Paul, once Saul, born in Darkness just as I was, and who came unto the Light, I wanted to spread the word of Christ to the heathens. Just as Paul spread the light to the Corinthians and Galatians, Ephesians and Philippians, Colossians and Thessalonians, Hebrews and Romans, I would spread Christ's Light to the Wagogo and Wayamba, the Wabisa and Wamwinyi. I would spread His light in Manyuema country and Bechuanaland, among the Barotse and Matabele.

The Light of Christ would shine over the Yao, over the very people who had sold me into slavery, from which action had come my salvation. From east to west, north to south, the light of Christ would shine with His Majesty, even unto the Ends of the Earth. For the light shineth in darkness, and the darkness comprehendeth it not. So shall it be, so shall it be. Amen, my Lord, let it be so.

3

Third Entry from the Journal of Jacob Wainwright, written at Chitambo's Village; in which Wainwright reflects on his Departure from the Nassick School and his First Encounter with Doctor Livingstone.

I knew of Doctor Livingstone long before I first set eyes on him at the Nassick school. Not only did his deeds and words feature most prominently in the newspapers that were circulated among us, both in our weekly assemblies and in our lessons, but I also held him as a beacon of what was possible.

I extolled his commitment to my natal land, so mired in darkness. In the speeches that he gave to audiences in England, and in which he talked to the great and the good of London, he addressed me too, a young native boy in far-away India. I listened closely as his words were relayed to us at assembly; I pored over his journeys in the *Illustrated Times*. I prayed for him and for the many that he was turning to Christ in our native land.

So when he came to the school when I was just a boy of fourteen, I could barely contain myself. It was in 1866 in the Year of Our Lord. He was then at the beginning of this very journey that has had its sorrowful conclusion in Chitambo. His visit to our school was a great occasion, so great an occasion that for two months before he arrived, we practised a special assembly in his honour.

The assembly had to be put off several times. Bad sailing conditions meant that Doctor Livingstone only reached India a month after we had first begun to expect him. When finally he did arrive, he was accompanied by the bishop of Calcutta. Then the Reverend Isenberg gave us news that lifted my spirits. The Doctor was not only passing through our school: he had come to recruit from among us Nassickers. He was to select from our number ten of us to accompany him to Africa.

I dared to entertain the great hope that I might be among the chosen, that I might be among those who would learn at the feet of the great Missionary, and be fired and filled with the Spirit that moved him to travel across the land and sea. Like him, I would cut through the forests and jungles of my dark natal land and light it up with the Power of His Shining Majesty.

Here was my chance at last, to go back to my own land as a missionary. This thought occupied me above all others, that here was the path laid before me that would take me back to my own people, to my mother and sister, if they are still living, and that I might forgive my uncle for his Sin in selling my brothers and me and killing my father. I would bring to all my people the Salvation that I had found and place them firmly within the Loving Embrace of my Lord Jesus Christ.

On the day after the great assembly, twenty of us were asked to stand before him. He had with him two men of our Race. My eyes took in every aspect of their appearance. The younger was dressed in English clothes, and the older in Arab dress of the Suaheli type. They were presented to us as James Chuma and Abdullah Susi, his long-serving companions. As our eyes met, Susi winked at me. I looked away.

As for the Doctor, he was, I must confess, a disappointment. He held his left arm rather stiffly, a result, he told us, of a ferocious lion attack in which he had almost lost both his arm and his life. It was hard to equate this small, wizened man before me, with his greying hair and stiff left arm, with the picture I had in my mind of a towering giant opening up a continent to Christ. Why, he was barely taller than I was, and I was only fourteen. In his grey frock coat and black trousers, he could have been any of my schoolmasters. Absent from his head was the cocked hat in which he appeared in all illustrations. Altogether, he was a much smaller and less prepossessing man than I had been given reason to expect.

I believe I made a better impression on the Doctor than he made on me, for I was introduced to him as a most promising lad. I had been practising for this moment. At first I thought I would stun him with the power of my memory for Bible verses. In the end, I chose to impress him with his own words, words that I had memorised from a speech he had made in the months before he sailed for India. It had been published in the London *Illustrated Times*. Now that I remember the words that I recited to him, in the sorrow of what has come to pass, they seem strangely prophetic.

I said to him, "'I beg to direct your attention to Africa. I know that in a few years I shall be cut off in that country, which is now open; do not let it be shut again. I go back to Africa to make a path for commerce and Christianity.'"

The Doctor laughed and clapped me on the shoulder. When he laughed, his whole face became animated, and his eyes twinkled with humour. I was a bright young lad, the doctor said, but I was too young, much too young for the work to be done.

I was crushingly disappointed. With great envy, I watched the chosen ones go: Abraham Pereira, Richard Isenberg, Andrew Powell, James Brown, and Simon Price. I could simply not understand why the Doctor had taken these unworthy fellows instead of taking me, or, if not me, then at the very least, William Jones, who, though not as able a student as I, was at least more gifted than all the others.

I swallowed my sorrow and instead vowed to work harder than ever I had. I read my Bible through, and read also the small stock of books in our humble library. And I prayed that I would grow both in my Spirit and in my body, so that when a similar opportunity presented itself, I would not be found too young or in any other way wanting.

I little thought that I would see the Doctor again.

My prayers were answered seven years after I met the Doctor. It was then that another opportunity presented itself. I was now approaching the age of twenty. The prediction that the Doctor had made in London had come all too true: he was shut off in Africa, lost to the world. Five of us from the school were sent for. We were to join a Lieutenant Dawson and the Doctor's own son, Mr Oswell Livingstone, on what they called the Livingstone Relief Expedition. Our one and only mission was to follow all reported sightings of the Doctor in the African interior until we found him, whether he be in this world or in the next.

The chosen five are the same Nassickers who are on this present Expedition: Matthew Wellington, John Rutton, Benjamin Rutton, John Wainwright, and I. We left Bombay on the SS *Livinia* in February in the Year of Our Lord 1872. The crossing was mostly in good weather, but there was a terrible storm in our second week.

The waters raged around us as the boat shook about, and it was as though I were a boy again, on the terrible dhow that took me into slavery. In my great fear, I sent up a prayer of Penitent Supplication to the God in whose hands the seas are, and all the lands too and the heavens over them, and in a matter of moments, the sea becalmed itself again, and all was tranquil. So have I always been favoured in the sight of the Lord.

Twenty-one days later, we landed at Zanzibar. We embarked to the Glad Tidings that our mission was no longer necessary: by the Grace of God, Doctor Livingstone had been found at Ujiji near Tabora. A Mr Henry Morton Stanley, a journalist said to be from the land of America, had been the agent of the Lord's Merciful Deliverance.

This necessitated an immediate change of plan. We were no longer to go with Lieutenant Dawson as part of the Livingstone Relief Expedition. Instead, we were to head into the interior on the instructions of this same Mr Stanley, along with further supplies to relieve the Doctor, and with *askari* and *pagazi* employed by Mr Stanley. And we were to be joined by Carus Farrar and Farjallah Christie, two other Nassickers who had left the school some years previously to find work in Bombay and Zanzibar. They were both living in Zanzibar when Mr Stanley recruited them.

The seven of us, with our *askari* and *pagazi*, reached Doctor Livingstone on 14 August 1872, in the Year of Our Lord, after three months of marching. And here I have been these nine months since.

Seven years had passed since I saw him, but it may as well have been seventeen. He was a broken shell of the man he had been. Indeed, if he had seemed unprepossessing to my child's eye, he looked positively wretched now. His skin was sallow and toughened. The little hair on his head was now completely grey, and his remaining teeth hung yellowly out of his mouth. He had clearly suffered much, and was a most pitiful sight.

And I found, to my great satisfaction, that the Nassick boys he had initially selected had all proved to be most unfaithful and abandoned him. Here was a chance to redeem our school! Here was a chance to show that it was I who should have been chosen all along. Here was a chance to bring a Lost Lamb back into the fold, for I could see at once that his experiences of the last year had greatly dispirited him and left him most dejected.

My joy was boundless, for in this I saw the workings of the Lord.

I know now that this was my mission all along. Especially after I started to watch him, and saw that he did not pray as often as I did, and when he did, he did not seem to have the same fervour that sometimes seized me. I saw that before I started on my larger mission to turn my people to salvation, I had *this* particular mission assigned to me, to shepherd this lost sheep to the loving Arms of the Shepherd. And so, here, through the Grace of Providence, I am firmly set on the course that Him Above has chosen for me.

4

Fourth Entry from the Journal of Jacob Wainwright, written at Chitambo's Village; in which Wainwright Reports on the Firm Resolution Made by the Whole Party, Recalls the Burial of the Doctor's Heart, and Prays that All May Improve by what they are Taught in the Sufferings of Christ.

I am most pleased to report that, after some contestation, the party are finally of one mind: we are firm in our resolve to take the Doctor's body to the coast for onward burial in England. We buried his heart in Chitambo's village. Halima, who is the most empty-headed of the women, has been inciting the others to chortle about other parts of his body that are to be buried. I am pleased to see that Ntaoéka, who is the only level-headed woman among them, refuses to join in Halima's more vacuous pursuits; she has a firm mind, and I made sure to tell her what I told the others, that what we were burying, and what we would always say we buried, was his heart, and only his heart.

I said the service as we buried that sacred organ. A person whom the Lord has blessed with an abundance of talent must, perforce, constantly struggle against the twin sins of Vanity and Pride. I have struggled, and, I hope, not in vain, to overcome, from an early age, the sin of Pride. But I must admit that my heart swelled inside me to hear the sighs and sniffles of the congregation before me, if I may make so bold as to so call such a small ragtag group of pilgrims.

It seemed to me then that all my life had been in preparation for this task. As I stood before them, I felt as though I was back at the Nassick school, pledging myself into His service.

And so it was that when I stood before the congregation at the burial of the Doctor's heart, I considered that this was perhaps the beginning of my ministry. Sorely distressing as the circumstances were, it pleased me nonetheless that I had found here my true calling, and that I was to be the Chosen Instrument by which the Lost Sheep came back to Christ, that I had been chosen to labour in the Garden of Christ. For with God, nothing is impossible. Ask anything in my Name, said Christ, and I will do it.

I would need to be ordained in England, of course, but here, in Chitambo, was the beginning. For though I was not yet ordained, I had the authority that comes from God, for He is an authority greater than any church. And in my heart, I blessed the Lord for the Blessings of His Loving Munificence.

I read the service for the Burial of the Dead from the Doctor's own Book of Common Prayer: 'Man that is born of a woman hath but a short time to live, and is full of misery. He cometh up, and is cut down, like a flower; he fleeth as it were a shadow, and never continueth in one stay. In the midst of life, we are in death: of whom may we seek for succour, but of thee, O Lord, who for our sins art justly displeased?'

Even as I spoke, it came to me that these words would be wasted on these men and women who understood almost no English. Apart from the Nassickers, as the Doctor called us, of the whole party, only Chuma and Susi, Amoda and Mabruki, speak the language, although the latter speaks it as badly as he does all other things.

If the rest of the party wept, it was not because of the power of my words. So I added some words in Suaheli, translating the book

133

before me, and adding my own flourishes. As I spoke, I was grateful again for the three books with which I have travelled, all from Reverend Wainwright.

My Readers will no doubt be aware that the Nassick school is an outpost of the London Missionary Society and, accordingly, is run on Congregationalist lines. From his letters to those of us who bear his name, it appears the Reverend Wainwright is particularly admiring of the Pilgrim Fathers, who, he says, had through their piety established their faith in a new land. He would that we become the Pilgrim Fathers of our own land and that we, in similar fashion, would assist in the establishment of the True Faith across all of Africa.

When I told him that this was my dearest wish, he sent to me three gifts in the form of books that he said were to be my guide. First is my confirmation gift, the Polyglot Bible, which I read each morning and again at night and whenever it is that I have periods of leisure. Then there is the book I have already talked of, *The Pilgrim's Progress* by Mr Bunyan, a steadfast and certain friend on my journey. On many a day, on the crossing from India to Zanzibar, only the comfort of those pages helped me withstand the heaving of the sea, a turbulence I felt as terribly as when I first felt it, as a child torn from my land and headed for I knew not where. Even in moments of peace, I find it the greatest pleasure to lose myself in those pages that have proved in all seasons to be the most nourishing food for my ravenous spirit.

That I could one day be given the visions to write such a treatise! But no, the humble powers that the Lord has given me are such that I am best emulating the Reverend Bean rather than the Great Dreamer. And by the Reverend Bean, I mean my *Book of Family Worship*. This is the third book that is always with me.

I have as yet no family with which to worship, being one who goes out to the world in the state of bachelorhood, but this *Book of Family Worship* has been an immense comfort to me, for the Reverend Bean has been with me as surely as My Lord Jesus is Faithful. The Reverend Bean consoled me as our ship traversed the seas. Across the untamed places of Africa, he has brought me comfort and succour. He gave me solace on restless nights.

It is astonishing that the Reverend Bean seemed to find a prayer for each occasion. There is a Prayer that we may have Grace to follow the Examples of Godly Men, that we may improve by what we see in the Sufferings of Christ, that we may always Set God before us. There is a prayer in a Time of Public Distress and a prayer at the time of the Assizes or on the Day of a Criminal's Execution.

There is a prayer on a change of weather, and even one that seems to have been written especially for the endlessly talking cookwoman Halima, for the Reverend Bean has been so thoughtful as to write, for those who need it most, a prayer for the Government of the Tongue. I have found the Reverend Bean's prayers immensely powerful, but there is sometimes, I believe, a need to fit the prayers better to our circumstances. The Revered Bean, in his wisdom, has anticipated most occasions on which prayers might be needed. But, having never been in climes such as those of Africa and India, he may not know that a prayer in a time of Great Frost may not be as important as a prayer in a time of Overpowering Heat.

Heat, I have found, indeed both at Nassick and here, and, particularly, extreme heat, can have a most woeful effect upon the mind. It is wont to induce languor, and nothing is as pernicious to the reception of the Lord as a mind that is languorous.

It is my humble prayer that I may do the same as the Reverend Bean, and fashion my own prayers. I flatter myself that I am, as

I showed at the burial of his heart, equal to any task, and that I can fashion any prayer appropriate to the occasion. But in those moments when my powers fail me, and the Gift of the Spirit deserts me, it is comforting to fall back upon those familiar words.

5

Fifth Entry from the Journal of Jacob Wainwright, written at Chitambo's Village; in which Wainwright Takes Inventory of the Doctor's Possessions, Makes a Note on the Leaders of the Expedition with a Reflection upon their Character, and Laments the Unnecessary Presence of Women in Expeditions.

It will be at least a fortnight before we are ready to start for the coast. I have counted the travellers and have noted that there are seventy altogether, including the men and children. I have attached to this record a full list of all who will travel with Doctor Livingstone's body, for I know well enough that a record will be required of all that transpired on the journey, beginning with a full list of all those with whom he travelled.

I must make particular mention of the expedition leaders. There are six expedition leaders responsible for their different departments: Chuma is responsible for navigating our route. Amoda is in charge of the *pagazi*, and Uledi Munyasere is in charge of Provisions. Susi is to take charge of the Doctor's Remains. Chowpereh, as *safire*, will lead the body of men from the front, while Mabruki is in charge of our twenty soldiers, the *askari*, and of their guns and ammunition.

At my insistence, I have been put in charge of the Doctor's papers. This is why I am now, together with the other Nassickers, preparing his papers, instruments, and other personal effects. As I have proved myself the natural leader among the Nassickers, it is I, not Farjallah Christie, who is to take command of the papers.

It is only right that it be so.

Of the seven of us from the Nassick school, it is I who is the most fit for this charge. Farjallah Christie and Carus Farrar are older than me by many years, that is true, but they are no scribes. Indeed, it was a surprise to see them among the men recruited by Mr Stanley, for they had left the Nassick school some years earlier and had both worked as assistants to two surgeons, Farjallah Christie in Zanzibar and Carus Farrar in Bombay. It was them who cut the Doctor open and it is fit that they have this task. And while both Benjamin Rutton and Matthew Wellington are as good writers as I am, they are not as responsible, and besides, neither has plans to be ordained. John Rutton is too young for any grave charge beyond carrying loads, and John Wainwright, well, we may both bear the surname of our benefactor, the Reverend Wainwright, but we are as night and day, for he is as far from being a leader as Mabruki.

I have just the right qualities for such a responsibility. The first seven years of my life aside, I have lived all my life with Englishmen, and have been trained and instructed in their ways of doing things. And so it is that I know how much they value exactitude. It is in that spirit that I enumerate his possessions.

The Doctor travelled with two large tin boxes for his papers and his instruments. Contained in these boxes were all the notebooks he had filled up. Many of these had already been taken to London by Mr Stanley, but even after that gentleman left our party, the Doctor had continued his usual custom of recording each day in his journal.

He wrote most prodigiously. His paper had been sadly depleted and was only replenished on Mr Stanley's orders, when we arrived, meaning that the Doctor had been forced to resort to such material as he had to hand, mainly other books and old newspapers, yellowed and damp, on which he wrote across the existing type. And when the ink he possessed had given out, he had simply used a substitute form of ink that he made from the juice of dark berries.

The only books he had spared writing over were a work by Ptolemy, his Bible, his Church Service book, and his *Book of Common Prayer*. I packed his Bible with reverent hands. On this journey, he said, he had read his Bible four times through, but it grieved me to learn that it had mainly been for want of other material. His Prayer Book I took and kept by me, together with his most recent notebooks.

He had three main books in which he wrote. Firstly was his small notebook for what he called his field notes. Inside, it had paper to write on, but the outside cover was made of metal, and could thus withstand every kind of weather. He often joked that if he ever had to take a bullet, he would prefer that it went through the pocket where he kept this book, for always it was on him. He would write even as he walked, stopping a moment to jot down something or other that he had just that minute thought of or observed.

He also had with him a journal in which he recorded the position of the stars. The third notebook was his journal. He told us that these were the journals that, when at leisure in England, he had turned into the books that brought him fame in his land. In these notebooks, he wrote at greater length the observations already made in his field notes. Here he wrote down all that he saw and thought.

I have appropriated to myself some of the notebooks that were given to him by Mr Stanley, and that were still to be used. It is in these books that I write this narrative of our journey. I am certain that neither the Doctor, were he alive, nor his heirs in England would find any reason to rebuke me for choosing to follow his example in this way, and using, for my own purposes, the notebooks and ink that, alas, he no longer has a need for.

I also oversaw the packing of his letters, carefully arranging them by date. In addition to this copious amount of paper, he also had with him a watch, two telescopes in their boxes, three sextants, and compasses. We also collected all his medicine into his medicine chest. We found a little money: a shilling and a half, three drachmas, and a half scrople. We put his beloved hat in its own box. Chuma tells me that it is the hat that he wore on every single day of each of his three long journeys, from the day he set foot on African soil to his last day on Earth.

I have looked into the notebooks and found that his mind wandered to many things. In some of them are observations of the waxing of the moon, the names of rivers, the heights of hills, maps, and botanical notes. And there are some personal memoranda there too, some despairing and lamentations, and observations about women that are most unseemly. If I could I would excise all such passages, for they add nothing at all. But to do violence to any of the pages is anathema to me. Wrong as they are, it matters that the words be received as he wrote them. And besides, to tear out a passage would affect another.

Now, to the men. As I have already intimated to the Reader, I have appended to this most interesting Journal my complete list of the sixty-nine men and women and children that make up the present party. Shocking as it will appear to my Readers, there are indeed women and children among us, many of them living and born in Sin, and I will say more on them in due course.

I confess that I do not know the expedition leaders as intimately as they know each other, for when I joined the Doctor, sent for by Mr

Stanley after he had found the Doctor in Ujiji, it was to find Amoda, Chuma, and Susi already with him, along with some others.

I was deeply grieved to find when I arrived that the Doctor had in his party men who were heathen, as well as men who were Mohammedan, like Abdullah Susi, who had been with him ten years or more. So long had the Doctor employed this man and not once had he thought to turn him to Christ!

Susi is a tall weathered man with a wiry frame and leathered skin. He is a carpenter and shipbuilder from Shupanga, on the mouth of the Zambesi, where, he says, his people build dhows that sail up and down the coast. It is also where the Doctor's wife, Mrs Mary Livingstone, is buried. He is a constantly laughing man who takes very little seriously, not even his own faith.

It is precisely that which makes him the sort of heathen that would have been easily converted, for though he professes to be of the Mohammedan faith, his is not that firm and stubborn cleaving to his faith, which is so common to those Mohammedans of India and Zanzibar, where, I fear, Christ's kingdom may never truly take root and spread.

He respects only those tenets of this religion as suit him, for a more wretched and debauched creature I have never met. There is no village we have passed in which he has not made approaches to a woman, sometimes more than one, and indeed, it is speculated that he has left bastards scattered between his home of Shupanga on the Zambesi and Zanzibar, and on every journey that he has taken with the Doctor.

Though he has a woman of his own, Misozi, I have watched him make eyes at the cook-woman Halima. She seems to encourage his reprobate attentions though she is attached to Amoda. I say attached, for it will shock my Readers greatly to learn that none of them are married to each other, though I encouraged that the Doctor marry them himself, for he is ordained.

When I was insistent on holding firm on this point, he laughed and said, 'Am I to read the banns on the march, Jacob? Are they to wed in a canoe as we cross a flooded river? On what paper am I to issue the marriage certificate? Will the broad leaves of the tree yonder suffice for the purpose if I dry them of moisture?'

Thus he mocked me as his men continued to live in sin.

As for drinking intoxicating brews of every description, only Adhiamberi, Mabruki, and a few of the lower *pagazi* are Susi's equals. And it is precisely because of his debauched nature that I despaired at the Doctor's failure. For what a rejoicing would there have been in my Father's Kingdom, what a sounding of trumpets, what a ringing chorus of angels would have greeted a sheep as black as this as it stepped over the threshold of the Celestial City! For in my father's house are many Chambers, and in none is there a more rapturous welcome than for the greatest of sinners.

Many of the *pagazi* of his faith are similar in attitude to Susi. The Mohammedans of this party appear willing to respect some tenets and not others. They have clearly no trouble having many women, but are not always inclined to obey the strictures on the consumption of intoxicating beverages and strong liquors.

Chuma, with whom the Doctor has worked the longest of all the men, is, in contrast, more thoughtful and quiet. As I recalled from having met him seven years before, his first name is James, and though he professes to be a Christian, I have never once heard him exclaim his faith with any great exuberance. He is most animated when he talks of maps and drawings, and mountains and rivers.

The other expedition leaders are Amoda, Chowpereh, Munyasere, and Mabruki. Amoda, a Suaheli from Zanzibar, is a big and powerful man of quick temper and irascible nature. Chowpereh is fast and foolish, while Munyasere is a huntsman happiest with a gun. They call him Uledi, meaning 'Master Craftsman'. Mabruki is a nothing of a man. He is a man of low inclinations, and is even more of a debauched reprobate than Susi. The less said about him the better.

I thought it right that I be made an expedition leader, for as the most competent penman, I was to be the scribe of the party. Amoda laughed at this and said, 'When the expedition becomes one about reading and writing, Uledi, we shall call on you.' When Amoda calls me Uledi, it is not the compliment that it is to Munyasere, but is said in a sneering manner that implies that I am lesser than he is.

Amoda is a competent man, that is true, but he is a hard taskmaster, and though the men respect his abilities, they often chafe under the yoke of his rule, for he has no respect for men who are not as strong as he.

I thought there was nothing more to be said of Mabruki, but I find myself making a further note on this most incompetent of men. He does not take seriously any responsibility, least of all that of being a husband. He not only abandoned two women, both of whom he left with child, but has also now taken up with a woman of our party called Ntaoéka, or perhaps I should say he has attached himself to her, for no law would ever recognise such a marriage.

He bears the full name Mabruki Speke because he once travelled with Lieutenant Speke, the Nile explorer. He deserted that mission, naturally, for he is the sort of man who would desert. But for the cunning that made him convince Mr Stanley that he knew more English than he actually did, and his comradeship with Bombay, the leader of Mr Stanley's expedition, he would have found no employment at all. He is a man full of tricks and deceptions. Happily for the party, in Farjallah Christie and Carus Farrar, we have two able marksmen, much more able than Mabruki ever will be.

Under these expedition leaders fall nine more gunmen, or *askari*, in addition to Mabruki and thirty-nine *pagazi*, many of whom were sent by Mr Stanley from Zanzibar, and were naturally keen to return to their homes in Zanzibar and the neighbouring islands of Pemba and Lamu.

As I have mentioned already, there are also ten women and their six children. It may surprise my Readers as much as it surprised me to learn that there are women and children on these expeditions of exploration. The reality of expedition life is that the men rest at villages so frequently, and sometimes for so long, that it allows all sorts of mischief to develop in their relations with local women.

When the time to leave came, it was not uncommon for one woman or another to attach herself to the party, and thus become part of the group. Nor was it uncommon for such women to find themselves with child a few months later. It is a licentious business, this travelling, with far too many opportunities for sin, for the men all have wives awaiting them at home.

It would appear that most of the leaders sanction this sort of licentiousness out of a misplaced sense of necessity, for without a certain degree of permissiveness, they may well find themselves with no porters. I was troubled to see that the Doctor appeared to not only sanction this behaviour, but to be a little too concerned with the matrimonial affairs of his men, even to the point of procuring women and making matches for them.

Such was the case with one of the young women who accompany us now, Ntaoéka she is called, and she is by no means ill-favoured. I have no time for frivolities such as women, but if she were in a garden, she might well be considered its most beautiful flower. She is a Manyuema woman who joined the party when the Doctor fell ill at Ujiji, before we arrived. The Doctor wanted another woman, mainly to keep Halima company, and though she offered herself as an assistant to Halima, the Doctor thought she was too good-looking to move within the party without a man.

'I asked her,' he told me, 'to choose between Chuma, Gardner, and Mabruki. She chose to be with Mabruki, though I would have preferred that it be Chuma. He needs a woman to straighten him up.'

When I am ordained, I will be able to more freely comment on how my parishioners live with their wives, but for now, it suffices to say that any person with eyes can see that Mabruki and Ntaoéka could not be more ill-suited. She is far superior to him, and is much too good, in fact, to be merely a woman of the road. If Mabruki has any sense, he will make her his wife, but that is unlikely, for he ran away from two women whom he left with child.

Ntaoéka's looks have often caused quarrels with the other women, particularly with Halima, the Doctor's sharp-tongued cook. The Doctor was at great pains to ensure harmony between them, though if you ask me, he would have achieved perfect harmony by sending them all packing. It does not help that both of them consider Misozi, who is Susi's road woman, to be their own particular friend. She is a veritable Pliable, and as did that gentleman with Stubborn and Christian, she bends one way, then another, first to one and then the other, and far from defusing the quarrels between them, she only makes them worse.

Ntaoéka too may as well be called Pliable, though her pliability is not offensive in itself, as it does not arise from a feeble-minded nature, but is rather of the kind that always aspires to be agreeable. In this, I feel, she has been failed both by the Doctor and by the man who styles himself her husband, a lazy scoundrel who is happiest when he is in liquor.

She could, with the right man, be moulded into a most excellent wife. As the Apostle Paul said, woman, submit to your husband. Of course, she must first accept Christ. And even if she had chosen Chuma, it would not have sufficed, for though Chuma was baptised James, his Christianity is not worn deeply, but rather on the surface. With a Christian husband, Ntaoéka could have been converted. Her name should be as beautiful as her eyes, Esther perhaps, or Ruth, so faithful.

It is heathen women like Ntaoéka that I am determined to save, for then they will save their children. It grieves me deeply to look at Ntaoéka and know that had she only met the right man, she could have been as faithful as Ruth was to Naomi. Entreat me not to leave thee, or to return from following after thee, she said, for whither thou goest, I will go; and where thou lodgest, I will lodge. Your people shall be my people, and your God shall be my God. And through her faith she bore Jesse, and through him was born King David, the vanquisher of Goliath and the ancestor of Our Lord Jesus Christ.

As I pause for a minute on David and his House, I have wondered often why it is that, in their Gospels, three of the Apostles trace the lineage of Jesus to David through Joseph, when he was, after all, only the husband of Mary, and not the father of Jesus. When I asked the Reverend Wainwright this question, he appeared most impatient with it.

Perhaps this is one of those mysteries like the puzzle of where Cain got a woman to take to wife when he was cast out of God's Grace and banished east of Eden. There were only four people created then, Adam and Eve, his wife; Abel, slain by Cain; and Cain himself. From where, then, came Cain's wife? Such are the mysteries that will, no doubt, be revealed to me through further reflection and study with those who have discerned these mysteries, and above all, through the operation of Grace.

Nor were these questions I could have discussed with the Doctor. He took far too little interest in such questions, as little interest as he took in the spiritual welfare of his companions. In contrast, he took far too keen an interest in the material goings-on of the party, and in who was sharing a bed with whom. I recall his coming to me a few months ago and saying, 'That poor girl, Jacob.'

'What poor girl?' I said.

I looked to where Halima was moving; she had just served him the dough cakes that were the only things his bad teeth could chew.

'Her people were here to say she was dead,' he said, 'but all they could think about was their goats.'

I became alarmed and thought he might have had too much sun. But it transpired that he was talking of a girl who had married one of the *pagazi* the week before, but whose family had spirited her away, only for her to die in their midst a few days ago.

'All that her people want are the goats they were promised in mar-riage,' the Doctor said. 'They come to me, Jacob, and ask for the goats. Oh, our goats, they lament, our ten goats. We want our goats. But no word of mourning at all for that beautiful creature. Oh, our goats!'

He had started to laugh at that point, and I knew by then that when the Doctor laughed thus, he laughed for a long time, some-times until he coughed and gasped, and tears ran from his eyes. In these moments, he had about him the same look on his face of the acrobat outside the cathedral in Bombay who whirled and whirled for no reason at all.

It was most disappointing. I had thought this man would be filled with the Light of the Redeemer, that he would stand steadfast before

147

all as one who brings with him the Radiance of the Saviour. And here he was, procuring women for his men.

I was astonished to learn on my arrival that the Doctor had gone as far as purchasing Halima for Amoda, for she had been the slave of an old Arab at Kazeh. If it had been a case of manumission, and he had freed her for her own sake, there would have been some glory in it, but to procure a slave in this way for one of his men seemed most un-Christlike.

And the Halima in question is a particularly troublesome woman, given to much levity and unable, apparently, to think seriously on any matter. Her propensity for causing quarrels among the women is great. The Apostle James may have been writing about her when he said: even so the tongue is a little member and boasteth great things. Behold, how great a matter a little fire kindleth! There is yet more reason, other than her clacking tongue, that Halima may cause more. Susi has not troubled to hide his admiration for the woman, he has not troubled to hide it from Amoda, nor from his own woman Misozi.

Were it only up to me, she and the other women would have gone long ago; there is nothing like a woman to hold back an expedition. When Mr Stanley sent us on the Expedition to relieve the Doctor last August, we marched at a steady pace. I am certain that was because we had no women in our party. With women involved, it is possible to lose a month or more simply from their dawdling. For where there are women, there are children, and the whole is enough to slow progress.

I expressed my doubts about the women and suggested that perhaps they should remain where they were. Misozi immediately rounded on me and said, 'And why should we stay behind? What are we to do, without our men?'

Halima cackled and said, 'Get new ones, of course.'

This is what I mean about the woman's tongue. They are God's creatures, women, and indeed, one should not forget that it was a woman who washed the feet of Christ with her tears; it was a woman who anointed His body at the burial and wept as He was going to the cross and sat by His sepulchre when He was buried. It was women who were first with Him on the Glorious Morn of His Resurrection, and it was women who were the first to bring the tidings to His disciples that He was risen indeed, from the dead He was risen.

But woman is also how sin came into the world. Through her weakness, Eve was tempted. The snake chose with the cunning of the Devil. Against Adam's firmness, the Devil would not have withstood. Were it all in my power, I would have fain sent the women away, every last one of them, and their children too, for I fear that the women will bring us nothing but strife.

6

Sixth Entry from the Journal of Jacob Wainwright, written at Chitambo's Village; in which Wainwright Contemplates the Pilgrimage before him and Prays that he may reach the Celestial City without meeting Stumbling Blocks, Humiliations, Temptations, and Other Evils, and Above All, that he and his Party may pass Safely through the Valley of the Shadow of Death.

The Nassickers have made good progress in ordering and sorting through the Doctor's papers and possessions. Under my direction, these have been packed into as few boxes as possible, while making sure that each container is not too heavy for one or at most two men to carry between them.

I bargained hard with Amoda to have some of the men handed over to my charge to carry the Doctor's possessions, for even if the Nassickers were to carry full loads, and not the half loads agreed to with the Doctor, there are simply not enough of us. This only led to a flaring of the old grievance. Amoda shared the anger of the inferior *pagazi* that we Nassickers were contracted to carry half loads for double the pay given to the *pagazi*.

He is particularly contemptuous of John Wainwright, who can be found breathing hard after marching of any length. It has been this way with him since we touched land. In our march down to relieve the Doctor, we had heard endless tales of John's weak heart, John's weak chest, John's weak legs, how John suffers headaches in the heat and John's back aches from carrying anything at all. We learned that we have to give him the smallest load; it was either that or listen to him complaining all the way. And I learned to be ashamed of this man with whom I was connected through our name. I could only be thankful that he was no real brother of mine, and made sure to correct anyone who assumed our kinship.

Amoda considered him lazy beyond redemption. He scorned my writing, but with John he seemed to scorn his very existence. 'All that one needs,' he said whenever any of John's complaints came to him, 'is a sound and thorough beating. One that will sort him out like it sorted out Chirango.'

There has already been some unpleasantness between the two. When the Nassickers first refused to carry the loads given them, the Doctor tried to force us into submission, but Matthew Wellington and Carus Farrar were firm in explaining that those were not the conditions on which we had been hired. The agreement was that all the Nassickers were to carry only half loads. For we were more than mere *pagazi*, we had other skills; for one thing, unlike the *pagazi*, we all spoke English. After some arguing, the Doctor had conceded the point, adding, with exasperation, 'Now I know that educated free blacks are to be avoided, they are expensive and too much the gentlemen for work.'

Amoda was particularly irritable as he considered that the papers we carried were entirely valueless. We could leave some of them behind, he said, but I pointed out how precious they all were. He expressed great impatience at this. 'I would rather carry food than paper,' he said.

With the Doctor gone, John Wainwright was entirely in Amoda's power. He had come to me to say he did not want to go on the march.

'Will you stay here in Chitambo, where you don't speak the language?' I asked.

He had nothing to say to that. All he could say was that he would not answer to Amoda.

I had my thoughts on persuading Amoda on the papers and hardly listened. In the end, I left it to Chuma to explain to Amoda why it mattered that all the Doctor's possessions should be borne along with him. With great reluctance, Amoda was brought round to my way of thinking, which was, of course, the right way of thinking.

The only thing we left behind was some of the old newspapers that had not been written over by the Doctor and that Susi suggested should be left with Chitambo, so that he could show proof, if it was ever needed, that the Doctor had been in that place and left his heart behind.

While we Nassickers carry the papers, James Chuma and Abdullah Susi are in charge of the body itself. They will rotate with others on the march. One of the *pagazi* sent by Mr Stanley, a certain Chirango Kirango, who had been a troublesome sort of fellow before being given a most deserved beating on the Doctor's orders, was eager to be one of the carriers, but he was given over to Amoda, Munyasere, and Chowpereh, who are to be responsible for supplies and ensuring food.

Thus have the responsibilities been allocated, and I have earned my place among the expedition leaders. All we wait for now is for the Doctor's body to be ready for travel. He died twelve days ago and has been drying since then, and Carus Farrar assures us that it will be just under a week, possibly less, before he is fully dry and we are ready to travel.

In the meantime, the leaders determined upon a path, and it is thanks mainly to Chuma, who is to be our navigator. There is no question that I am the most superior man here, the best read and the one with the best English, but I must own that Chuma is no mean cartographer. This of course is not due to any superior intelligence, but due to his having spent a lifetime travelling with the Doctor.

He has drawn a rough but detailed map that shows where he believes Chitambo is in relation to the sea. He has pointed out to us that the easiest course would be for us to head east as the vulture flies and head straight for the coastal town that is nearest to us, which is the town of Kilwa on the Indian Ocean. We would then commission dhows to sail up the coast to Zanzibar, or else walk along the coastline until we find a convenient crossing, though Susi, who knows everything there is to know about the sea, says the tides in that part may make sailing upwards difficult.

Amoda has advised against such a course as it is likely to be beset with innumerable difficulties. It is not the tides or currents that trouble him, but getting to Kilwa itself. For this place is the nearest slave port to where we are.

'Getting to Kilwa would mean that we find ourselves on the same routes that are used by parties of slave traders.'

The men nodded as they considered his words.

'Sure, we have ammunition,' Amoda continued. 'But we have just twenty guns, and several flintlock muskets besides. It is not worth it to attempt to fight slavers all while we make our way through these strange lands.

'Add to that the fact that we are carrying the Bwana's body, an act which is likely to be regarded with great suspicion by all we meet, whether slavers or not. Where we can control matters, we should do so.'

Thus it was agreed that we should take a route that is less likely to be used by slavers, even though such a route may be more tortuous. Accordingly, we are to hold east as far as we can, in a northerly direction, getting as far northeast as we can. When we then find ourselves in the familiar territory of Chungu's and Kapesha's lands, which Chuma, Susi, and Amoda went to with the Bwana two years previously, we will then head north, towards Unyanyembe and the Arab settlement of Kazeh in Tabora and from there to Bagamoio, the town by the coast from where we will cross the sea to Zanzibar.

'There is something we must keep well in mind,' Susi said. 'It would be well for us if the journey were to end before the start of Ramadan. The *pagazi* as we all know are mainly of the Mohammedan faith. It would not do well for them to march while they are fasting.'

Munyasere and Chowpereh nodded as Susi spoke.

'Ramadan begins in the month of November,' Amoda said, 'and here we are, at the start of the month of May. The journey will have finished long before then, that I can swear on the lives of my sons. If we follow the route drawn for us by Chuma, it will take no more than three months of steady marching, four at the most.'

We were all assured by Amoda's confidence. For my part, I began to pray as hard as I could that I would pass Our Lord's birthday, the Christmas feast, in England. I must own to feeling mounting excitement at the prospect of entering the great city of London, to which I have never been, but which shines before the eye of my mind as brightly as did the Celestial City in the mind of Christian.

For in London is my Mount Zion; in London I will be ordained, and ready finally to begin my mission. I know not whether this journey before will take me through the Palace Beautiful, the Delectable Mountains, or the Land of Beulah, but I can, at any rate, pray that I will not meet Apollyon or Beelzebub, or pass through Vanity Fair, nor climb the Hill Difficulty, get mired in the Slough of Despond, or enter the Valley of Humiliation. Above all, I pray with all my might that neither I nor any of my companions will pass through the Valley of the Shadow of Death.

7

Seventh Entry from the Journal of Jacob Wainwright, written at Mua-namuzungu's Village; in which the Livingstone Expedition sets off, preceded by a Mournful Farewell to Chitambo and his People before Marching into the Interior, where Wainwright prays for the Blessings of Providence and Redemption.

The Livingstone Expedition, if I may be so bold as to give this name to our small band of Pilgrims, set off from Chitambo's before dawn on the sixteenth day of May 1873, in the Year of Our Lord. It was exactly fifteen days after the Doctor's Death. Such was the determination of the party that we were all up before the cockerels gave the cry.

Then we made our final call on Chitambo, who came back with us to our settlement. As he watched the preparations for our final departure, he told us we were to pass through his brother Mua-namuzungu's village. He had already sent a messenger with word, he said. Indeed, we had seen the man being instructed in his message, and heard him reciting it over and over again to himself, so that he remembered it.

I am told that it is the way that the chiefs in these parts send messengers to each other. Their men carry messages of considerable length over great distances, and deliver them word for word. On even longer distances, two or more will go together, rehearsing and reciting to each other the message that they bear.

We thanked Chitambo for sending this emissary and gave him strict injunctions to keep the grass around the grave of the Doctor's heart cleared, so as to save it from the bush fires. And he was to be sure that no man would cut down the tree under which his heart reposed. We showed him as well the signpost that we had built out of two high thick posts, with a crosspiece which we covered with tar.

We left the rest of the tar with him, so that he and his people might use it should the need arise. We also left with him a large tin biscuit box and some newspapers. 'On this is printed the white man's knowledge,' we said, 'and if, in future, travellers from their lands should come this way, you and your descendants are to show them this, that they may know that one of them has been on your land.'

As he promised to do all this, he looked at us wistfully and said, 'My people too were travellers once, and they went all the way to the sea. But these Engerese, if they come, they should not be long in coming, because there might at any time be an invasion of the Mazitu. And if that happens, I and my people will be forced to fly further north into the forests beyond the Lualaba.'

Then he added, 'The tree might be cut down for a canoe by some-one, and then all trace of it would be lost.'

We assured him that they would come soon, the English, but we knew as well as he did that it was a guarantee we could not make.

Our mournful burden secure, we walked past the line of thatched houses, past the Chief's enclosure, past the cattle pens, and past the granaries, where chickens pecked at stray grains on the ground. The sky above was a brilliant blue. At the head were Amoda and Chowpereh, as the *safire*. Majwara blew at his horn and beat the drum. Chitambo's wives ululated in echo. Majwara blew the horn again. The party gave a loud cheer as Chitambo's people shouted.

Chitambo gave a last wave. Turning our backs on his people, we faced north and followed the winding river out of the Bangweulu swamps and into the unknown.

We had agreed that the caravan would travel in the same manner that we had adopted on our approach to Chitambo, the only difference being that instead of a living man who marched in our midst, the Doctor would be a corpse.

In front, leading us as the *safire*, was Chowpereh, with Munyasere next to him. As the leading guide, Chowpereh carried the blood-red flag of the Sultan of Zanzibar, while, next to him, Munyasere held aloft the Doctor's flag, the Union Jack. As he had been appointed Her Majesty's honorary consul, the Doctor had the right to carry before him the flag of his nation. The two flags, fluttering in the breeze, were a gladsome sight before us; they served, we hoped, as protection from the people through whose territories we passed.

Amoda cautioned us that they only protected us in those territories where their authority was recognised. At present, we were too deep in the interior for them to make a difference. We were so far beyond the reach of the Sultan of Zanzibar's power that his name was but the stuff of fable. Nevertheless, it did us good to see those familiar emblems before us.

Behind Chowpereh came our ten *askari* bearing twenty guns and rounds of ammunition, as well as their own loads. They each carried a flintlock musket in addition to their rifle. Then came Majwara, as the *kirangozi*, who set the pace of the march and beat a steady rhythm on his drum that gave strength even to the sorest feet. He occasionally blew his horn to lift our spirits.

After Majwara came us Nassickers, with the Doctor's papers, and behind us Nassickers came the Mournful Burden. It was carried in rotation by different *pagazi*, with Susi always making sure that only men of the same height carried it to avoid overburdening the shorter of the bearers.

Chirango, who is far from being the first to volunteer for any unforced labour, offered to carry the Doctor, eagerly presenting himself and offering to carry the 'White Bones', as he called them. He was declined, and came immediately to me that he might carry the 'White Papers'.

We had enough men for the papers, I told him, and so Chirango took his place among the lower *pagazi*, but with a smiling affability that was most pleasing to behold. I must say that such a spirit was a surprise, for he has not always been the most obliging of men.

In the rear, Misozi, Halima, and the children kept up a steady chatter that was occasionally broken up by singing. The women's load was light, for they carry only their possessions and cooking implements. They also share the carrying of the children when they are too tired to walk.

Amoda was keen to encourage the party to act as normal as possible. As he said, it was important that this be seen as any other travelling party, so though our task was mournful and our burden heavy, Majwara's horn blew cheerfully and his drum beat steadily, those who attached bells to their feet and loads jingled them, and the women and the *pagazi* sang. It could have been any other march.

As our line marched, occasionally, I walked back to be with the women, that I might say a word or two to rush them along. Indeed, I have said women are liable to slow down an Expedition, but I must confess that I found their singing pleasant, particularly that of Ntaoéka, who has a sweet and true voice. It transpired that when we came to a particularly swampy part of our path, a few times, I had to help her cross the stream, for she asked for my assistance most pleasantly. I looked to where her man, Mabruki, was; he had already crossed with the other *pagazi*.

'Will you help only Ntaoéka and leave the rest of us standing?' said Halima. Faced with that, I had no choice but to help all the women, and their children, across the stream while Halima cackled that I looked stronger than I appeared under my clothes. As I carried Halima's child, Losi, across, I was pleased to see Chirango drop his own package to come to my aid.

The swampy bit of ground passed, we marched well for a full day, spent the night in a clearing, and marched again until we reached Muanamuzungu's village just before sunset.

Chitambo, as promised, had sent word of our arrival to Muanamuzungu, who was his brother. They looked as unlike as brothers could look; where Chitambo was fat and genial, his brother was slim of figure and of serious mien. Indeed, when men of these parts talk of their brothers, it is not always certain whether they refer to men of the same blood, or whether it is simply a word loosely used to denote men with whom they have an alliance.

He welcomed us warmly, however, though it was clear that without Chitambo's approbation, he would have sent us packing. He had already given thought to where we would sleep and showed us to five huts on the edge of the settlement that his people used to store grain after a harvest, but at that time stood empty as it was not harvest season.

We were to settle there for the night, he said, but he was stern in insisting that in the morning, he wanted us gone. We assured him of our intentions to leave as soon as was possible and made preparations for the night. The women cooked an evening meal, we sat and ate, and soon, exhaustion crept over all the party and the camp fell to sleep.

8

Eighth Entry from the Journal of Jacob Wainwright, written at Mua-namuzungu; in which the Party fall Gravely Ill from a Disputed Illness and Wainwright prays for Relief from Grave Afflictions.

After such a determined departure, it sorrows me to report that we have been delayed this entire month by a most grievous illness that has afflicted the whole party. We remain a few days' walk from where our Expedition started, in the land of Muanamuzungu.

I was myself afflicted most severely and was completely unable to pick up my pen, let alone to write with it. It is for this reason that I have not been able to transmit to this journal timely information on how the party came to be struck down. Indeed, it is only today that I have been able to make up for this lamentable lapse.

On our leaving Chitambo, we were, as I have narrated, welcomed warmly enough by Chitambo's brother Muanamuzungu. But already on the first morning after our pleasant night on his land, the whole party lay stricken.

It is a strange illness. I have felt it most in my limbs and muscles, as have many of the others. The symptoms we all share are intense pain in the limbs and face, a great lassitude, and, in the most severe cases, a complete inability to move. Throughout our illness, Muanamuzu-ngu has been as kind to us as his brother Chitambo was welcoming.

The most afflicted appears to be Susi, who has suffered greatly. For him, the disease settled first in one leg, and then, just as he thought he had recovered, it moved to the other. Chuma has pain in his thighs and groin and cannot walk at all. A *pagazi* called Songolo is also gravely ill; he feels it most in his limbs. Chirango has also been struck. Despite his own illness, he has been tending to me most assiduously.

I am pleased to report that he has expressed some interest in coming to know more of the Mercies of Christ. He may come to be my first convert, a most important convert too should he be restored, as he hopes, to the throne of his land. I am hoping in time to dissuade him from playing the heathen instrument that he plays every night and that he calls the *njari*. There is something unseemly about the sound it produces. Indeed, when he plays it, it appears to induce a sort of trance in his listeners. Altogether, I have found it all too unsettlingly similar in effect to the pipes of the snake charmers at the Bombay market.

A quarrel threatened to break out between Chirango and Carus Farrar earlier. Carus Farrar and Farjallah Christie, as the men in the party who know the most about physical ailments, have been, when they are not themselves prostrated, seeking to find means to relieve the whole party. To this end, they have been trying to trace the course of the disease, in the hope that identifying its source may help in seeking if not a cure, then at least its alleviation.

Chirango has been loud in his belief that the whole party are suffering the effects of overeating. 'Indeed, much meat was consumed when we arrived,' he said, and he pointed to the dangers of eating offal.

Carus Farrar contradicted him sharply: he believes that the explanation for the whole party, and not just one or two, falling ill lies in the marshy swamps through which we have been wading. The mischief, he believes, has been done by the continual wading through water before the Doctor's death; an illness that came from the water settled then, he believes, possibly from the leeches that clung so tenaciously to us as we crossed, and has been waiting for some slight provocation to flare up. He believes that our tramp to Muanamuzungu, which was almost entirely through the same marshy swamps, turned the scales against us.

Farjallah Christie is in agreement with this conclusion, which he says is well supported by the general absence of illness in the children. Of the children, only Majwara has been afflicted. Halima was most insistent, indeed most hysterical in this matter, that Losi and the smaller children be carried through the swamps, for fear that they would be drowned. It was a long slow progress, carrying first the children, then the goods. That the children have largely escaped unscathed is proof, Carus agreed, that the damage was done by the brackish, swampy waters.

At this, Chirango begged most humbly for their forgiveness and said he would say nothing further to contradict them but do all he could to assist. 'Chirango,' he said, 'though the most ill among you, ill enough to know what ails him, trusts to those of you who have swallowed the White Man's knowledge, though he has seen many examples of such cases.'

The women were struck in a similar manner; we can only give thanks that our weakness means that we do not require much food, and thus only eat once a day, with the food being sent over through the kindness of Muanamuzungu. In the meantime, he asked that various of the families take in the six children in our party, on the understanding that they were to help around the homestead in exchange for their food.

Halima is firm in her belief that witchcraft is the source of our troubles, and that at the bottom of it all is Chitambo's witch doctor, whom she says she saw talking to Chirango on the day the Doctor died. I was quick to dispel her heathen suspicions. Indeed, if Carus Farrar and Farjallah Christie are right about what ails us, then these Bangweulu swamps have truly been a Slough of Despond, and Muanamuzungu has been that good figure, Help, who thrust his hands into the Slough to pull us out.

In addition to this illness, we soon had to contend with another crisis. While we were thus stricken, the heavens opened and a most unseasonal rain fell upon the land, and on us. Rain is most unwelcome to all travellers, but it was particularly unwelcome to us, for it endangered all the work that had gone into preparing the Doctor's body for the travels ahead.

For the moment, all was safe, for the body had been put in its own hut, together with our packages, and was in no immediate danger from the rains. But it was clear that if the rains continued not only here at Muanamuzungu but also in the future, protective measures would need to be taken to ensure that no damage undid all the careful work of two weeks.

By this time, fortunately, Amoda had recovered sufficiently to take command in the matter. It is to his credit that he came up with the idea to have the canvas covering tarred. Amoda recalled that we had left our remaining stock of tar with Chitambo. All that was needed to do was send for it, and as Chitambo was about two days' walk, it would be a matter of four days before a messenger went thither and returned to Muanamuzungu.

Chirango, who had up to that point been thought gravely ill, insisted on going, protesting that he was well enough to travel, and indeed, he rallied quite remarkably and accompanied Wadi Saféné and Asmani as they made their way to Chitambo's village.

They returned five days later with the cask of tar, and with

Chitambo's sorrowful protestations at the delay that kept us here. Amoda oversaw the coating of tar over the canvas surrounding the body. This seemed to answer all purposes. Fortunately, in this interval the rains entirely ceased. But the rains had brought with them yet another crisis.

The rains had fallen with darkness on Muanamuzungu's suspicious mind, for they had come at a time that they were not expected. The Chief held counsel with his rainmakers and his other men of native medicine and they told him that the rains were an ill omen, a portent of what was to come.

He thus expressed the strongest inclination to see us depart his land. He had given permission for us to camp one night only, possibly two, he said, and after that, his brother had assured him, the strange men who carried with them the bones of the dead would soon be gone from his land. But now the whole party had fallen ill, and like as not, we would have more dead bodies to carry away and he could not allow death to come from strangers to his people.

We were now under the greatest of pressure to move. We met with a stroke of fortune when Carus Farrar, who had become stronger, shot three large buffaloes. We presented these to Muanamuzungu and his people, who protested that it was too much meat and we were to have our share of it. There was much laughter and rejoicing at this unexpected feast. After that, Muanamuzungu was mollified to a considerable degree and exhibited towards us the greatest kindness. Not a day passed without his bringing us some present or other.

The women had sufficiently recovered to make themselves useful in preparing some of the meat for our own travels. Halima, Misozi, and Ntaoéka between them dried as much of the buffalo meat as they could. As I passed them at work, Halima shook a string of meat at me and said, 'Ah, if we had only sliced the Bwana small-small like this, he would have dried in no time.'

The woman is incorrigible. I left them to their laughter but was pleased to see that Ntaoéka did not laugh as giddily as did the others. I like the name Judith for her, if she were ever to convert. Judith is just the name I would choose for her.

In his flush of generosity, and gratitude for the two buffaloes, Muanamuzungu gave us a cow and a donkey. The cow was in milk, which led to Halima's excitedly telling us about the spiced tea with milk that they drank at the Liwali's house. She would see what she could devise on the road. To my great regret, Muanamuzungu also sent two large drums full of *pombe*, which were gladly taken up by the men. We agreed that we would set forth at dawn the next day.

We were now fully recovered. Ntaoéka and Misozi departed for the village to bring back the children, in order to prepare to depart. They were scarcely back from their short walk when came news of a shocking nature. A woman of our party, Kaniki, who had attached herself to Chirango, had taken violently ill and had sunk under the illness. Another three were stricken, Susi and his woman Misozi, and Songolo. They had taken ill after drinking the *pombe* sent to us by Muanamuzungu. All four were so unwell and vomited such copious amounts that they could barely walk.

It looked as though the illness had spread from the limbs to the bowels. And just as it looked like Susi was recovering, his woman Misozi succumbed to her illness, and within hours, just like Kaniki, was dead. Barely two hours later, Songolo too succumbed.

The whole party were plunged into deep mourning. Though Susi promised to rally, the three deaths were so distressing to Muanamuzungu's ease of mind that the goodwill we had procured through the gift of the buffaloes had all but dissipated. As unquestioningly as he had embraced us, he now turned on us. We were bearers of ill fortune, he said, and he wanted us off his land at once. And we were to take our dead, all of our dead, with us. We were to leave at once.

9

Ninth Entry from the Journal of Jacob Wainwright, written at Chis-alamala; in which the Expedition reaches the Luapula and Wain-wright Prays to Him Above to Incline our Hearts to those who do not yet know His Name and enter the Hearts of all Men that they may turn from Sin.

We have relocated to a small hill that is far from, but within sight of, Muanamuzungu's land. Though Susi and Amoda pleaded with Muanamuzungu most urgently that our party be allowed to rest a little more, he was resolute in his wish to see us leave his land.

He relented only as far as pointing us in the direction we were to go in. 'When you reach that hill,' he said, 'you will have left my land. The Luapula will be before you, but where you go, I care not, for you have brought death to my land and I want you gone before you bring the death you carry to my people.'

Susi repeated to him the words of his brother and said, 'Recall the wise words of your brother Chitambo, who said to us that death often comes to those on journeys, even when they do not expect it.'

'My brother,' said Muanamuzungu, 'is a fool.'

Armed with spears, his men lined up along our path to make sure that we left his land. What a contrast there was between our departure from his brother's land and this!

As his final act of spite against us, Muanamuzungu took back the cow he had given us as a gift. He grudgingly allowed us to keep the donkey, and it was on this creature that Susi lay as he could not walk at all. Seven of the *pagazi* were too weak to serve as porters, and even the Nassickers had to become *pagazi* and assist in the carrying of loads. John Wainwright was the loudest in complaining, but I made sure to tell him that this resentment had to give way to the necessary exigencies of our situation.

We were further burdened by having to carry the corpses of Kaniki, Misozi, and Songolo as far as we could outside Muanamuzungu's territory. Chirango volunteered to carry so many packages that he was left with a heap, which he then had to request assistance to carry. We managed as best as we could and made slow progress.

It took half a day to reach the small hill that was the boundary of Muanamuzungu's land, and a true Hill Difficulty it proved to be. At the first opportunity, we conducted burial services for the fallen three. Before that there were some arguments as to what should happen to the bodies. The women were long in arguing that we should do to the bodies what we had done with the Bwana. Halima wailed loud and long. Misozi, she said, would not rest happily because she had always feared turning into a *shetani* ghost. Amoda, rather more roughly than was warranted, told her not to be stupid. It was bad enough to carry the Doctor's body; how could we carry four bodies at once?

Chuma was gentler in his opposition and pointed out the gathering clouds above. 'We were fortunate to get sun to dry Bwana Daudi's body in Chitambo,' he said. 'These threatening rains mean that the best course would be to bury them at once.'

It was hard to tell whether Susi mourned Misozi, for he was prostrated by his illness. Halima certainly mourned for her, giving voice to her grief, though it seemed to be more from guilt than any other feeling, for certainly, she had not always been kind to the woman.

As for Chirango, the man conducted himself with a dignity that was most pleasing to see. He displayed great sanguinity at the death of his companion, the woman Kaniki. 'It is how fate has always been with me,' he said. 'I am heir to a kingdom that is lost, and now my woman has gone before she could give me just one seed.'

I was most gratified that Chirango asked me to say a few words over her body. There is no mind more fertile to the reception of His word than one ravaged by a new grief, or recovering from an affliction, and here was Chirango, in both these interesting states. I did not hesitate to suggest to him that he might seek solace in He who comforts all.

But it would seem that I was planting in a field already furrowed. My words at the Bwana's funeral appear to have had a most penetrating effect on Chirango. What I said had struck him so forcibly, he said, that he wanted to know more about my God, for he had not yet found any god who truly suited him.

Though I naturally frowned on his belief that he could try on and discard a god as one would choose a garment, I was pleased to see that, as far as my mission went, I had, at least, one prospect. 'The first commandment, Chirango,' I said to him, 'is thou shalt have no other gods than me. There is only one God: I am the Lord your God, He says.'

It came to me then that I was the most appropriate person to render a translation of His Holy Word into Suaheli. What a thing that would be. What souls would be turned to God then, if they understand the Word in their own language! Perhaps I could do in the Suaheli language what my former headmaster, the Reverend Isenberg, had done in the Abyssinian tongue. But I soon turned my thoughts in the direction of the more urgent matter of conducting a service over the bodies of our fallen companions.

Having buried them and rested three nights in a clearing, we resumed our journey and headed in the direction of the Luapula. Chirango stuck by me while I told him of the glories of God's Kingdom. Even when it was his turn to carry the Doctor's body, he insisted that I walk close to him.

A pang struck me when I considered that but for the death of his wife, I might have had two converts in the party, but I soon put the thought out of my mind when I considered that without Kaniki's death, Chirango might not have been so receptive to His word. The Lord moves in mysterious ways, His wonders to perform! Call to me and I will answer you, he says, and I will show you Wonders you have never heard of.

It was in this way, with me talking while Chirango listened at my side, that we caught sight of the Luapula. We headed to the village of a chief named Chisalamalama, who offered us canoes for the passage across the river in exchange for beads and cloth. As we sat around the fire that night as Chirango plucked at his instrument, Chuma said, 'Bwana Daudi would have wanted to know from Chisalamalama if this river was one of the fountains that he was looking for.'

Halima wanted to know why the Bwana wanted to find this river so much. 'Though I have cracked my head on the matter,' she said, 'I still cannot fathom why it is that he wanted to find the beginning of this river so much.'

Susi said, 'Have you never known the glory of coming to some spot that you think you are the first to see?'

Halima said, 'There are no such spots, for there have been people everywhere. Ancestors, my mother called them. We all have Ancestors who lived before we did, and it is their Spirits that look after us.'

'But not everything that is there has been seen,' said Amoda, 'and Bwana Daudi was one of those who seek that which is hidden.'

'I agree with Halima,' Ntaoéka said, 'I do not see what business all these men have in coming all this way, digging up bones and digging up this and digging up that and discovering places where people already live.'

'It is because you have not been caught by the wanderlust,' said Amoda. 'Susi there, though he winks at every woman and smiles in every direction, he will never settle in one place. Once a man takes to travelling he will go far.'

'I want to escape the land altogether,' said Susi. 'It is my dream that I will have enough money to buy a dhow and fit it up for a long voyage. I want to sail down the coast, from Zanzibar to Shupanga, my home.'

'I do not understand it at all,' said Halima. 'All I want is a small house somewhere, where I can cook my fish and grow a fruit tree, maybe two.'

The music stopped as a soft voice called out, 'Maybe if you go with him you will understand. I am sure he would take you with him. It is clear what he thinks of you, for it is as though he eats you with his eyes.'

Amoda and Halima glared at Chirango, but he said, 'I mean to say, if you go with Amoda – your man – for he is greatly travelled and has seen many things that he can show you.'

I must confess that though I would not express my sentiments in the crude, unlearned terms used by Halima, travelling for its own sake seems like a most wasteful way to spend time. It is the thing I least understood about the Doctor. Sidi Mubarak, whom everyone called Bombay, and who led Mr Stanley's expedition, often said that Lieutenant Burton, who was the leader of his First Expedition, had confessed that he knew every time he left on an expedition, it was on a fool's errand, and one driven by the Devil.

I know not whether it is the Devil who drives these men to such deeds, but it is certainly a great pity that men of such industry and determination seem entirely unable to direct their talents into a more industrious path. This Lieutenant Burton, it seems, was a most gifted man who spoke more than twenty tongues. He had also travelled extensively among the Mohammedans, even to the point of having penetrated Mecca. That such energy and industry should be expended on something as frivolous as mere travel and exploration for its own sake is a sorrowful pity. If he had converted but just one Mohammedan on his journey, what a gift there would have been to the world!

It is the same with the Doctor. Had he but only been labouring for God! Now, if the government of his land could only send ordained priests, to preach and convert, baptise and catechise, then afterwards to oversee the building of churches and schools across the breadth of Africa to bring this entire race to the Light of Christ, and to uplift all who come within it from the poverty of ignorance, that would be a mission worthy of any expedition. But this ever-present hunger to discover, and to rename that which is already named, is, I confess, something I cannot comprehend.

Imagine the gains that could be made for Christ if a man like Susi could be converted. He could then sail with me, with a small party of porters; he could take me up and down the coast, perhaps even as far as the land of my birth, not for the mere animal pleasure of travelling, but because Christ commands it.

As I was cogitating thus while the others talked around the fire, from the darkness without came the tortured sound of an animal in great pain. We jumped up and ran in the direction of the noise. Amoda snatched a log and set fire to the grass, for it was pitch-dark. In the light of the burning grass, we saw a most horrible sight.

A lion, with its mouth dripping in blood, was standing over our poor donkey, which was bleeding from its neck. Munyasere, who had had the foresight to take up his rifle, fired at the beast, and on his shot, the lion turned and fled.

We were now gravely alive to the immediate danger in which we all stood. We could not decamp there and then, for who knew into what further danger we might wander. Under Munyasere's command, the *askari* took turns to guard the camp that night, with their rifles at the ready and their muskets loaded.

At daylight the next day, a trail of blood showed that Munyasere's shot had taken effect. At the end of the trail lay the lion; it had fallen dead some distance off, but as we could see quite clearly tracks of a second lion, and possibly, Munyasere said, a whole pride, we agreed to decamp as soon as possible. Munyasere skinned the beast.

'This hide,' he said, 'will accompany me all my days.'

As she cast a hungry eye over the meat, Halima was most regretful that we could eat neither the lion nor the donkey. 'Not even the juice of a thousand limes could make this palatable fare,' she said.

As we made our way across the Luapula, I made sure to stay close to Chuma. Though I have no interest in matters geographical, I was only too aware that notations of features of the land, particularly if they could lead to further elucidation of the Doctor's search, could only make my own Humble Journal a more Interesting Object to its Readers.

So I questioned Chuma closely on his observations and wrote down what he said.

Here then, in Chuma's words, is the Luapula. At the point of our crossing, the Luapula is double the width of the Zambesi at Shupanga, a full four miles. A man could not be seen on the opposite bank, the trees look small; a gun could be heard, but no other sound, like shouting, would ever reach a person across the river. The distance at the deepest point is about four hundred yards.

I can also confirm that the passage took fully two hours across an enormous torrent. In the process, we lost three packages with meat and meal, a loss we all felt keenly, particularly Halima, who seemed to lament this loss more keenly than she had lamented Misozi.

Chuma is now convinced that the Doctor was wrong in his estimation. This river has nothing at all to do with the Nile, for it carries the waters of Bangweulu towards the north. If Chuma is to be believed, the Doctor's southwards march was in vain. For if this is the fountain of Herodotus that he had hoped to find, it is most certainly not the source of the Nile.

After crossing the Luapula, we found ourselves in a great, dense forest. Under the trees was a most shocking and grievous sight. Here and there rested small piles of human bones. This was, alas, all too familiar; on the downwards march to join the Doctor, I had seen such pitiful piles of bones, as well as corpses lashed to trees.

This is the only protest that is within the power of the Captured: they simply refuse to walk further. As they cannot be carried, pulled, or pushed, it is a powerful act of protest. But so infinitely black are the hearts of their Captors that when this happens, they tie the Captured to trees in tight bonds and leave them there to perish.

On matters spiritual, I found myself disappointed in the Doctor. But on the matter of the Great Stain that is on this continent, I find that we are as one. During a moment of repose that night, by firelight, I read the Doctor's journal entry after the Massacre at Manyuema, and I will confess freely that it made me weep. 'As I write,' he says, 'I hear the loud wails on the left bank over those who are there slain. Oh, let Thy Kingdom come!'

Let Thy Kingdom come indeed, Dear Lord, let it come, and let it come today! Let it come to Manyuema; let it come to Zanzibar and to Kilwa, and to Lamu and Pemba, let it come to the land of the Yao and to all who profit from this grievous trade. Come down, Lord Jesus, and ransom this captive land. Let Thy Kingdom come, so that never again will we see men die tied to trees, all because the spirit in them cries out against the endless darkness of slavery. Let Thy Kingdom Come, dear Lord, let Thy Kingdom come.

10

Tenth Entry from the Journal of Jacob Wainwright, written at an Abandoned Village northeast of the Luapula; in which Wainwright prays that the Lord may turn the Hearts of All Men who hold the Weak in the Grip of Terror and Tyranny.

We currently find ourselves quartered in a small village that has seen most of its inhabitants flee. An air of stillness hangs about this abandoned place, for the people we found here were mainly the lame and the old. Those who are at all young appear to be either diseased or crippled, with some bearing on their faces the dread mark of the Small Pox.

On the first night we were here, as I came from the nearby stream where I had completed my ablutions, the woman Ntaoéka accosted me. For reasons that are beyond me to understand, we often find ourselves alone in the same places, and even when we are moving in groups, I seem to always be aware of her presence close to me.

'Regard,' she said. 'Is this silence not strange?'

I did not know what she meant, for we were in a forest in which birds were calling to each other and a nearby stream was babbling pleasantly.

'I mean that there are no children's voices. Our children are the only ones here,' she said.

The moment she said this, I understood what it was about the place that had so unsettled me on our arrival. In our travels, when we approached any village, it was normal to hear the sounds of occupation: women's laughter as they pounded and ground their corn, the crowing of the cocks and clucking of chickens, and the high voices of children.

And yet here, for the first time since I arrived on African soil, I find myself in a place in which there is no sound of children at all, neither their laughter, their play, nor their crying. I do not pay particular attention to children when they are there, I have said already that women and children are enough to slow down an Expedition, but certain it is that their high chattering voices make a normal part of everyday life.

As I walked around the village I saw abandoned musical instruments, mats, mortars for pounding meal, that were lying about unused and becoming the prey of the white ants. When I remarked upon these things to an old crippled man who was listlessly staring up at the heavens, I got only the laconic answer, 'Those were left there a long time ago. No one uses them now.'

I have never in my life met with a more wretched group of people. They make no effort at all to stir themselves beyond doing the necessities to keep the body together. They eat, they sleep, they barely work, for they believe there is no point to any effort because they believe that the Mazitu will come and destroy it all over again. Even the presence of the Doctor's body has not stirred their lassitude. We expected that they would be alarmed that we carried such a thing, and had made up our minds to dissemble as to what it was, but all they did was to point us to where we should store our packages, along with the body.

Truly, the Lord is needed here, more than in any place I have been. In this miserable and pitiful place, we are now more than ever alive to the danger that we may meet slave traders on our journey.

Though we have been careful not to take the most direct route to the coast, which would have seen us heading for the slave-trading port of Kilwa, it seems to be the case that even this far inland, we may yet encounter the slave parties of the four most fearsome traders, who are Casembe, Mirambo, Kumbakumba, and Tippoo Tip.

These four have been fighting each other over the control of territory in the interior. It would appear from the news that has made its way to our ears that Casembe has been defeated in a great war with Mirambo and Kumbakumba. It also appears however that Casembe is not his name but a title, like king or sultan. So this one Casembe may have been defeated but there is very likely another Casembe who will rise to take his place.

In addition to these loathsome traders, it was forced on us to consider that we may also encounter a fierce warrior group from the south called the Mazitu, the same tribe of warriors that Chitambo had warned us about. As Chuma explained, on many occasions as they journeyed with Doctor Livingstone, they came across villages that had been emptied and depleted by these Mazitu.

As is the case with those who are most feared, the Mazitu are known throughout these lands by many names. In some lands, they are the Maviti, in others the Madzviti, and in yet others the Matuta or Watuta, each name invoking fear and terror in those who hear of it. They have amassed great power through conquering neighbouring lands, so that even just the whisper that the Mazitu were coming was enough to send people scurrying further into the interior until they heard the menace had passed.

This is what has happened in this village, which has been abandoned by its chief. Along with his courtiers and advisors, and the able-bodied of the whole village, the Chief abandoned the village as soon as they heard the rumour that the Mazitu were coming. I worry that Chitambo may well do the same, and abandon his village, along with the grave of the Doctor's heart, if the Mazitu make their way there.

As for food, our supplies are close to being exhausted, and the people of this place have but little to give. What they have given, they have given freely, however. Amoda had some work to do to persuade them that we could not take them with us, for they would fain have joined us if they could.

I will not forget their miserable faces as we left. For it is not certain that they will meet with another travelling party soon. All I could do for them was to lay a benediction on every head, and pray the Lord to keep them, and us too, as we moved away from this place of misery and hopelessness. My final prayer was that the Lord would, in His own time, turn the heart of every slaver, and of every man who holds the weak in the grip of Tyranny and Terror.

11

Eleventh Entry from the Journal of Jacob Wainwright, written at Chawende; in which the Expedition overpowers a Village, Occasioning a Lamentable Loss of Life, and Wainwright reflects on the Unexpected Munificence of Providence.

After the miserable conditions of that last village, I am pleased to say that here in the stockaded village of Chawende, we are at last sheltered in some comfort. Though not quite the Palace Beautiful, Chawende has given us the greatest ease we have enjoyed since we left Chitambo.

It is, altogether, a most impressive place. Secure within high walls made of an ingenious combination of thatch, mud, and wooden poles is a great number of well-built huts, of both the round and square variety that we have seen elsewhere. Entrance can only come from one direction, through large wooden gates that we have secured with rope made from strong bark.

How we came to occupy this village is a tale most distressing, and indeed, it might be well if, when it comes to publication of this Journal, I should omit this section altogether in narrating our travails, as it would reflect no credit on any of the party. But as my own conduct is entirely blameless and can attract no reproach, it may well be that the record should stand as truthfully as it can, so that it may be known to what exigencies the party was driven.

After crossing the Luapula, we walked a great distance. Firstly, we passed through the village of a man named Kawinga, whose reputation appeared to rest on his great height and his rumoured possession of a gun, a rare instrument this deep into the interior. The height was indeed remarkable – we found him to be a strikingly tall man, of singularly light colour – but the gun in question, which rested above his seat, was more a talisman than a weapon, for it was nothing but a rusted piece of metal. And if ever it had any bullets, Kawinga had never heard of them. The magic of the word 'gun', however, secured his power over his land.

We did not stop long with him, for we feared that seeing what a real gun not only looked like but, more important, was capable of, he might consider it necessary that he have more than one, and thus lay claim to those of our *askari*. All we asked from him was for directions to the next village, that of Nkossu, where we had heard report of their having many herds of cattle.

We found as we marched that we got hungrier as we talked of food, but on this occasion, we gave rein to our thoughts as we imagined the feast that awaited us at Nkossu. It was with a cheerful step that we moved on.

Alas, the report of Nkossu's cattle was as exaggerated as rumours of Kawinga's gun, for the animals were untamed and exceedingly wild, and seemed to roam where they pleased. The three best hunters of the expedition, Wadi Saféné, Munyasere, and Carus Farrar, loaded their guns and prepared to fire on the creatures. Their actions attracted a great deal of notice, and soon a crowd of Nkossu's people had gathered to watch the proceedings.

To the great excitement of the crowd, Munyasere felled one creature. Not to be outdone, Wadi Saféné fired in echo. This was when the accident happened. Wadi Saféné, firing wildly, hit one of the villagers. The man let out a great bellow of pain as the people around him scattered in fear. The bullet had struck him in his right thigh. Carus Farrar dropped his gun and rushed to attend to him.

It can only have been due to the Merciful Intervention of Him above that the man sustained no great injury. The bullet had gone right through the flesh, and would cause no lasting damage, Carus Farrar said. After treatment using some of the Doctor's ointments, the man was soon hobbling about and showing his wounds with evident pride and delight.

Seeing that no real harm had been done, the Chief said a fine of three strings of blue beads would have to be paid to the wounded man's father, and also demanded that we leave behind the beast we had slain as our fine.

From Nkossu we walked for many days, looking for a sheltered place at which to set camp. Our supplies were dangerously low. Bitterly did we regret the cow Nkossu had fined us. Not only were we passing through a barren landscape, we were doing so in the bone-dry month of July.

In the two months that we had been on the road, the skies had turned blue with no clouds. The streams that we passed were parched, the trees bore no fruit. Thus it was that the march from Nkossu saw us with an ever-diminishing supply of food, which we augmented with the few berries that came our way.

Quarrels were now a daily feature of our march. Petty disputes were threatening to break out into open warfare. Amoda and Susi almost came to blows over a small matter, and were stopped only by the intervention of Chuma. Two of the *pagazi* came to blows because one of them had looked at the other in the wrong way.

The Nassickers were getting even more fractious than the children, and there was great unpleasantness between Benjamin Rutton and John Wainwright, for the latter claimed that the former was carrying a trunk in such a manner as to unfairly tilt all the weight towards him. The women were no better, for whenever any of the children fought, their mothers picked up the quarrels, with Khadijah and Laede fighting over their children on more than one occasion.

I am certain that the discord in the party was due to the hunger that was now pressing on all of us. The *pagazi* who had no women and children in the party were becoming fractious about sharing rations with the weaker members of the expedition. A small group of *quat*-chewing *pagazi*, led by Ali and Asmani, were threatening mutiny, for they had consumed most of their leaf and would not march without more. It took all of Amoda's efforts to keep the group peaceable.

On the night before we reached Chawende, we made a meagre repast of some fish caught by Susi, and a yellow fruit with sharp thorns that Halima assured us was a prickly cucumber. 'It tastes particularly good if you eat it with lamb stewed with limes and cardamom spice,' she said, a statement that was of little use to us on that particular day. Indeed, if we could all have fed from Halima's descriptions of the food that her mother cooked when she was in the Liwali's kitchen, we might never have hungered.

We gathered as much of the fruit as we could. It would have kept us going, but we found when it came time to eat again that the powerful heat had wilted and rotted it.

'I am sure,' Ntaoéka said, 'that this would not smell at all if we only had limes to dress it with. It would taste so good with limes.'

'Ah, if only we had limes,' added Laede. 'The Liwali had so many limes.'

'Limes that would make even this rotten fruit the best feast ever eaten.'

At this, Halima flew at both women, and it took Amoda and Susi to separate them from each other. Chirango, meantime, was narrating to me all the food that he planned to buy for the party when he got his reward in Zanzibar.

While Halima dreamed of past feasts and Chirango of future ones, for my part, I could not help but wish that I had in me the power of Our Lord Jesus Christ to turn fish and bread into a meal to feed the party before me, just as he had once fed the five thousand on two loaves and five fishes. I soon put such blasphemous thoughts from my mind.

Instead, I said out loud the Reverend Bean's prayer to Him Above to have compassion and give us seasonable weather for the fruits of the Earth. I also prayed that the Lord from whom comes our Daily Bread relieve us from hunger. The answer to my prayer came in an unexpected way. It is indeed true that the Lord's Purposes will Ripen Fast and Unfold Every Hour, but this answer to my prayer came at great cost.

We were fortunate to meet a hunting party that told us of a village that lay directly north of our path. We pressed on to ask for admittance but met with the keenest disappointment when we were refused entry. No doubt the intelligence that we were carrying a body had reached this place, for it seems to have spread with the greatest rapidity in all directions: every hut and hamlet that we reached was shut against us.

Desperate for shelter and food, we marched on. By the time we approached Chawende's town, we had exhausted all provisions, even the rotten fruit that those with stronger stomachs had been eating. We had also walked further than we had on any day since leaving Chitambo.

Pressed on by hunger, we marched until we reached the approach to Chawende's. It was most pleasing to see that Chawende's promised to be more than a village; it seemed to be an impressively built and stockaded town protected by large wooden gates. Munyasere and Chowpereh went on in front to inform the Chief of our presence and to ask leave to enter his town. We waited for them. And waited. We waited an hour and they did not return. Two hours, no return.

By the third hour, we were all impatient for news. The children were wailing with hunger, the women petulant as they failed to comfort them. John Wainwright, who at first had been sighing and weeping silently, now picked up and then threw down his load, and in great hysterics said he was not moving anymore.

Then Mariko Chanda and Toufiki Ali, the two men whose turn it was to carry the Doctor's body, laid it down on the ground and said they would not move any longer with this blasted corpse. Another man said the same, and another, and another, until all of the *pagazi* who marched between the body and the *safire* were threatening to revolt. It was clear to me that they had been dissatisfied for a while, but Amoda chose to lay their actions at the feet of John Wainwright. As he was still protesting furiously, Amoda walked up to him and hit him hard in the stomach. John doubled over with a howl of pain.

In the silence that followed, Amoda said: 'If you do not shut yourself up this instant, I will whip you until your skin falls off. I am as hungry as you, and as tired as you, but weak as I am, I have the strength of all the men here and I will whip you all the way to Bagamoio.

'You see Chirango there?'

He indicated Chirango, who had been watching the scene as helplessly as anyone else.

'What happened to him is nothing compared to what will happen to you if you do not shut that mouth.'

Amoda was addressing himself to all the *pagazi*, but his eyes were on John Wainwright. 'It is only the thought of the recovery that you will need afterwards that prevents me from doing it now. So instead, your whipping will wait until we get to Bagamoio.'

John collapsed to sit on his load. He was silent now, but still he wept silently, but enough to produce tears and mucus that he wiped from his nose with his hand. It was a most unedifying sight. I was about to go to tell him to pull himself up, and that he was a Nassicker and a Christian and he was letting down the school with this disgraceful display, when Amoda declared that he would go himself to see what was happening.

He and Chuma set off after Munyasere and Chowpereh. Again we waited. No better success seemed to attend this second venture, so shouldering our burdens, we went forwards as a body in the track of the four messengers.

We were almost at the gates of the stockaded town when we saw all four come in the opposite direction to meet us. They walked together with five men whose faces looked most unfriendly. They had sought to enter the town but found it a very large place and extremely well protected. There were two other villages of equal size close to it. Much *pombe* drinking was going on, and they had refused to entertain the request of our first two messengers.

When the second messengers had arrived, Amoda had made straight for the Chief. It would appear that Amoda had approached the Chief with his gun in hand. A man who it seems was Chawende's son had become drunk and quarrelsome, and made this a cause of offence. Swaggering up to Amoda, he had, with great insolence, asked how he dared threaten the Chief with a gun.

This man had ordered our men's expulsion from the compound and sent five of his own men to ensure that they left. When the four reached us, we made a show of walking in the direction opposite to the town, until the five returned from whence they came.

By this time, our whole party were foot-sore and heart-sore; the women fussed, the children cried. We were as close to starvation as we had been since we left Chitambo.

The following events might have been avoided, perhaps, had there not been hunger. But there was nothing to eat, and no likely looking place or materials to build shelters. The expedition leaders also later confessed that they were also actuated by another fear, that if we were to camp anywhere close to this town for the night, these drunken people who already had cause to be offended with us were likely to plunder the baggage.

It was resolved among us to make for the town and plead our case. We were flatly refused admittance, those inside telling us to go down to the river and camp on the bank. We replied that this was impossible: we were tired, it was late, and nothing could be found there to give shelter. We met only with derisive laughter.

It is said often enough that a hungry man is an angry man, and truly I saw the meaning of that statement that day. The men pushed in, to the surprise of those on the other side. Saféné got through, and Munyasere climbed over the top of the stockade, followed by Chuma. They opened the gate wide to let the rest of the party through.

I tried to call for peace, as did Amoda, but our voices were drowned in the general tumult. Those at the back of the column pushed with such force that most of our party were moved into the stockade. At that, a man inside drew a bow and fired an arrow at Munyasere, who managed to duck the arrow. It fell harmlessly to the ground. Amoda, seeking to restore some semblance of order, fired a gun into the air. The sound of the fearful weapon threw the townsfolk into a panic as they ran for the gate. There was pandemonium as the remnants of our party fought to get in while they fought to get out. Munyasere fired, as did Wadi Saféné. More arrows flew through the air.

Susi gathered Halima, Khadijah, and the children and led them to the shelter of a nearby hut before running to Chowpereh to take from him his musket. He and Chuma then followed Amoda as he commanded that Mariko and Ali put the body of the Doctor, along with all our goods and chattels, inside an empty hut. Mabruki was already in the thick of it, without once checking to see if Ntaoéka was safe.

'Come with me,' I said, and took her hand. It was soft in mine. As I held it, it appeared to me that my heart was beating faster and my blood was coursing at a rapid speed through my body. Laede then grabbed my other hand, and with both women screaming in my ears, and John Wainwright hard on my heels, I shepherded them to safety.

Now, I am no coward, and can, in a good cause, fight as well as any man. It brought me a little shame to see that John and I were the only men standing among the women, away from the fray before us, but I reassured myself that, unlike John Wainwright, I was not driven by lowly cowardice. No: I kept away because my true duty was to watch over the women and children, and to pray that our men would get safely through the affray. Though the men ribbed me afterwards for not joining, I am certain that it was my prayers for the Lord's Merciful Intervention, and my watching over the women, that allowed us to prevail.

From the granary in which we sheltered, I watched as the scene descended into the general mayhem of men fighting with fists, spears, and anything else they could find. Chirango aimed a blow at the man nearest to him. A hurled spear just avoided hitting Matthew Wellington in the back. On Munyasere's order, our *askari* fired their guns. At this sound, there was a panic of running as Chawende's men called a retreat. Their drums beat the assembly in all directions. But they were not in full retreat. The drums appeared to be a signal for reinforcements. Soon, an immense number of men swarmed towards the town with bows, arrows, and spears. Abandoned in the fight, the Doctor's body lay on the ground with the other packages. Things were becoming desperate.

At Munyasere's signal, the *askari* charged out of the gates and fired with disastrous results. As bodies fell to the ground, the villagers ran, leaving behind their spears and shields. Having got rid of every last man, the *askari* bolted the gates to the town and gave a roar of triumph.

I am sorry to say that there was great joy as the men whooped and plundered the village of all the food they could find. The townsfolk had clearly been feasting, which meant there was a great deal of meat and *pombe*, which our men had no hesitation in drinking. The air that had rung with the noise of battle now rung with cheers and whooping celebrations, with the ululation of women and the squawking of chickens attempting to evade the pot.

Thanks to the Mercy of God, our lives were spared, save that of two of the *askari*, Nchise and Ntaru. Nchise was shot with an arrow to the neck through the palisade and died on the spot, while Ntaru was shot in the bowels and sank soon afterwards.

A few others who were hurt here and there had their injuries tended to by Carus Farrar and Farjallah Christie. I find myself thankful yet again for the Doctor's medicine chest. I tried but could not succeed in urging the men to give a soberer reflection to the whole affair, for the victory, despite the deaths of Nchise and Ntaru, had gone to their heads and they were crowing with the sense of their own power.

It was as well, however, that Amoda insisted that a guard should be up to keep watch, for that night, a party approached from outside the stockade and threw small balls of fire within the compound. None landed on the thatch of the huts, however, and it was no time at all before the small fires were put out. A volley of gunfire soon scared off those outside.

And so it is that we have been here ten days now, in which time we have enjoyed peaceful occupation of the town. Eight days after we took the town, a man approached and called out at the top of his voice that he came alone. He crawled on his stomach before Amoda and asked for peace.

'We have taken our dead and buried them. We ask for your mercy. It was all the fault of the bad son of our Chief, who brought all this upon us.'

We were great wizards, he had heard, for we carried not only the power of the gun, but also a powerful medicine in the form of the body of a white man.

Amoda said, 'That is true, we will show you the body that we carry.'

The man looked absolutely petrified at the thought. They would leave us in peace, he said, but we were please to leave the town whole. For now, they would seek far and wide medicine men who would perform cleansing rituals after we left. If a man of sufficient power could not be found they would have to abandon the whole town.

Amoda's deception was a wise one, though it pains me to admit it. By owning up to the witchcraft and aligning it to great power, he had bought for us a truce, and some rest. As I tried to find sleep that night, it came to me that from every perspective possible, our whole enterprise was so desperate, so foolhardy, that it had accumulated its own stock of determination. I could only hope that this was the last provocation that we would meet.

12

Twelfth Entry from the Journal of Jacob Wainwright; in which the Expedition remains at Chawende's, and in that Palace Beautiful, Wainwright is sidetracked by the Pleasantness of By-Path Meadow.

We have been at Chawende's for an entire fortnight. Certain that we will enjoy undisturbed occupation of the town, we have resolved to remain here while the weak and injured recover. The Doctor's body rests in an empty granary, and indeed, without its mournful presence ever before us as we march, I sometimes forget that he is among us at all.

It has been a period of great peace, the only peace any of us has known since we began travelling with the Doctor. We have access to a flowing stream, and are able to wash ourselves, and our clothing. There is plenty of food and grain, the women cook, the chickens are in a flutter as they run from the pot. And I am most especially pleased to report that a small Congregation of the Faithful is now flourishing in this wilderness.

Even without being ordained, I find that I am doing better than the Doctor, who thought it a great joke that he had only ever turned one soul to God. 'It was a chief in Bechuanaland, Jacob,' he said, 'a man called Sechele. He promised to turn his face to Christ. Send away all your wives but one, I told him, for Our Gracious Lord can only receive you if you have but the one. And this Sechele did, for he sent them away, but I cannot say it was much of a success, Jacob, because when I visited him again some years later, the wives were all present, and one more besides, all showing most troubling signs of their expecting.'

I marvelled at the opportunity that had so lamentably been lost. Had the seed of the Lamb only taken root in his heart, what a reaping would there have been! The Doctor also talked of meeting a great chief he called Sebituane, who was the Sultan of a people called the Makololo. He called him a great friend and talked of many conversations they had had after he cured his son of malaria.

Here again, another lost chance to win a soul to God!

In my mind I saw it, the light shining from the centre of Bechuanaland, the light blazing from all Makolololand, across the entire continent, as heathen after heathen was washed in the blood of the Lamb, removing Sin and Darkness, and above all, Slavery, the Dark Stain that has blighted many a life. I wondered that the Doctor did not see how costly was Sechele's return to his heathen ways, how grave an error to let the other heathen chief, Sebituane, live his life without so much as an attempt to say to him, 'Look out, Heathen Chief, you are in Lamentable Peril; for the burden that you carry upon your back shall surely sink you into Tophet, where a Great Fire waits to consume you.'

I pray every night for the Influence of the Holy Spirit over these Heathen Chiefs, that they might come back to the Flock of the Lamb. And I prayed for all heathens, and most especially for my own father and mother and sister, wherever they may be, and that I might one day be in the position of great influence, an advisor to a chief or sultan, to a king loved by his people, that I might, through such an office, bring all his people to the redeeming love of Christ.

I am certain that as long as Christ is my Champion, I will succeed where the Doctor failed, and win lives to God, as I am doing now.

In addition to Chirango, here in Chawende I now have eleven other adherents who are interested in the new faith. Chirango, whom I hold dear in my heart as my First Convert, has been a most able and obliging assistant. I baptised them in the river all on one day, in the old way of the Baptist John. It is true that I have not yet the power to deliver the sacraments, but I am certain that when I get to England, they will overlook that and rejoice over the Lost Sheep I have regained for the Shepherd.

I renewed my prayer that before our time together was over, I would have converted many in the party, and most particularly, that I would win for my Lord the soul of the Mohammedan Abdullah Susi.

I find that those of no real faith are more likely to convert, while the more stubborn among the Mohammedans are harder to sway. The battle we endured and the fear of what awaits us outside have been most conducive to turning minds to Christ.

I initially made the mistake of rather emphasising more than I should have God's Mercy, and the gift of His Grace. This unfortunately gave my congregants the lamentable idea that it is perfectly possible for them to sin, then confess to the evil of their sin, pray for the forgiveness of their sin, then sin again, confess the sin, and pray for the forgiveness of sin in an endless cycle of sin, confession, repentance, forgiveness, and sin. It is a Papist idea, and one that I am not keen to encourage.

I have found that it is when they are in the most terror that their minds are most receptive. And so it is that in our services, I emphasise less the teachings on forgiveness and lay stress on those readings where the Mighty God shows His Wrath and not His Loving-Kindness. They will come to love my Lord Jehovah as I do, but first, they must earn their own salvation with fear and trembling.

'Fear God,' I tell them, 'and keep His commandments, for this is the Whole Duty of Man. Let all the Earth fear the Lord; let all the inhabitants of the world stand in awe of Him.'

And I speak to them of the Wars of God. I thunder to them of the Lord of War who smote the Ammonites and Hittites, who brought fire and brimstone on Sodom and Gomorrah and turned Lot's wife into a pillar of salt.

I tell them of how He smote the men of Bethshemesh, even as He smote of the people fifty-thousand and threescore and ten men, and the people lamented, because the Lord had smitten them with a great slaughter. For as it is written in the Psalms of King Solomon, He makes wars to cease unto the end of the Earth; he breaks the bow and cuts the spear; he burns chariots in the fire.

When I preach thus, they get into a fever pitch of ecstasy, shaking their bodies all while their voices tremble. Such is the power of my words when the Spirit moves me. It is as though I speak words of Lightning with the conviction of Thunder.

Away from my small congregation, things are not as peaceful. I had anticipated that the women would create many a difficulty, and I have been proved correct. Halima and Ntaoéka in particular are always coming to blows, for without the poor dead Misozi between them, they have been going over some long-remembered grievances. It is also a frequent bone of contention between them that Halima believes that Ntaoéka is frequently unkind to her child, Losi. As if a creature of Ntaoéka's gentleness could ever be unjust to any person.

Chirango was so troubled by the situation that he interceded with me. In his respectful voice, he said, 'Mwalimu, you must do what you can.'

This is what he calls me now, Mwalimu, meaning 'Teacher', and I must say it is a word that falls pleasantly on the ear. He continued, 'I thought the best thing would be for her to come to you, that she spend time praying with us and coming to know the Lord.'

I thought he meant Halima, for certainly, she was the cause of the quarrel, but it was not her of whom he spoke. 'It is Ntaoéka that you should talk to,' he said. 'You may have influence over her that her own husband does not.'

I looked at him sharply.

He blinked his eye, licked his lips, and said, 'You could find a way to talk to her, Mwalimu, to comfort her, for she is sorely troubled by the harsh words Halima has directed at her. I can, if you wish, talk to her for you, and will ask her to join us at our service tonight.'

Chirango was true to his word, for Ntaoéka came to the next service. My heart rejoiced to see her listening closely, and it seemed to drop to my feet when, on opening one eye, I saw that hers were fully open, and were on me. I thought again of all the names she could take if she converted, Elizabeth perhaps, the mother of the Baptist, or Eunice, the mother of Timothy.

We were to meet again for morning prayers.

We were now so secure in our possession of the town that we could wander in and out of the gates without fear. The nearby stream had many trees overhanging it that created a pleasant and shaded place, and it was there that I met with my congregants, far from the derision of the others.

To this place we walked on the first morning that Ntaoéka joined us. But it was to find that someone had got there ahead of us, for there was a small bundle of clothes gathered in the water, next to a rock that was halfway into the water, and on which the women frequently washed clothes. Ntaoéka had the same thought, for she said: 'I wonder who it is who washes clothes at this hour.'

We looked around to see who had risen at this early hour but there was no other person to be seen. Ntaoéka walked over to the pile of clothes, and as she did so, I felt a terrible foreboding. I called out for her to stop just at the moment she leaned over to inspect the clothes.

She rose with a fearful scream. She rushed back to where we stood. I instinctively held out my arms to her as she said, trembling, 'It is a child. I think it is a child.'

I left her and went to look for myself. It was indeed a child. The clean heels of small feet that were turned towards me in the water told me that. The body was face-down. I turned it over to find to my horror that it was not a local child, as I had thought.

It was Losi. It was Halima's little girl.

I have said before that I prayed for something to still Halima's tongue, but not for anything would I have had that it be the death of that child. Her grief was dreadful to behold. Her instinct was to attack the person who had brought the news. Ntaoéka had killed her child, she screamed. When her mind was more settled, I explained to her how it had come to be that we discovered the child, but it was some days before Halima could see Ntaoéka without wanting to attack her.

We none of us could understand how a child that small had passed through the gate, but it would appear that the gate had perhaps been left open the night before. Certainly, we had found the latch had not been pulled through when we left.

The hardest thing was to persuade Halima that we had to bury Losi in Chawende, close to the stream where she died. Amoda particularly pushed this point: he could not understand, he said, what woman would mourn a child who is not hers.

The others were gentler with her. She had always liked Farjallah

Christie, who is the only man here who cooks. He explained to her that drowning was like falling asleep, and recruited Carus Farrar to say the same to her. I have heard it said that drowning is a horribly painful death, but I am sure that the Lord was able to forgive this lie, for it was one that came from kindness.

It was Carus Farrar who persuaded her to let them bury Losi. She could have been from anywhere, and it was better that she be buried here, close to her people, than that she be marched all the way to Bagamoio. She had been a light in her life, he said. She should not be a burden in death. Halima agreed, and so the child was buried. We agreed to wait another week before we moved.

13

Thirteenth Entry from the Journal of Jacob Wainwright; in which the Expedition Remains at Chawende's, the Congregation of the Saved continues to Grow, and Wainwright enters the Land of Beulah.

The world has now stopped spinning and spinning, though I am still spinning with it. I had thought to name her Judith or Esther or even Martha or Elizabeth, but she is Beulah, for in her arms I was in the Land of Beulah, a place of sweetness and beauty, light and great delight. In that land of wonder, birds sing continually and flowers bloom, the sun shines day and night, far from Doubting Castle and Giant Despair and as far as it is possible to be from the Valley of the Shadow of Death.

In the distance gleams the Celestial City, for the Land of Beulah is on the border of Heaven, where the Shining Ones proclaim: 'Behold, your Salvation comes, behold his Reward is with her, take your Bride.'

And she will be a beautiful bride.

I have just this minute returned from a walk down to the water to bathe myself, the same water where Losi drowned just a week ago.

It is this same water that I have been using in my baptism rituals. My heart sang when Chirango brought Ntaoéka to me to baptise.

'She is ready for you, Mwalimu,' he said. 'She has heard all that you have said about the Mercy of the Father and like me and the others that I brought you, she wants to be Saved.'

I asked her earnestly and seriously if she accepted Jesus. There was no time for catechism, but filled with the rightness of my actions, I baptised her in the way of the Baptist John. I dipped her fully in the deepest part of the river. Her clothes clung to her form as I prayed over her. The same jolt I had felt when I held her hand came over me, but it was soon replaced by a fervour of gratitude that it was I who had been chosen to lead this Child of God to the arms of the Lamb.

Truly, the Lord is with me. First, I had ensured that the Doctor went to his peace at one with his Maker. Then, I had converted Chirango, and eleven other men. Now, here was this beautiful creature, the first woman that I had won for Christ.

The grass seems greener, the sky more blue than it has ever been, and for the first time, it strikes me how wonderful it is that God has chosen to make not one bird, but several varieties of bird, not one tree, but several varieties of tree, not one flower, but several varieties of flower. And the grass, even the grass. Who would have thought there were so many types of grass, so much variation in the shades of green? Truly the gift of Creation is a joyful thing.

I begin to understand at last what the Doctor meant when he said, 'I see Him in His creations.' I begin to understand why it was that he could sit for hours on end doing nothing but study a group of ants, lying on his stomach in the dirt as the creatures moved in and out of his vision. The Doctor's preoccupation with such things has been an eternal puzzlement to me.

I asked him once, 'Is Christ's concern with the ants, or that we seek the Kingdom of God here on Earth, that we turn heathen souls to Paradise, that we instill in the hearts of all men the Fear of His Holy Name?'

'I understand Him through navigating His rivers and seeing His greatest creations,' the Doctor replied.

He talked to me then about seeing the great waterfall on the River Zambesi, about hearing from a distance a sound as though of a thousand million falling rocks, of being covered in a mist of rain as he approached finally to behold a sight like he had never seen before.

'Scenes as lovely as that,' he said, 'are surely proof of the workings of His Great Majesty.'

The memory had brought tears to his eyes; actual tears shone in his eyes. I have tears in my eyes now. Of all God's creation, is the wonder of Woman. How magnanimous is the All-Seeing, All-Knowing Lord who created Woman that she be the Helpmeet and comfort of man for all his days? How wondrous is it that he found Adam sleeping and from his side took a rib, then closed the place up with flesh. And from that rib, God created woman. How wonderful is Woman, how magnanimous is God?

On the night of the day that I baptised her, she came to be my sleeping mate. The men had drunk the *pombe* that was presented in supplication by the placating villagers and were sleeping soundly. I was half-asleep in the hut I shared with Chirango, with my thoughts drifting off, when I felt a soft body next to me whisper, 'It's me.' Her breath was warm in my ear.

'Mind, Chirango,' I said.

'He is not here,' she said.

And without being told, I knew why she was there and what it was that I had to do. Like Adam and Eve before us, we were naked but knew no shame. Ntaoéka, so beautiful, beautiful beyond comprehension, Bone of my Bones and Flesh of my Flesh. A rush of gratitude gushed out of me. And in an instant, vistas were opened up for me as to how I should lead my life.

Afterwards, I said to her, 'We must kneel, we must.'

And there, in our nakedness, we knelt in fervent prayer. In the morning, she was gone. But when I saw her again, and she looked at me, smiled, and looked away, I knew that it had been no fever dream, that she was real and she was mine. All that morning's reveries passed before my mind as I saw the life we would have as we overcame the many hazards in our path. She would be my Helpmeet and with her at my side, I would have all the strength I needed to dare and more.

I went over again the many names I had thought of for her. No, she would not be Esther or Ruth. She would be Rachel. Most certainly Rachel, the best-beloved wife of Jacob and the mother of his beloved sons. Our first child shall be called Joseph and our second Benjamin, and between us, we shall create a new tribe in faith and piety.

She brought food to the expedition leaders, and when she served Mabruki, he barely looked at her. Mabruki. I had forgotten about him, that he had – but no, I would not think of that. After all, Ruth had lain with another man before she met Jesse, the father of David. And Bathsheba had lain with Uriah the Hittite and David had loved her still. It mattered not that Ntaoéka had known another man. That was a thing of sin. With me she would be reborn, with a new name. Her sins would be washed away and together we would start our lives. Let he who is without sin cast the first stone, said Our Lord of the woman taken in adultery.

I had prayed on the matter and I knew in my heart that the Lord had sanctioned our union, that He would sanction our marriage, for as soon as we reached Zanzibar and were able to marry, we would marry in a Christian Church. Until then, it behooved me to be self-denying, to be self-sacrificing. Until we married, I would sacrifice the bliss of her arms. In any event, it would be difficult to find ways and means and places to meet without all the others' knowing.

It was with this in mind that I accosted her as she walked to the stream. I took up her pail as though to assist her. In my ecstasy I shared with her all that I saw. She would be my Helpmeet, my fellow labourer. We would marry in Zanzibar, then I would be ordained in England. After that, we would return to Africa to labour in Christ's vineyard. She would be more than my wife, she would be a missionary's wife, an instrument of God, and Salvation.

Then we espied a hidden copse and lay behind it for a blissful while. What a glory is woman. Afterwards, I took up the thread I had started to unwind. 'It would be a life of great hardship and sacrifice,' I cautioned, 'but what is that when we are doing the work of Christ?'

'I am not Christian,' Ntaoéka said.

'I will make you a Christian,' I said. 'And together, we will convert all of God's children who live here in Africa, who live in darkness, without the light of His Grace.'

'Do you not plan to go to England then?' she said. 'Halima said you were to go to England, then live there or in Zanzibar.'

'I will go to England,' I said, 'but only to be ordained so that I may return here, where God is calling me. With you by my side I know I will succeed.'

In my fervour, I grabbed her hand and put it against my heart. As I did so, I heard a rustling in the grass behind us. With a beating heart, I turned to see who approached.

'Accept my pardons, please, I had not seen you there.'

The voice belonged to Chirango, who had appeared from behind a tree without either of us seeing him. Ntaoéka's hand was suddenly hot in mine. I dropped it at once. He smiled and bowed and licked his lips. Without a word to either of us, Ntaoéka went back in the direction of the town.

I thought Chirango gave a knowing smile as she left but I am certain that he will not betray me. I have not had the courage to ask him where he was the night she first came to my sleeping mat, and where he has been the nights since then. I consoled myself that this unseemly subterfuge can only be for the few weeks and days that are now left of our march. At the end will come lightness, of that I am certain.

As it happens, I did not need to broach the matter, for he immediately said, 'You are the only friend I have on this journey, a friend from the first. Be assured all your secrets are stored safely in my heart.'

'There is no secret,' I said at once.

'No, indeed,' he said, 'but there are things that are not to be revealed to all, or all at once.'

'It is a matter, you understand,' I said, 'not of my own skin.'

'I quite understand,' he said. 'It is about a certain Person, whom we can call the Person in Question.'

As he spoke, he leered at me. This was the very last thing I would have called her, for his innuendos and leering made the matter seem much more seedy than it was.

'It is a matter of honour, because we would not want any unpleasant rumours to get back to Mabruki.'

'We would not indeed,' he agreed. 'We would not want any rumours spreading about the Person in Question.'

I was finding it harder and harder to look him in the eye.

'Or indeed,' I said, 'to any of the others.'

'Indeed not.'

'I will also,' he said, 'talk to the Person in Question and assure her that the secret is safe. That is, of course, if that will please you.'

What could I say? To make a conspiracy between the three of us in this manner was, of all things, the very last thing I wanted, but what could I do? The conversation had not gone in the direction I would have wanted, but certain I had his confidence, I let him go on his smiling, bowing way.

It's not my protection I seek, but hers. It filled me with distaste to keep such a matter a secret, but I was not one to question God's plan when it was clear before me. This was what He had willed, and if there must be some duplicity, it was of the kind practised by my namesake Jacob when he covered his arms and face in goatskin, and appeared in the guise of his brother, Esau, to his father, Isaac, weak in sight and old in age, and from him got his brother's blessing.

See what good came out of that deception, for Jacob was the father of the Twelve Tribes, and who better to have such a blessing than one who gave birth to the nation of Judah, from which sprang King David, and through his line, Our Lord Jesus.

And if it is a sin for a man to lie with a woman to whom he is betrothed and whom he will marry in a matter of weeks, then I comfort myself with the certainty that it is perhaps as well that I know what it is to sin, for I have, until this moment, been completely without blemish. It is surely right that one who is to be a clergyman should know, first-hand, what it means to be a sinner.

14

Fourteenth Entry from the Journal of Jacob Wainwright, entered at Kumbakumba; in which Wainwright suffers a Great Shock as the Party receive Succour through an Unlikely Alliance.

We have now entered the town of Kumbakumba, where we are encamped in uneasy comfort. My Readers will forgive me if my thoughts run on and my words are incoherent, for I have suffered a great shock. I am finding it impossible to match what the Doctor writes in his journal with the intelligence I have lately received concerning his conduct.

'The strangest disease I have seen in this country seems really to be broken-heartedness, and it attacks free men who have been captured and made slaves.' Thus enters the Doctor in his Journal of the twentieth day of December 1870, in the Year of Our Lord.

In this entry, he narrates the story of a man he calls Syed bin Habib, whose elder brother was killed in Rua from a spear that was pitched through his tent into his side. This Syed then vowed vengeance for the blood of his brother and assaulted all he could find, killing all the elders of the village from which the fateful spear had come and making the young men captives.

As the Doctor tells it, Syed secured a large number of captives, who endured well enough in their chains until they saw the broad River Lualaba roll between them and their free homes. A third of them died just three days after crossing, having ascribed their only pain to the heart and placed the hand correctly on the spot. One boy of about twelve years was carried, and when about to expire, was laid down on the side of the path, and a hole was dug to deposit the body in. He too said he had nothing the matter with him, except a pain in his heart.

The Doctor says this broken heart syndrome attacks only the free who are captured and never those who are born in captivity. 'The sights I have seen,' he writes, in another entry, 'though common incidents of the traffic, are so nauseous that I always strive to drive them from memory.'

It is when I compare the Doctor's words with his conduct that I find myself in shock. For all the Doctor's moving protestations against this most noxious of trades, I have confirmed with my own ears that the things that were said around the fire at Chitambo, the things I ascribed to drink and *pombe* and false memory, are all too true. I have confirmed beyond all questioning, and beyond all proof, that the Doctor received sustenance and aid from Slave Traders.

I have been looking to his own Journal to see if I could find any words to vindicate him from this grave charge. I have found entries that speak of a heart made sore by the sights that he saw. And yet the man who wrote these words received the assistance of Slavers.

In another place, shortly, uncharacteristically so, given that he was not ill, he writes only, 'Went two and a half hours west to village of Ponda, where a head Arab, called by the natives Tippoo Tipo, lives; his name is Hamid bin Mohamed bin Juma Borajib.'

It transpires that Kumbakumba, the Lord of the Town where we are encamped, is the brother of that same Tippoo Tip, he is the brother of this 'Mohamed bin Juma', this Tippoo Tip, whose wealth has grown from the anguish of the Enslaved. This is the same Kumbakumba who boasted to me of his and his brother's long-standing friendship with the Doctor.

Chawende gave us much-needed rest. Those who had been ill were recovering, even Halima, who was chastened by grief. It was with great reluctance that we left the stockaded town, but we were now well supplied for the rest of the journey. It cannot be another month before we are in Tabora, then it will be a few more weeks to Bagamoio.

Over the next few days, we camped wherever a resting place could be found. There were more stops than movement on this section of the journey, and where there *was* movement it was more in fits and starts than steady marching. I am pleased to report that thus far, I am the only one to hold out against a most dismaying fashion. The Nassickers have taken to wearing their nightshirts in the day. It is cooler to be dressed this way, they argue, but I have been insistent that dignity matters more than comfort.

I have had but few opportunities of any kind to speak with Ntaoéka, though Chirango has been most helpful in procuring these few opportunities for me. What a friend he has been to me. He has come on in a way that is delightful to see.

We passed one more night in the plain before reaching a tributary of the Lopupussi River called the M'pamba. It was a considerable stream that took an average man up to the chest in crossing. The five children were carried over, just as they had been carried through the swamps of Bangweulu. I could not help thinking of poor Losi, who had been the sixth child, but who now lay under the soil at Chawende's.

We drew near to Chiwaye's town, which was very much like Chawende's in appearance: a strong and fortified town stockaded by a ditch. As we approached this place, we were stopped most rudely by six men who tried to pick a quarrel with us for carrying flags. Fortunately, a man of some importance, who seemed related to their Chief, came up and stopped the discussion. There may well have been some mischief done, for our *askari* were in no temper to lower their flags or guns, knowing their own strength well by this time.

We did not stop in the town itself, but camped in a clearing just outside it. Up to this point, our course had been easterly, but now we turned our backs to the Lake, which we had been holding on the right hand since crossing the Luapula, and struck north.

At last, we were on the familiar track to Kapesha's town. Amoda, Susi, and Chuma had stopped here with the Bwana. Our feet were light as we now could see where we were going. Those of us who had not been here before were willing to put our trust in those who knew the path.

I had further reason to be thankful. Now that we were among men who had known the Doctor as a living man we could put behind us the distasteful pretense of sorcery that we had been forced to adopt at Chawende's. We could walk in the Light and say we carried the corpse of the man they had met only last year.

I had not been with the Doctor as he travelled through these lands. So I looked back to the Doctor's notes to see that indeed, Kapesha had been civil and generous to the Doctor, and had given him men to guide his party to his elder brother Chungu. When we met Kapesha, that good man was most sorrowed to learn of the Doctor's death. He insisted that the Doctor's body be placed on an elevated platform so that his people could file past it to pay their respects.

He was most gratifyingly moved to share his remembrances of the Doctor, even to the point of producing for our perusal a small bottle of powder that the Doctor had given him. From Kapesha, we went through the lands of Chama and Kasongo, finding everywhere great fear and desolation prevailing in the neighbourhood from the constant raids made by Kumbakumba's men.

At last Kumbakumba's town came in sight. We had no choice but to pass through his land. I say his land but the truth is that he has no land; he simply holds the neighbouring lands in his control through fear of being raided. Though his given name is Mohamad bin Mousad, according to the Arab style of naming, he is more commonly called Kumbakumba because that word means 'the Gatherer of People'. To avoid being raided, Kapesha, Chungu, Chama, Kasongo, and the other chieftains within his sphere are compelled to pay to him tribute in the form of ivory tusks.

Amoda thought it wise to send two men ahead to inform him of our presence. He came himself to meet us, attended by a great retinue. Though filled with the strongest repugnance, I was immensely curious about this man. I had expected a man of great stature and fearsome size, so I was not prepared for the small round man who approached, his dark face beaming with cordiality.

He spoke with great affection of the Doctor, whom he called Daudi Taabibu; indeed, he spoke of him as a friend. He ordered that guns should be fired in his honour. Afterwards he ordered a great feast for us. As we ate, he narrated to us all his recent doings. He was full of power and boasts, for, as we had learned in the abandoned village some months before, he had killed Casembe, possibly the only other man, other than Kumbakumba, whose mere name inspired fear in his neighbours. He told us in gruesome detail how Casembe had perished, and rejoiced in a most bloodthirsty manner as he narrated his final sufferings.

It was not necessary for any of our party to look at each other to know that we shared a single resolve: that we be quit of this odious man's company as soon as it was at all possible. And yet he had a civility I hardly expected. He showed us every kind attention during our five days' rest.

He was particularly curious about me and the other Nassickers. Unlike the other Nassickers, I was dressed as normal, in my suit and waistcoat, for I wanted Kumbakumba to be in doubt about the kind of man I was.

'A black English,' he said as he peered at my face. 'Or are you just a Shensi dressed like an English?' The word he used for me, Shensi, is an offensive term in his Arabic language for persons of the Black Race, for it means 'savage'. This is how they separate themselves; the Shensi are not human, but merely savages, to be tamed and sold as cargo. He then looked at me as though I were under inspection and declared, to my great astonishment, that I must be a Yao.

He clearly did not expect me to answer, for he turned away after this declaration and made a guess about where the others came from. He had theories about all the unfortunates. 'The Wanyamwezi make good porters, the Manyuema compliant house slaves; the Wagogo are difficult to tame, just like you Yao.'

'I was in bondage as a child,' I said at last. 'But I am a free man.'

He was delighted with our presence, for it supplied him with a new audience for his stories. He took particular delight in narrating how he and his brother Tippoo Tip had started as traders. 'We hired a hundred Wasaramo men to come as porters but made the mistake of giving them a quarter of their ten dollars' salary. We should have known that when the Shensi get a little money, you never see them again.

'They took off, and there we were with cloth to take to the interior and ivory to bring back but no porters to carry it all. So Tippoo Tip and I took two men with fifteen guns and we overpowered the Wasaramo. Took two hundred men captive and bound them, in specially made irons. They carried our packages to the interior, and back again, and we have never had to pay a porter since then.'

Then, in a characteristic we learned was typically his, he moved to another topic and began long and sentimental reminiscences of the Doctor. 'I shall send word to my brother Tippoo Tip to say Daudi Taabibu has died; he will be plunged into severe mourning.'

He narrated long stories of how the Doctor had been saved from starvation, and indeed, had been lost looking for Lake Meroe until Tippoo Tip came to his rescue. The Doctor had then travelled with Tippoo Tip and his slaves until he had reached where he wished to go. From there, the Doctor had passed into the care of Mohammad bin Saleh, another Slave Trader.

I felt it necessary to defend the Doctor.

'He had integrity,' I said.

'Integrity.' Kumbakumba laughed as though he was mocking me. 'There is certainly some integrity in saving your own skin.'

That night, I looked again through the Doctor's notes. In one entry, he says, 'To-day we came upon a man dead from starvation, as he was very thin. One of our men wandered and found a number of slaves with slave sticks on, abandoned by their master from want of food; they were too weak to be able to speak or say where they had come from; some were quite young.'

In yet another he writes: 'Slavery is a great evil wherever I have seen it. A poor old woman and child are among the captives, the boy about three years old seems a mother's pet. His feet are sore from walking in the sun. He was offered for two fathoms, and his mother for one fathom; he understood it all, and cried bitterly, clinging to his mother. She had, of course, no power to help him; they were separated at Karungu afterwards.'

As we left Kumbakumba, we saw sobering proof that this land was indeed in thrall to him. We saw five gangs of slaves bound neck to neck by chains. Here and there were groups of corpses and heaps of skeletons. A flare of anger filled me when I thought that the Doctor had sought the assistance of such a man. He had eaten with this man, had laughed with him. He had eaten food bought with the tears of slaves.

We left as quickly as we could, for none of us wished to stay a minute longer than necessary in his noxious company. But there was other news that hurried us on. From Kumbakumba had come news of the most interesting kind. A party of Englishmen, headed by Doctor Livingstone's son, were on their way to relieve his father, and in fact had left Zanzibar some months previously, and were reported to be approaching Bagamoio.

15

Fifteenth Entry from the Journal of Jacob Wainwright; in which the Expedition, having met with an Enterprising Chief, crosses the Wilderness of Chungu and the Mountains of the Lambalamfipa.

The news of the approaching Englishmen gave purpose to our journey at a time we needed it. Notwithstanding Kumbakumba's geniality and hospitality to our party, it said something about the miasma of evil that surrounded him that the terror of his name died away the further northeasterly we travelled.

We saw again the sights that have become so familiar to us but that, no matter how often we see them, remain as odious as the first time we saw them: the bodies tied to trees, slave sticks, skeletons. My congregants and I said prayers over each body, but that was all we could do for these poor souls. Would that we could have done more.

We were welcomed with delight by the young chief Chungu. He came to meet us, dressed in Arab costume and a red fez. He had nothing but good memories of the Doctor, for when the Doctor had explored these regions before, Chungu had been much impressed with him. It delighted me in the extreme to see that he willingly cast off all superstition and regarded the arrival of the Doctor's body as a cause of real sorrow. He insisted that his people mourn the Bwana, and so for a whole morning, they gathered to keen over the corpse.

Chungu's country lay in a territory that was most propitious for the hunter. Munyasere, along with Wadi Saféné, Carus Farrar, and

Asmani, had some luck in hunting, and a fine buffalo was killed near the town. According to the laws of Chungu's land, he as Chief had a right to a foreleg. Our men pleaded that this was no ordinary case, and that hunger had laws of its own. Munyasere and Saféné begged for our party to be allowed to keep the whole carcass, and Chungu not only listened but willingly waived his claim to the Chief's share.

I was pleased to have the opportunity for intercourse with Chungu, for I found that he spoke Suaheli well and clearly. Indeed, I found him to be a man of a superior mind and fine understanding. He had heard, he said, of the wonders of Zanzibar and wanted some of those things here in his land. He had spoken too with the Doctor and had been impressed by knowledge that came from books.

He appears to be a worthy leader, this Chungu. He took me on a tour of the villages that are under his control. I found them to be places of great industry. The women are constantly busy making homespun cloth, which they dye themselves, while from the numbers of hunting dogs and elephant spears that one sees all around, no further testimony is needed to show the character that the men bear as great hunters.

The only shadow over the week we spent in Chungu was Chirango. Though we had agreed that the best moments for me to spend with Ntaoéka were those moments just after our prayer meetings had ended and the dark surrounded us while Chirango kept watch, I found that every time I approached Ntaoéka, even outside of the times we had agreed, he was there, offering his smiling assistance.

We had a good rest at Chungu's before departing amicably from him. The steep descent to the Lake now lay before us. It was a light march to get down to the neck and indeed, the men carrying the Doctor's Body for this section of our journey could well have sprinted with it all the way down. As we rounded the southern end of the lake of Tanganyika, I made note of Chuma's observations that the Lovu River ran in front of us on its way to Tanganyika, while the Kalongwese flowed to Lake Moero in the opposite direction.

We stopped to wash ourselves in the waters of the Lovu. As I completed my ablutions, I noticed the figure of John Wainwright, who stood far off from the others, gazing sightlessly at the water. I approached him and said his name. He did not answer me. I called his name again, and still, there was no response. I moved to touch him on the shoulder. He gave the startled look of one coming out of a trance.

In a voice quite unlike his normal one, the kind of voice one hears in a dream, he said, 'Would it not be wonderful to go into this river and see how far it goes, to follow it all the way to its end?'

'You are beginning to sound like the Doctor,' I said. 'If you ask Chuma, he could tell you where it goes, without your having to go into it.'

'Going into it is exactly what I wish to do: to fall into this water and let it carry me where it will.'

'But you will drown,' I said.

'That may not be a bad thing,' he said. He looked away from me and though I tried to talk to him, I could no longer reach him. I left him standing there, looking at the water.

I returned to camp to find the men arguing about whether they could eat a creature that Munyasere had shot. There had apparently been much celebration when Munyasere killed the beast. It was a creature such as I had never seen before, with a hairy brown hide and white sharp tusks protruding from its mouth. Chuma said it was known as a wild pig.

On hearing Chuma's pronouncement, the Mohammedans of the party were extremely unhappy. No pig in the world looked like that, they argued. When Amoda said that it was not like an ordinary pig, but was a creature that ate only grass, the Mohammedans appeared greatly relieved. They turned to Wadi Saféné for his ruling. Before his travels, Wadi Saféné had spent three years in a *madrassa*, and he is the closest that the Mohammedans in the party have to an *imam*. He also acts as the *muezzin* of the party and leads them in all the prayers.

'If it eats grass,' Wadi Saféné said, 'then it is no pig; for no pig eats only grass. If it eats grass, it cannot be *haram*. In any event, the Prophet Mohammed, peace be upon His name, says that it is no sin to eat a pig when such an action will save a man who is starving to death. But I am certain that, from what Amoda says, this is no pig.'

Toufiki Ali and the other Mohammedans were quick to give their approbation, for such an interpretation meant that this was a pig that could be eaten by every Mohammedan. For my part, I believe it was hunger that allowed them to overcome their scruples, because, with its pig-like shape and long snout, from which protruded two small horns, the creature was certainly ugly enough to be a pig.

We cooked the animal over an open fire. Pig or no pig, it made a fine meal, though we all regretted the want of salt. The cooking smells must have attracted hyenas, for we saw a pack of them prowling on the edge of the camp. In the firelight, their eyes glinted in their sand-brown bodies.

'You must watch this fine trick,' Chirango said. 'This is how we take care of hyenas back home.'

From the ground, he took up the animal's hide, still dripping with fresh blood. In his other hand, he carried a spear. Walking a short distance away, he hung the hide from a tree branch and planted the spear in the ground just below the hanging hide.

He came back to the fire and said, 'Watch.' Soon enough, we saw a hyena approach the tree. Tempted by the smell of blood above the tree, it jumped up to get at the hide, and fell onto the protruding spear. It gave a loud bellow of pain. It attempted to flee, but the spear held fast. In panic and terror, the creature tried to move this way and that as it sought to free itself from the merciless spear. The animal would have died an agonising death if Susi had not taken up Munyasere's rifle and walked in the direction of the creature. A shot soon sounded and the cries died out. Chirango treated it as a great joke, but I must confess that I was unable to look at him.

16

Sixteenth Entry from the Journal of Jacob Wainwright, written in Baula; in which Wainwright has a Consultation of a Curious Nature with the Doctor's Cook as the Party of Englishmen Approach.

We have now reached Baula, and are just days from Unyanyembe. There is news that the party of Englishmen are close at hand. The Arabs we have met here tell us that among them is Oswell Living-stone, the Doctor's son. The men have been reported to be on the approach to the Arab settlement at Kazeh.

It is more than likely that when they hear of the charge in our midst, they will join us and take over the expedition until we reach the coast. Seen from every perspective, the approach of the Eng-lishmen is most welcome, for it will resolve a matter that has been pressing since Chawende. It is now known in these parts that we are carrying with us the body of a dead white man, and with that knowledge has come ringing accusations of witchcraft and sorcery.

Only the news of the attack at Chawende has protected us, for it is known that we are armed. But as Munyasere reported just before we reached Baula, the supply of ammunition is dangerously low. If we should meet another attack such as that at Chawende, it is not certain that we will prevail.

We were almost tested as we crossed the Manyara River, which Chuma informed me was making its way to Lake Tanganyika, for we met with a party of Wagogo men who were hunting elephants.

We were relieved to see that they were armed only with their dogs and spears. Although they treated us well, exchanging honey and other food for beads, we thought it best to keep these men in ignorance of the fact that we were in charge of the Doctor's dead body.

We managed to convince them that we were merely a party of traders on our way to the coast. The prospect of the white men in our party is thus to be welcomed, for this will go some way to insulate that fear, for it is often believed that the witchcraft of the whites is superior to that of the blacks. Many in these parts believe that the whites live under the water, which explains their pale skin and waving hair. Then there are those who believe that the whites are cannibals; indeed, the Doctor himself often joked to me about the many mothers who had forced better behaviour on their children by threatening that the Doctor would eat them if they did not behave.

It is the thought of such superstitions that strengthens me in my resolve. To think of the lightness of Christ chasing away the Darkness of Satan! The Brightness of My Lord, the Redeemer, chasing away the Fear of Superstition! But that is for another day.

Just as we came to the Likwa River, we saw a long string of men on the opposite side filing down to the water. They were elephant hunters and ivory traders, and had come straight from the coast through Unyanyembe. The Doctor's death, they said, had already been reported there by natives of Fipa. With no small satisfaction, we learned from them that the story we had heard that the party of Englishmen had reached Unyanyembe was true.

Chuma has reminded me of a matter most pressing. In just under two weeks, it will be the Mohammedan Fast of the Ramadan. It will weaken the party considerably if the majority cannot eat while marching. I have known in Bombay that the Ramadan is a period of great lassitude, with eating possible only after the sunset.

Chuma had persuaded the Nassickers, without informing me, that they were to observe the Ramadan. I was extremely displeased not to have been consulted, but as he explained, it is to build the morale of the party. For how can we march as one body if one-third is eating and the other two-thirds are not? This threatened to be the subject of a great quarrel until Amoda came up with a solution.

Chuma's idea was a generous one, Amoda conceded, but there was yet another way to mitigate the ill effects that the fast would have on the group. This was to march at double the pace, so that by the time Ramadan came, we would be as close as we could be to settlements. Then those who chose to fast could fast, while the rest could do as they chose. This we agreed, and so it is that we found that our pace quickened until we were melting two days of the previous outward journey into one.

I have been commissioned by the expedition leaders to write an account of the distressing circumstances of the Doctor's death that is to be transmitted to the party of Englishmen. Four of the men will travel ahead with the letter, while we follow behind.

Heading my letter 'The Livingstone Expedition', and dating it 10 October 1873, I addressed myself thus: 'To the party of Englishmen,' I wrote. 'You will have heard the sorrowful news of Doctor Livingstone's demise. We are now approaching Unyanyembe and have heard of your presence there. Our party are low on provisions. Please advise us whether we should approach the town, and if so, whether we should fire guns. Yours, Jacob Wainwright, Scribe.'

Chuma took this letter and with Adhiamberi, Mariko Chanda, and Munyasere pressed on to deliver it to the English party. The rest of us were to await his return here at Baula. From here we will make our way to Kasekera, and by then, we will know from Chuma what awaits us in Unyanyembe.

About an hour after Chuma and his small party left, Chirango came to where I sat under the shade of a tree and said, 'There is one to see you, Mwalimu.'

In delight, I thought it was Ntaoéka. The quick pace of the march had meant that our prayer evenings were momentarily suspended, and thus I had had but little chance to commune with her. But there had been chances here and there, for Chirango had contrived in different ways to make some meetings happen.

But it was Halima who walked up to me in a state of great agitation. She has been a lot less animated since the death of Losi, and has gone about with a subdued air, but here she seemed to be the old Halima again, though she spoke rapidly, and in great agitation.

She began without preamble. 'You are a man of learning,' she said, 'you have learning that is almost as much as the scribe who was sent to help the Liwali once. But he was nothing to look at, you know, weedy and hunched he was, with a voice to scratch the ears.'

'Halima,' I said.

'. . . ended up married to a niece of the Liwali's, didn't he, but they did not last long in Zanzibar. The heat affected him something awful. It is not for everyone, Zanzibar, particularly when the sun is high in the sky. Even the cats suffer, I have seen as many as two dozen dropping just like that, all faint from the heat, and then they swell up and burst, and, oh, the smell. He called it Stinkibar, Bwana Daudi did, it is the first English word he taught me, and he said it was because Zanzibar smells so much. Stinkibar.'

I looked at her without speaking as she continued, 'But what are you doing, talking to me about smells and dead cats?'

'I have no particular interest in cats,' I said.

'Well, then, why you want to know about them is a mystery, but enough of that. I have something of great moment to talk about with you. I want to ask you about what awaits me in Unyanyembe.'

'What awaits you in Unyanyembe?' I asked.

'Bwana Daudi's son. He is sure to claim me for himself, or per-haps even to sell me to someone else, perhaps to another white.'

She then narrated her familiar history of being owned by first this master, then that one. Did the law not say that a slave was the prop-erty of the heirs once the master died, that is how it had been when her second master the *qadi* died and she ended up with the Arab merchant who had bought her from one of the *qadi*'s sons. Now that Bwana Daudi had died, she was surely the property of his son, who had no doubt come to Unyanyembe with the sole purpose of claim-ing her, along with all of Bwana Daudi's guns and books and clothes and strange instruments and what have you.

I looked at her with pity and exasperation, but it was the Doctor that I felt most angry with. 'Did he not tell you that he bought you as a form of manumission?'

'What is manumission?' she asked.

'You know surely that there are four principal ways in which an enslaved man can get freedom: through being freed by a mas-ter, through manumission by another person or his own efforts, and through a court petition if there is particularly cruel treatment to him by the master.'

'Well that has nothing to do with me then.'

'What on Earth do you mean?'

'You keep saying a slave man can get his freedom. You talk only of the men. What of me?'

'It is the same thing for women,' I said. 'The same rules apply to all slaves, children too, though naturally, children are unable to man-umit themselves.'

I spoke thus but I must own that I was not entirely certain on this point. I had never heard of a manumitted slave woman; certainly, all of the freed slaves who made their way to the Nassick school were boys. Perhaps my hesitation showed in my voice, for I saw that she was unconvinced.

'Did Bwana Daudi not explain to you that he was buying your freedom in the same way that he bought Chuma's or Majwara's freedom? He did not buy you for himself, he bought you for yourself. It was not purchase. It was manumission.'

This was clearly an entirely new idea to her, that she was free not because the Doctor was dead, but because she had been free since the Bwana had purchased her in Kazeh. I could certainly understand why Amoda would not lay stress on this matter, but I could not comprehend why the Doctor had not explained better to her. But perhaps he had, and the contemplation of her freedom was simply too big a question for her weak mind to take.

I believe I managed to persuade her that neither the merchant who had sold her to the Bwana nor the Doctor's son had any kind of claim on her, nor was it at all possible that a man who lived in England would make a journey from that land that had abolished slavery just to claim her.

'You have done me good, that you have,' she said. 'If I can do you good in turn you let me know, indeed, I can do you good right now, for you must know all that goes on between Chirango and Ntaoéka.'

As I looked at her in some puzzlement, Chirango came up to join us. Seeing him, Halima once again mumbled her thanks and walked off. Chirango's face indicated that he wished to enter into some sort of intercourse with me. But I made an excuse about needing to pray until he finally walked off. I am trying to stay as far from Chirango as possible.

That matter of the hyena showed a most unpleasant side of the man. I have not held a service in many days. I do not know whether it is he who has changed, or I. It must be me, for he is as obliging as ever but something in his manner feels oppressive to me. It is almost as though he is too obliging, too agreeable, too willing to come to my aid, to the point of being suffocating. Every time he smiles, it is as though my heart contracts in fear.

17

Seventeenth Entry from the Journal of Jacob Wainwright, written in Baula; in which the Expedition Divides as the Party plunge into Deep Mourning and searches in Vain for a Lost Companion as Wainwright Prays to Him Above to Teach us to Number our Days, that we may Apply our Hearts unto Wisdom.

Before Chuma could come back with the others, Mabruki and Chirango came to report a most shocking discovery. They had gone down to the stream to fetch water. There they found a man lying on a rock, his back to the heavens and his face in the stream. They called to him, but there was no response. Worried, they moved to turn him over. It was Amoda. He had fallen to the rocks and broken his skull.

Farjallah Christie and Carus Farrar consulted each other in whispers and looked troubled. 'The way he lay would indicate that he fell forwards, on his stomach, but he cannot have died from that fall because there was a large gash behind his head.'

I could not take in what they said, for it made no sense at all. 'You cannot surely be saying he fell forwards and still managed to crack his head from behind?'

'That is exactly what it looks like,' Farjallah said. 'And that is why it makes no sense. He cracked his head so hard that it would have been impossible for him to turn himself in this way.'

The meaning of this hit us all at the same time as Farjallah put into words what we were all thinking.

'His head was bashed from behind.'

It was more troubling still when Carus Farrar said, 'And so it means that one of us has killed this man.'

'We will have to establish where everyone was at dawn, for this is when it happened.'

'Perhaps it was a stranger,' said Mabruki.

'A stranger from where?' said Farjallah.

'It is not possible that this is the work of one of us,' I pleaded. 'Surely, it is more likely that he fell to his death?'

I felt hot and cold at once at the thought of revealing where I had been. For I had been with Ntaoéka. As though he was reading my mind, Chirango came to my side and in a low voice said, 'Not to worry, Mwalimu. I was praying with you both. We all prayed together, then after some time elapsed, we all parted, is that not so?'

I looked at him, and there was a look in his eye I could not understand. A thought came to me that I was putting myself into his power, but I brushed it away.

'You need not worry,' he said. 'I have a small hare of my own that I was chasing. You are not the only man satisfying a woman unsatisfied by her man.'

I felt cold to my bones, and as though I had done the dirtiest thing, but I did not want to know what he meant. I knew only that he had saved me from the ignominy of revealing where I had been.

As soon as the news spread throughout the camp, we became eager to leave this place. Halima is splitting the heavens with her wails, for though Amoda was not the best of companions, it was still a shocking way to go.

Just before we could bury Amoda, Chuma and the others returned with the news that we were to bring the Doctor's body to Unyanyembe.

While the men dug the grave, and made sure that it was at right angles to the direction of the Mecca, Laede and Ntaoéka heated water so that the Mohammedans among the *pagazi* could bathe Amoda's body. Halima was too prostrated to do anything of assistance.

Susi, Toufiki Ali, and Wadi Saféné led the Mohammedans as they gathered around Amoda's body and rubbed the water over his body three times.

'It should be the family of the deceased who do this,' Susi said, 'but we are good enough, for he has been like a brother to us.'

They did what they could with his poor wounded head, but it was clearly beyond cleaning. Then they wrapped him in the whitest cloth that we could find, a dust-coloured Americano bolt. It was meant to be for trade, but no one could begrudge poor Amoda. They wound it twice around his body to make a simple burial raiment, for there was no more cloth left after the first wrapping. They then laid him out on a bed made of grass, and the whole company trooped by to pay him homage.

Now, I have made clear throughout this account that I do not hold with Mohammedan beliefs, but even I must admit that I could not but be moved, for the ceremony, short and simple as it was, had its own dignity and solemnity.

Wadi Saféné led the prayers. In a voice of trembling beauty, he called out: '*Allāhu akbar!* In the name of God, the Entirely Merciful, the Especially Merciful. It is You we worship and You we ask for help. Guide us to the straight path. *Allāhu akbar!* Pour Blessings upon Mohammed Your Prophet. *Allāhu akbar!* O God, O God, forgive our brother Amoda and have mercy on him, keep him safe and forgive him, honour his rest and ease his entrance; wash him with water and cleanse him of sin. O God, admit Amoda to Paradise and protect him from the torment of the grave; make his grave spacious and fill it with light. *Allāhu akbar!*'

His voice trembled on the air as the men raised his body and carried it to the open grave. Gently, they placed him in the hole, laying him on his right side, so that he faced Mecca. They placed soil under his head, under his chin, and under his shoulder. Then they sprinkled earth over him as Wadi Saféné said, 'We created you from it, and return you into it, and from it we will raise you a second time.' All the *pagazi* then placed soil over his body.

It is certainly clear why the Mohammedans are not keen to convert, for there is a simple beauty to their rituals. Even where one does not understand it, the words have a raw eloquence that goes straight to the heart. I shudder to think how the party will bear up without this most able of commanders.

As soon as Amoda was buried came another complication: John Wainwright was missing. Mabruki and Munyasere put together a small detachment of men to try to locate him. It was no secret that he had been unhappy for some time, and indeed, Toufiki Ali said he had heard that he purposely went off rather than carry a load any further.

It seemed to me that this was most unlike him. True, he always was a lazy sort of fellow, and completely lacking in the Nassick spirit, but for him to simply take off in this manner without a word to anyone was most surprising. It seemed to me that this was also entirely out of character. If he had gone, it would not have been in this secretive, furtive manner, but it would have been in a manner that sought to make as much of his going as possible.

The men were divided into small parties to enquire into his whereabouts, but they all came back to say there was no further news of him.

'Is it not clear,' Chirango said, 'that it was this John who killed Amoda?'

I had not thought that this was possible, but looking back to the fractious relationship of these two men, it seemed all too likely. Another fear followed as I remembered our strange conversation just outside Chungu's country: that he might have not only taken a man's life, but also committed the ultimate sin of despair and taken his own life. My heart grew heavy as, in my mind, I saw him a few months before we reached this place, standing by the Lovu, looking into its waters, and wishing that he could follow it to its end.

We did all we could to find him, of that I am certain. Not only were small groups sent in different directions to trace him, we also set fire to the grass around us, that he might see the smoke, and, as a final measure, Munyasere ordered that the guns were to be fired twice a day so that he could hear them if he was close.

None of this was sufficient to gain intelligence of him, and so, with regret, and after five days' search in all directions, with no tidings to be gained, we gave him up as lost, and made our way to Unyanyembe. By the time we were ready to set off, the whole party had become convinced that John Wainwright had killed Amoda and vanished into the vastness of Africa. And not a single person spoke up in his defence.

18

Eighteenth Entry from the Journal of Jacob Wainwright, entered in Kazeh; in which the Livingstone Expedition Meets Lt Verney Cameron's Expedition and the Doctor's Body is mourned in State.

The pall of grief hangs over the party. Amoda has truly been our Great-Heart, slaying the giants of Despair and Sloth, the centre of our expedition, the large man with his laugh and voice, his strength. The night of his burial, the party sat around a large single fire.

Even those *pagazi* who had suffered the most under his yoke, the men he had upbraided for their slowness and laziness, expressed their deepest sorrow. Halima found comfort only in Majwara. Together they sat in silence while he polished his drum.

Amoda's death almost made us forget that Chuma had arrived with news of the Englishmen, but once we buried Amoda, we turned our minds to that matter. Chuma and his three companions had reached the Arab settlement without let or hindrance. There they had found that the white men were indeed on an Expedition to relieve the Doctor. But instead of Oswell Livingstone, the Doctor's son, they found that the party were led by a Lieutenant Cameron, whom Chuma put in possession of the main facts of Doctor Livingstone's death by showing him the letter that I had written.

There are three white men in his party, Chuma said. Lieutenant Cameron is travelling with another lieutenant, a man called Murphy, and a medical doctor called Dillon. Chuma reported to us that all three men questioned him extremely closely, and in fact, with great suspicion. Thinking that his knowledge of their language was not equal to theirs, they had explained in his company that we should 'all be d—— to the D——' with our 'd—— fool' mission of an expedition, and I hope I have not offended the delicacy of my future Readers by implying these words, for they are the very words used by them. Chuma is not sanguine as to whether they will accompany us to the coast. In addition, they also cast severe aspersions as to whether it really was the corpse of Dr Livingstone that we carried.

At this intelligence, Carus and Farjallah immediately said they had thought there would be such doubts, even if we reached the coast, but they were certain that any proper postmortem examination of the Doctor would reveal beyond all doubt that it was indeed the Doctor: particularly remarkable would be the injuries he had received in his lifetime, and most especially the broken arm that had been occasioned by a lion attack when he had been a younger man in the Barotseland. Such an examination, however, could not be carried out in the wild, so we were all in suspense as to what course of action the white men would recommend.

All the party felt a keen disappointment on learning that the reported arrival of Mr Oswell Livingstone was entirely erroneous. Still, we had received our orders: we were to march on with the body to Kazeh.

And now the greater part of our task was over. We wound our way into the old well-known settlement of Kazeh, where a host of Arabs and their attendant slaves met us. If she still retained any fears of what awaited her in Kazeh, Halima was silent. I know little about matters of love between men and women, and I doubt that she felt love towards Amoda. But even her heathen heart will have been shocked by such a death. I was pleased to see Ntaoéka was being her usual helpful self and supporting her.

Here, indeed, we felt the power of the white man, for it was no longer necessary to conceal what we carried. In Kazeh, the expedition leaders and I faced the three men. Cameron was a large man with much hair about his face and small serious eyes.

I could see that Doctor Dillon, a small round man who was red in the face, was not going to make much progress on this expedition. Murphy was a quiet man who deferred in everything to Cameron, who was clearly the leader of the party. Lieutenant Cameron expressed doubt about whether the risk of taking the body through the Ugogo country ought to be run. It was most likely, he suggested, that the Doctor had felt a wish during his life to be buried in the same land in which the remains of his wife also lay. Was it not better that he be buried in Africa than that we continue with our mission to the coast?

We could have handed over the body right there and then, and left them to do what they wished with it, but we were all, when we consulted each other, actuated by the thoughts of our fallen companions.

Was their sacrifice to be rewarded by our burying the Doctor here in Kazeh, by our taking an action that we could have undertaken at the very beginning of the journey? I thought of all the men who had died, the women too, and John Wainwright, who had simply disappeared without a trace; of Nchise and Ntaru, shot with arrows at Chawende. Most of all, I thought of Amoda, our strong, fallen comrade, whose wisdom had guided us this far.

I am pleased to say that the others saw the matter as I did. A few of the men still talked of the reward that awaited us in Zanzibar, but it was clear to most that reward or no reward, this was no longer just the last journey of the Doctor, but our journey too. It was no longer just about the Doctor, about the wrongs and rights of bearing him home, or burying him here or burying him there, but about all that we had endured. It was about our fallen comrades. In their honour, for their sakes, for all our sakes, we vowed to remain committed to our first conviction, that it was right at all risk to attempt to bear the Doctor home.

Lieutenant Cameron was angered considerably by this decision and fully expressed himself on the matter.

'D—— your stubbornness,' he said. 'Do as you will. I will have no further part in the whole business. I wash my hands of it.'

Having no further need to concern himself with Doctor Living-stone, he decided that he would continue into the interior. We were importuned further by their desire to examine the boxes. As I have narrated, we had carefully packed up everything at Chitambo's – books, instruments, clothes, and all which would bear special inter-est in time to come from having been associated with the Doctor in his last hours.

He then insisted on opening the boxes of instruments. I had the duty of asking the Nassickers to unpack for him the chief part of the Doctor's instruments for him to appropriate.

Chuma in particular was most aggrieved to see them go: the aneroid barometers, compasses, thermometers, and sextants, for he had been the Doctor's apprentice for so long that he had come to know each one and treat them as his own, for these were the instru-ments with which the Doctor had made observations extending over seven years.

The plunder, though most regrettable, did have the effect of lightening the load considerably. Susi and Chowpereh were more alarmed when Cameron turned his attention to the guns carried by our *askari*. He wanted ten of them, and five muskets, as well as most of our ammunition. We were not able to persuade him otherwise. It was our choice to continue with the journey, he said, and that was no reason to take the guns.

We then asked if we could, in exchange for the weapons, have some goods to trade our way to the east, for we were severely low on resources.

He said he had nothing at all to give us, for he needed our supplies for himself. To leave us unprotected, unprovisioned in this way! Readers of this account will make of the man's character what they will, for I will say no more on this subject. I leave his punishment to Him above, for Vengeance is mine, says the Lord, and I will repay.

Dejected and discouraged, we gathered to plot the way forwards. As we huddled together, an Arab with the bronzest teeth and the yellowest eyes known to man came to pluck the sleeve of Susi. 'I have something to show you,' he said.

Curious, Susi, Chuma, and I followed him to a small house at the end of the row. From a large chest, he extracted four large bales of fine Americano cloth.

They had been left by the Doctor on his way down, as a reserve stock, he said. Lieutenant Cameron, he said, had been most insulting to him, and he did not wish him to have it. Susi laughed as he shook hands most cordially with the Arab.

This was treasure indeed, and very glad we were to receive it too. Our spirits somewhat revived, we arranged that we would collect the cloth the day on which Cameron left for the interior, lest he claim it as he had the Doctor's instruments and guns. The next morning, we parted company with Cameron's party. But we found that though Cameron had lightened our load, he had further burdened us with a most unexpected charge: he had left Doctor Dillon behind with instructions that we were to take him with us to the coast.

As the news of our new travel companion spread through the party, I could read on every face the one emotion that gripped them all, which was complete and abject dismay at the prospect of this man's joining us as a travel companion. Indeed, I could almost feel every heart sink along with mine.

Though God has made man in His general image, He has in His infinite wisdom chosen to give each man his own particular shape. But there was no question at all that the shape that He had given Doctor Dillon made him entirely unsuitable to an expedition such as this.

On a ship on the high seas, which is how he had got here, he might perhaps have been perfectly at home, particularly if such a journey brought with it a fine stateroom and nightly dining at the Captain's table, but everything about his figure, from his red face, his rotund stomach, and his small plump hands to his sweaty swollen neck, suggested that he was not one made to wander the African wilderness. But Cameron had left early for the interior, and had, just as he had in the matter of the guns and the doctor's instruments, left us no choice in this matter. And thus it was that Doctor Dillon joined us that morning as we departed Kazeh.

19

22 October 1873

Nineteenth Entry from the Journal of Jacob Wainwright, written out-side Unyanyembe; in which Doctor Dillon proves Himself a Travel Companion even More Burdensome than the Most Petulant Child.

If our progress was slow before Doctor Dillon joined us, then we are moving at a snail's pace now. I am sorry to report that the entire party's misgivings about Doctor Dillon's suitability as a travel-ling companion have been proved to have foundation. He is now become such a burden that I would that we could, like Christian and Hopeful in *The Pilgrim's Progress*, have let him go at the Place of the Unburdening.

It is now clear why Lieutenant Cameron had no wish to travel further with him, for Doctor Dillon is a most difficult man. We have lost John Wainwright, true, but we have replaced him with Doc-tor Dillon, who is by far the more unpleasant companion, for while poor John only snivelled, complained, and malingered, Doctor Dil-lon is actively disruptive.

When he is not lagging back, or refusing to move, he is raining on our ears ceaseless complaints about the food and the weather, about the insects and the noise of animals in the night, about the children's laughter during the day, about the men's singing on the march. Most of all, he can't bear the sound of Majwara's drum or Chirango's *njari*.

And as he has decided, correctly as it happens, that my English is the best of the party, these complaints are all falling on me. He has given me a long and detailed history of his passage on Her Majesty's Ship *Enchantress*, the ship that brought him to Zanzibar; of the many fevers he fell into on African soil; of the dysentery and malaria he suffered.

He has been a doctor with but one patient, himself, and though his ministrations to his own person have been as careful as they have been plentiful, his physique appears too weak to withstand these climes. Such a companion is most unpleasant to travel with, particularly when he feels himself master of us all. It is as though we are on the Dillon, and not the Livingstone, Expedition.

The morning after we set off, he refused to rouse when Majwara called the reveille. It was much too early, he said; in their party, they only started to march when the grass was dry of dew. Even with that late departure, we had to stop in the middle of the morning of the first day's march for a long halt. In their party, Doctor Dillon said, they only walked until the lunch hour. This was enough to shock Halima into clucking over such laziness.

Two days into the march from Kazeh, he said he was quite unable to walk, and demanded that he be carried in a litter. His feet were swollen, he said, and his legs quite unable to support his body. This request occasioned significant anger among the men while Halima and Ntaoéka gave us their opinion that the man was not nearly as sick as he seemed.

I feared that he would not get on with Chirango, who carried the front of the litter, while Mariko Chanda carried the back. At one point as we walked, Chirango hit a stone and stumbled. Doctor Dillon was jolted in the litter and came down with a thump. Beckoning to Chirango, Doctor Dillon gave him a slap that shocked us with its power. Chirango seemed unfazed, and only smiled and bowed, before picking up the litter and striding with it so powerfully that Mariko Chanda had to scamper to pick it up.

Susi told Chirango to give the litter to another of the *pagazi*, but Chirango seemed so determined to make up for the jolt that he had given Doctor Dillon that he gave him nothing but smiling refusals. The Power of Christ truly moves in Chirango, and in him, Our Lord's humility is made manifest.

Doctor Dillon was proving a terrible distraction from bigger problems. As I have said in an earlier entry, not only had Lieutenant Cameron appropriated the Bwana's instruments to his use, he had also, most crucially, taken half our guns, and almost all the ammunition of our *askari*. Of the twenty guns they had carried, just ten were left, and three muskets besides.

There was no disguising the fact that we were now completely undefended. Nor would we be able to hide the activity in which we were engaged. Carrying a dead body, and a white man's body for that matter, was sure to stir up a certain hostility.

Soon we were approaching a cluster of villages with whom we hoped to trade, left to defend ourselves only with stratagems. The news of our mournful burden had already arrived at the first village we reached. They turned us away. We marched to a second village, and here too we were turned away. We were just a party of traders, we protested, carrying nothing but goods to trade. They did not believe us.

On we marched, until we reached the village of Kasekera. To the villagers here, we feigned that we had listened to the Englishmen and abandoned the task of carrying the Doctor's body. We had changed our minds and sent the body back to Unyanyembe to be buried there. Devoid of fear, the people of Kasekera asked us all to come and take up quarters in the town, a privilege that had been denied us so long as it was known that we had the remains of the dead with us.

Doctor Dillon continued to cause us trouble. In the evening after we left Kasekera, we camped near a flowing river. Once he had eaten his meal, he ordered his tent erected and disappeared within its folds. The rest of the party sat around the fire at night, listening to music made by Majwara's drum, accompanied by Chirango's *njari*.

We were so absorbed in the music that we did not hear Doctor Dillon leave his tent. It was only when he spoke that we saw him. 'Will you stop that infernal din,' he said. 'I can barely hear myself think.'

He lurched himself at Chirango, and took up his *njari* and smashed it to the ground. The outer calabash broke and shattered into three pieces, and the board with its metal keys fell with a clang. He picked it up and flung it into the river. We all stood in silence as he raged. His passion spent, Doctor Dillon turned on his heel and walked back to his tent.

'I fear the fever has got to him,' Carus Farrar said.

Chirango said nothing, but stood looking at the flowing river, as though to see where his instrument had fallen. Though he waded into the river to look for it at dawn the next day, though he dived into as many sections as he could, he did not find it. Instead he took the pieces of painted, broken calabash that were all that remained and packed them with his things.

20

Twentieth Entry from the Journal of Jacob Wainwright, written just outside Kasekera; in which Wainwright enters the Valley of Humiliation.

Darkness, darkness, all is darkness, all is despair. I am in the grip of the Giant Despair, tightly held. I am shut up in his Doubting Castle. I have sinned against the Light of the World, against the Goodness of God. I doubt my own salvation. I have grieved the Spirit and He will flee from me. I tempted the Devil and he is come to me. And as the Devil is wont to do, he has used the agent Woman, Tainted Eve, Double-Faced Jezebel, and Traitorous Aholibah, Whorish Aholah. She has felled me as Delilah did Samson, as Jezebel felled Ahab, as Eve felled Adam.

For I was not in the Land of Beulah after all, but had been ensnared to the Enchanted Ground on Vanity Fair, where an Enchantress made me lose my way. Such despair I feel. Mabruki called the expedition leaders together for an urgent consultation. He had received news of significant import from Mariko, he said, he wished to discuss a matter of import, for he had been greatly dishonoured. A member of the party had been lying with his woman Ntaoéka under the cover of darkness. He looked over to where I sat with the other Nassickers and pointed his finger.

My eyes closed in prayer. I had not been aware just how hot the day was, for sweat began to prickle at my forehead. Before anything more could be said, Ntaoéka ran up to stand a few meters from where Mabruki stood.

'It is true,' said Ntaoéka as she looked in my direction.

I felt as though the eyes of the whole party were on me.

'I chose Carus,' Ntaoéka said.

I opened my eyes to see that Carus Farrar had risen to stand beside her.

'I chose Carus, and I am carrying his child.'

For a minute, they seemed suspended before me, Mabruki stupefied, Ntaoéka defiant, Carus contained. My eyes closed again, as a lance of pain shot through my side.

Ntaoéka said, 'Yes, it is Carus that I want, and there is nothing anyone could do to make me change my mind. I am a free woman, am I not, I am no bondswoman. I am not Halima.'

Halima flared up in anger and asked, 'Is a bondswoman not a person?' to which Ntaoéka retorted that this had nothing to do with Halima, and nothing anyone said would change the way she felt about Carus.

I escaped the quarrelling voices and walked down to the stream. Their shouting voices rose and fell as though from a place far off. I do not know how long I stood on my own, I know only that at first my breath came in short painful stabs, then in longer breaths that sent agony through the whole of my being. I could not see anything around me, for my vision was blurred. Though I could no longer hear it, her voice rang in my head. I chose Carus. She chose Carus.

She waylaid me as I walked from the stream. I held up my hand, that I might not see her, but she stood in my way. 'I cannot be what you want me to be,' she said.

I walked on as though I had not heard her. 'And you know what you made me do, what you told me to do. How can I love such a man?'

I stopped and looked at her without speaking.

'Chirango said I was to lie with him, at your request.'

My heart froze as the meaning of what she said hit me. Then she said, 'Carus and I are to be married and go and live in the Cape, and I will learn English.'

The rest was drowned out at the sound of that name. She had chosen Carus Farrar. As thoughts of her with Chirango threatened to fill my mind, I forced myself to think of her with Carus Farrar. She babbled their plans as I walked away. He and Farjallah plan to ask Doctor Christie in Zanzibar to help them to be trained as doctors. He has promised her frocks and frivolity. 'I cannot help it,' she said. 'I am carrying a child, and that child must have a father.'

No, she cannot help it. She cannot help being a false Jezebel. No, she cannot help it, for she is a daughter of Eve, and sister to the temptress Jezebel. She is Samaria, Aholah, and Aholibah. She is all the whores of Jerusalem. She can't help that she played the harlot, she can't help defiling herself with men whose flesh is as the flesh of asses, and whose issue is like the issue of horses. No, she cannot help it.

I am sure they laugh at me, she and Carus. This Chirango business is nonsense, of course it is nonsense. It is something that she has made up, it can only be that. He is my first convert. I know in my heart that he would not do such a thing. To whiten her name and that of her lover, she will not scruple to blacken the name of a Christian.

I have always known that Carus resents me, that he resents my gifts. I have known that he does not like me, neither he nor his friend Farjallah, for I am younger than him but was so well favoured at school. He does not like that I speak the Doctor's language better than he ever will, that I read the same books, that I know of what the Doctor thought.

He is much my senior in years, and so he must have looked in envy as a much younger man became the Doctor's confidante. And he is to be a doctor too, to be trained in medicine just as the Doctor was trained. But it was not enough. Oh, but it was less than enough! For matters of the spirit are not the same as matters of the body. This body is but a shell. We have no abiding city here, but seek a home that is far away, and here on Earth we leave our bodies so that, thus lightened, our souls can take flight. Though he knows how to cut human bodies, I know how to cut to the human soul.

This evening, after a meal I could not eat, Carus came to me where I sat with the other Nassickers. As the others ribbed him and joshed him about, I stood up and gave him a stony look. 'Mabruki is being very good about it all. I suppose it helps that he can hardly take her to be his wife.'

'Excuse me,' I said as I walked past him, 'I have more important matters to think on than which bed a harlot plans to sleep in this week.'

On my way to I knew not where, I met Chirango, who gave me a smiling greeting. I walked past him without acknowledging him. I walked on alone in the raging cauldron of my hate.

21

Twenty-First Entry from the Journal of Jacob Wainwright; in which the Mohammedan Feast of Eid Approaches as Wainwright Dons the Armour of God and Sets Forth to Do Battle Against the Authorities and Principalities of Apollyon.

Jehovah Jireh. The Lord is my provider. Jehovah Jireh. Christ is my protector. His Grace is sufficient for me. His Grace is sufficient for me. Yes, it is sufficient. His Grace is sufficient. I will lay the reins on the neck of my lusts. In the Blood of the Lamb I shall write on my heart: *sola fide, sola gratia, sola scriptura*. With the fire of the Holy Spirit I shall brand those words on my soul. By Faith alone, by Grace alone, by Scripture alone.

His Grace is sufficient for me. His Faith is sufficient for me. His Salvation is sufficient for me. I will pray with the Spirit, eat with the Spirit, walk in the Spirit. For this battle is not one of Flesh and Blood.

It is a fight against the Authorities and Principalities of Evil. It is a battle I fight for my Lord and King, against all that is Dark in this world, against the spiritual forces of Evil. For they have sent to me the Temptress Woman. They have sent Aholah and her sister Aholibah, who lust after men with the flesh of donkeys and issue that flows like that of horses. They have sent the Jezebel who whispered to me in the dark just as the snake whispered to Eve and she whispered back in the garden long ago. And through her came the Fall of Man.

I will stand against her plots, stand true against the Devil's schemes. I will put on His Armour and, thus clothed, set out to meet Apollyon, that scaled, tailed Demon who is enemy to all that is Pure. Satan will not defeat me, Beelzebub will not defeat me. Around my waist, I wear the Belt of Truth; over my chest the Breastplate of Righteousness; on my feet, the Gospel of Peace; on my head, the Helmet of Salvation; and in my hands, I clutch the Shield of Faith and the Sword of the Spirit. And I will stand firm against every one of Apollyon's flaming arrows.

Do not be afraid, my Lord God Jehovah says to me. For I have named thee JACOB, and thou art Mine. I have bought you and made you free. When you pass through the waters, I will be with you. When you pass through the rivers, they will not flow over you. When you walk through the fire, you will not be burned. The fire will not destroy you. For I am the Lord your God, the Holy One of Israel, who saves you.

And I will pray in the Spirit, and eat with the Spirit. I will drink with the Spirit and sleep in the Spirit. I will walk in the Spirit and live in the Spirit. And I will conquer. The fire will not consume me, for I am washed in His Blood. The fire will not destroy me, for I am made Pure by His Love. I will conquer. In the name of my Saviour, I will conquer.

And soon, Tainted Jezebel, Apollyon's Minion, will be but a memory to me. She will be a memory like the uncle who sold me into bondage is a memory to me, like the whips that marched me weeping to the coast are a memory to me, like the dhow that took me across the terror of the high, high waters is a memory to me, like the bodies jumping into those waters as the great ship bore down upon us are but a memory to me. I am an Heir to Salvation. I am cloaked in His Grace and shod in His Truth.

I will pray in the Spirit, and walk in the Spirit, and live in the Spirit. And I will conquer. And, just like Christian in *The Pilgrim's Progress*, I will enter the Celestial City and walk with the Shining Ones. I shall pass over. And All the Trumpets shall sound for me on the other side. And the Trumpets shall sound.

22

Twenty-Second Entry from the Journal of Jacob Wainwright; in which Wainwright celebrates his rebirth, casts aside his Stupor, and Rededicates Himself to the Service of He who by His Incarnation Gathered into one All Things Earthly and Heavenly.

For some days, we were wandering in a great dense forest, where the only shelter is under trees. Beyond the bare knowledge that we are somewhere between Unyanyembe and Bagamoio, I do not know where we are, nor do I care to ask. When we emerged from the forest, we reached a large, featureless plain.

Between the forest and the plain, we moved slowly, for the weather has been most inclement. The rain has been falling constantly. My thoughts are as muddled and dark as the overcast sky. My mind is vexingly slow and dull. I appear to have been woken unwillingly from a deep slumber before falling again into stupor, only to be woken again in protest.

I eat when the others eat, I walk when the others walk, and I sleep when the others sleep, though the food has no taste and the ground seems to float beneath my feet. My sleep is plagued by horrible visions of unclothed women. When I walk, or talk, it is as though I am in a daze or just emerging from a fever dream. When I am spoken to, the voices come to me as though from a far-off place, while objects take on an unreal quality in my sight.

When I am not marching, and often even then, I find myself in the grip of a great lassitude. I feel a great disinclination to all labour or thought. It is for this reason that I have made no entries in this Journal.

Even the manner of my dressing is altered. I have now given in to wearing my nightshirt in the day. My suit feels heavy in the heat. And when it rains, it hangs on my body like a clammy curse. I have also lately taken to wearing a turban around my head to protect it against the sun, a sight that pleased the empty mind of Halima, who insisted on calling me a right-looking Mohammedan.

It was that comment, together with seeing my face in a stream, that finally woke me up. Were those my eyes, so dull and lifeless? Was that my mouth, so downcast? Though the pen is heavy in my hand, I forced myself to take it up. And it was as I wrote down the date that it came to me that today is my birthday.

No, I do not have her.

And I never will.

But I have my freedom.

I have my life.

I have my Christ.

The fire will not consume me. Despair will not consume me. I take up my pen on this most blessed of days to give thanks to Him Above for the life that I have. And I pray for a Shower of Blessings to rain upon all the men who sailed aboard the SS *Daphne* on the day of my rescue all those many years ago.

I pray Blessings on the heads of Reverends Wainwright, Price, and Isenberg and on all my teachers. I pray for all the boys who remain at the Nassick school, freed from human bondage. And I pray for all the Pilgrims on this journey, both the deceased and the living, and, yes, even for she whose name shall never pass my lips again, though she has smote my heart.

Though we are far from any human settlement, we are in a land that is not unknown, for everywhere we see the small piles of bones under trees, a true sign that slaves have been on this route. The sight of those poor yellowed bones has done its work on me. I fasted and prayed for two days and found myself with Ezekiel in the Valley of the Dry Bones.

And the hand of the Lord came upon me, and He brought me out by the spirit of the Lord and set me down in a valley full of bones, and He said to me, Can these bones live? And I turned to them and said, O dry bones, hear the Word of the Lord. The Lord shall put breath in you, and lay sinews on you, and you shall live. And you shall know that He is the Lord.

And so it is my birthday. On this day, I rededicate my faith in God. On this day, I renew my mission. I swear to Him who guides the weak, for weak I have proved to be, that I will put aside all that has distracted me and rededicate myself to His service.

On this day, of my twenty-second year on Earth, I pledge that I will do everything I can to get to England. And when I am there, I will be ordained, and then I will have my own mission.

I shall return to my homeland, where I shall do all that is in my power to fight the reason that these forests are dotted with aging bones. I shall do all in my power to fight the detestable traffic in humans that demeans every person associated with it. I shall save the people who sold me into bondage and cast me out those many years ago.

My mother will not know that the Jacob Wainwright who stands before her, so full of knowledge and great learning, is the same Thenga that she bore all those years ago. If she is alive. But they are alive, of that I am certain, for that is my fate and my mission, to save my people, and to bring them to Salvation just as I was brought to salvation on this day, the day of my rebirth. And the Dry Bones shall live.

23

25 December 1873

Twenty-Third Entry from the Journal of Jacob Wainwright; in which the Party Discover the Duplicity of a Trustworthy Companion and Wainwright Rues his Wilful Blindness.

Will this dangerous and toilsome journey ever end? We are walking with Death, eating with Death; we carry Death in our midst. At present, we are in the Forest of Slaves. Here lie the doomed, dozens upon dozens of them, their bones lying in heaps at the bottom of the trees to which they were tied. Their skulls roll along the forest in a high wind and knock against each other. The trees themselves seem to send up a smell of rot and corruption.

We are at the mercy of Providence; we are tossed about by the vicissitudes of fortune. In the last week, I have been fortifying my faith by proclaiming His name in Antiphons.

O Leader of the House of Israel, giver of the Law to Moses, come to rescue us with Your mighty power!

O Root of Jesse's stem, sign of God's love for all his people, come to save us without delay!

O Radiant Dawn, splendour of eternal light, sun of justice, come and shine on those who dwell in darkness and in the shadow of death!

And today of all days, most precious day that it is, my Lord Jesus Christ's birthday, I proclaim, O Emmanuel, our King and Giver of Law, come to save us, Lord our God!

For today finds us burying another body as we continue to bear our toilsome burden on this wretched, endless journey. It is the Doctor's corpse that calls death into our midst. Losi is gone, Kaniki is gone. Songolo is gone. Misozi is gone. Nchise is gone. Ntaru is gone. John Wainwright is gone. Amoda is gone. And to that number we now add Chirango.

We are walking with blood and bones, we are walking with mangled bodies, here in the Valley of the Shadow of Death, we are walking with Sorrow and with Strife.

The sorrows of Death have compassed us, and we shall not see the land of Milk and Honey. I wish to God we had never borne the Doctor away. I wish we had heeded the Mohammedans. I wish, above all, we had heeded his own words and buried him in the ground at Chitambo. Better still, we should have left him to be eaten by wild animals, or flung him into one of those rivers he was endlessly discovering.

Truly, I wish to God I may never see again the shape of his body as it is carried between two men. Because the cost that he has wrought on us is too great to bear, for anyone to bear.

24

Twenty-Fourth Entry from the Journal of Jacob Wainwright; in which the New Year finds the Expedition still on the Journey and stalked Everywhere by Death, and Wainwright comes Face-to-Face with the Flatterer and Worldly Wiseman.

I have not written a word since that last entry. Instead I have been praying penance for allowing myself to be conquered by the Giant Despair. Though I have read His words over and over, and prayed again and again to Him who cures all for His counsel and wisdom, and though I have said so many times the Reverend Bean's Prayer against the Sin of Despondency that I know it now by heart, I am unable to shake completely the heaviness that rests in my chest.

After days of hunger, and marching in relentless rain, more than half the *pagazi* have deserted. Led no doubt by Asmani, for he is gone, they have taken the most valuable packages and simply vanished in the night. No one bears them any ill will, for we would all desert if we could.

For we have been travelling with a great evil among us. We have harboured a snake in our midst, one which has spread great venom and destruction among us. To my own personal disappointments, I must add the firm and certain knowledge that I have nested at my bosom a Worldly Wiseman, a Flatterer in possession of a cursed tongue that speaks words of honey that drip with poison, and who comes in the guise of a Friend of the Spirit. And with this has come certain knowledge of my Wilful Blindness. I have allowed the Flatterer to take Comfort under my Protection.

On the night before that last despairing entry, Chuma had woken up to relieve himself in the place we had assigned for the purpose, far from the camp. It was long past midnight but not yet dawn, and the whole camp slept. On his return to where he slept, he heard what sounded like a muffled cry.

The sound came from the tent where Doctor Dillon was quartered. Chuma went in that direction, and just as he was about to call, from the tent emerged Chirango. On seeing him, Chirango said, 'I was just checking on the Doctor. Everything is well.'

Chuma was made suspicious by Chirango's manner. He tried to enter the tent, but Chirango stood in his way. But Chuma is a larger man than Chirango; he fought his way into the tent and met a most horrible sight. Doctor Dillon was lying on his bed, his eyes staring ahead sightlessly. His throat had been most mercilessly cut. One look at Chirango told Chuma all he needed to know, and indeed, had he not rushed out to give a cry that roused the rest of the party, he might have met Doctor Dillon's fate.

As it was, he gave a great cry that woke the camp. In the tumult that followed, Chirango tried to flee, but was tackled to the ground by Munyasere and Adhiamberi. Chirango, wild-eyed, made a charge to escape, but the men held him fast.

It took some time before any of us could understand what it was that Chuma was relating to us. And when we did, only one question was on every mouth. 'Why? How came it that he killed this man?'

Chirango said, 'And why not? Why was he here, why were they all here? I would kill them all if I could. And he is not the first either. I have killed more than him.'

My stomach turned to water as I said, 'Amoda.' I spoke as though to myself but I must have been louder than I thought.

'You killed Amoda?' Susi said.

'And not him only,' Chirango said. 'Why did he whip me?'

'He did so on Bwana Daudi's orders,' Chuma said.

'Pwana Pwaudi's pworders. Pwana Pwaudi, Pwana Pwaudi. Will you listen to yourself? How is he your *bwana*? How is he anyone's *bwana*? And that other one, the one with the boiled eyes whom you call Bwana Stanley. And you talk of Bwana Dillon too. Bwana pwana. How are any of them your *bwana*?'

Gone was the pleasing self-effacing Chirango of the humble demeanour. In his place was this man whose rage seemed to waft from him in waves and threaten to consume us with its power.

'Your Bwana Daudi is lucky that he died when he did, because I would have killed him too. As I killed Losi and Misozi and Kaniki, I killed them all, it was to be Halima too, but it is all the same to me.'

'You killed Losi . . . ,' Halima wailed.

'And Kaniki knew I had bought poison from Chitambo's medicine man, and I killed John Wainwright because he helped me to kill Amoda.

'And it is all because of that man you are carrying so slavishly. Who was he to come to my land? To bury his woman on my land? This Stanley, this Cameron, this Speke, this Grant. Who are they, who are any of them, who are they that they go so freely to any of our lands? This man Dillon raises his hand to me, and you all do nothing. Nothing.

'He slaps me without consequence. He destroys my instrument, and you do nothing. I have told you again and again, but you will not listen to how the Portuguese drove my ancestors off their own land. They wasted my kingdom, stole my land. And now this Cameron goes inland. More of them will come, mark my words. This Nile source that he wanted to find, that they all want to find. They will find it, and other river sources, and in the process, they will see that there are other things to be taken. And they will want us to worship their gods, like we have not our own.'

His one eye bulged so much that it seemed in danger of falling out. In a voice of great anguish, he cried out, 'Look at me, look at me, look at me. I have nothing. Nothing. Blinded, and for what? For one string of beads? Blinded for taking a string of beads from a man who has not paid me for my labour?'

In the stunned silence that followed his words, he looked directly at me and said, 'And you are the worst of them all, Jacob Wainwright.'

My stomach lurched as I scrambled for the words to deny what I knew was coming. 'You are the worst,' he said. 'For you have allowed them to enter your soul and hate yourself. You have discarded your gods for theirs. You loathe your own skin, and your own kin. You want to dress like they do, and speak like they do, but you will never be one of them.'

I breathed in relief. I had to say something to stem the words that might come next. To my great relief, the expedition leaders moved off to discuss the matter away from the group. Halima was weeping into her cloth, with Laede and Khadijah consoling her. The others were dissecting in stunned voices the information they had received.

There was a clear consensus among the leaders: we could not take him with us, that much was certain. But nor could we leave him behind, because he would come after us while we slept and kill us. And the blood that he had shed had to be avenged. While we pondered what we were to do with him, we tied him to a tree; the night grew long as around the fire we talked.

'We could leave him tied there,' said Munyasere.

'It would be a week or so before he died, because the body has reserves of food,' said Farjallah.

'Without food or water, that would mean we leave him to die,' said Carus. 'We cannot do that to him, it would make us no better than slavers.'

I did not want to agree with the man, but my soul revolted at the notion of leaving him tied to a tree. Perhaps another party of travellers would, in time, come across him as we had come across other corpses and skeletons and assume that he was just one of the many slaves tied to trees. It was a horrible thought, to think of him there, for who knew how many nights it would take for him to die.

But it was just as clear that we could not take him with us. For where would we take him? And to face whose justice? Would the Sultan's courts, the *qadi*'s courts even try him?

Finally, Chowpereh suggested a plan. There were ten guns left, and three muskets. Ten men, to be picked by lot, would load their guns and each would fire at Chirango once. That way, he would not only die quickly, it would never be known who had fired the fatal shot. No man would bear the burden of this guilt. This would be done at first light without alerting the rest of the party.

At first light, the ten men assembled. It was clear that no one had slept. Susi took up Amoda's gun. Chirango did not act like a man about to meet his Maker. His voice dripped with malice as he said, 'But surely, you want to know all about it. Halima wants to know how Amoda begged for his life. Still, Susi, you must be grateful, for I have cleared your way for you. Indeed, you should thank me, you and Halima, for I have done you a great service. I took Misozi's life with one hand and Amoda's with another. Now you can lie with one another all day long like the slut Ntaoéka lies with—'

From the right side of my vision, I saw a blur break through the line of men. I heard a guttural scream. For a wild moment, it looked like Susi was embracing Chirango. Chuma and Chowpereh ran to pull him away. Chirango's head drooped. Susi stepped back. As he did so, we saw that he had driven a knife into Chirango's stomach.

I had not realised until then that I was holding my breath. Susi pulled the knife from his stomach. Chirango's body twitched and spasmed. Chirango gave a look of puzzled astonishment. He opened his eye and his mouth, made as though to speak, and then was still. I breathed at last.

25

Twenty-Fifth Entry from the Journal of Jacob Wainwright; in which Journey's End approaches as the Expedition Heads for Bagamoio.

We have moved a little from the place of Chirango's death. We would fain have moved further, but we are awaiting Susi's return. And the end of Ramadan approaches. We are all faint with hunger. I admit that I have found a new respect for these Mohammedans, for I do not know how they can march without food.

Halima has been prostrated by Chirango's revelations. She believes it is the spirit of Misozi that has come back as a *vembwigo* from the land of the dead to punish her. First Losi, now Amoda: she is convinced that Misozi wants her revenge. She is out of her mind with fear and grief. She is babbling about her house in Zanzibar, and the door that she will make, and that Susi was supposed to live with her there, but now he can't because Misozi will not let him.

Susi was last seen walking back to Kasekera. Chuma and Mun-yasere followed him there. They found him trading cloth and beads for calabashes of *pombe*. He was deep in liquor and belligerently refusing to come with the party. There was only one thing to be done. Four men carried him back when he was at his drunkest. As soon as he came to himself, the whole party took turns to talk to him. I prayed for him, Chuma shouted at him, Laede and Khadijah wept, we have all talked ourselves hoarse.

And we have all said the same thing, the same thing I said to him:

'It was not murder, what you did. You acted to save us all.'

But Susi will not listen to anyone. 'When you have killed a man, only then can you come to me and tell me what is a murderer.'

'In that case,' I said, 'let Christ be your salvation.'

Susi laughed then, the laugh of a demented man. I left him, the others took over. After three more days of waiting, we resolved to continue with our mission. It was Majwara who said, 'Leave me to talk to Susi, I will talk to Halima too.'

He led the unresponsive but complaisant Susi to where Halima sat under a tree. From afar, we saw the three of them talking. They sat thus for more than three hours. We do not know what, if anything, was said, for none of them ever spoke about it.

The next day, on the morning before we left, we were joined by Susi. He indicated to Mariko Chanda that he was to help him carry the Doctor's body. Halima took her place in the caravan, next to Laede and Ntaoéka. Majwara blew his horn and beat the drum, and on we marched, until we reached the glorious sight that told us we were almost there, until we reached the sea. I have not had many happy associations with the sea, but I must own that no body of water has ever looked so beautiful as the sea did that day.

The moment we saw it, Majwara let out a great cry. '*Alḥamdulil-lāh!*' he shouted. '*Bahari, bahari!*' An answering cry went up as the group spoke like a man in possession of only one word, and that word, 'the sea', 'the sea'.

For one happy moment, we were all children again. We dropped all we carried and embraced each other in giddy dances as Majwara let out a positive frenzy of drumbeating. Chowpereh took up Majwara's horn and blew it. The flags waved in a riot of colour. Then we ran as a body to play and dance in the sea and splash each other with its waters.

Amoda would have scolded us for tarrying, but perhaps he might also have been overcome by the sight of our journey's end and done no more than frown. As it was, there was no Amoda to rebuke us. That whole day, we swam and fished and lay in the sun. It was the first truly merry day that we had spent together since Amoda's death.

Against the blue ocean touching the even bluer sky, against the warmth of the sand and gentle lapping of the water, the evil wrought by Chirango and the sorrowful troubles of the journey receded behind us.

We agreed that we would camp there for the night before following the coast up to Bagamoio. That night, we lit two large fires on the beach and roasted fish we had caught during the day. There was even more singing, and much laughter too.

The following morning, Halima insisted on washing and drying the clothes of everyone left. 'We cannot walk into Bagamoio looking like a party of miserable rescued slaves,' said she.

The weight of her loss still sat upon her. It seemed no harm to indulge her in this small vanity. Bagamoio was but a day away; what harm could another day do? The women spent the day washing clothes and plaiting their hair.

Early the next morning, before dawn, we struck out for Bagamoio, choosing to walk along the coastline. This was a most pleasant part of the journey. We did not need the drum now. The waves and the gulls above gave us encouragement on our march. The children ran in delight to the cows that lay in the sun as birds pecked and picked at their ticks and fleas. In the distance, coconut growers climbed the tall trees and lowered their prizes.

The sea was in our every view, the ground soft beneath our feet. Now and then, we hailed fishermen who were taking their dhows out or fixing nets in a stream of chatter. The news soon spread of our strange party with its woeful bundle. By the time we reached Bagamoio just before the hour of eleven, we had gathered a crowd of followers that was twice as large as our own party.

And that is how we entered Bagamoio, praying and sorrowing with twenty-five people less than when we left Chitambo, fifteen deserters and the ten dead. We headed for the church. Chuma and Susi made a sign to the others that they would carry him inside themselves. A Sunday service was in progress. The people rose in their pews as we walked to the front. The priest stopped in midsentence and stared. '*Mwili wa Daudi*,' Chuma said. On the cold stone floor of the church, they laid down the body of Doctor Livingstone.

III

BAGAMOYO

'Thy slave Kafur came to us, bareheaded with torn garments and howling: Alas, the master! Alas the master! A wall of the garden hath fallen on my master and his friends the merchants, and they are all crushed and dead!'

'By Allah,' said my master, 'he came to me but now howling: Alas, my mistress! Alas, the children of the mistress!, and said: My mistress and her children are all dead, every one of them!'

Then he looked round and seeing me . . . he cried out at me. . . . 'O dog, son of a dog! . . . O most accursed of slaves! Get thee from me, thou art free in the face of Allah!'

'By Allah,' rejoined I . . . 'thou shalt not manumit me, for I have no handicraft whereby to gain my living; and this my demand is a matter of law which the doctors have laid down in the Chapter of Emancipation.'

The Book of the Thousand Nights and a Night,
volume 2, translated by Richard Francis Burton

The sounds of exclaiming laughter and excited chatter are loud enough to reach me at the top floor of my house. From the high window, I can see a crowd of people. They stop in admiration and wonder as they point at my door. Whenever I enter or leave the house, I often find that I have to work my way through a gaggle of onlookers. In their chatter, I hear my name, only now, it is not just plain Halima, Bwana Daudi's cook, of whom they speak, but Bibi Halima, the freedwoman who has her own house.

My mother, Zafrene, and my little Losi are surely clapping with joy together with my ancestors when they hear me called 'bibi' almost as often as I once called others 'bwana.' I wish I could know for certain that Losi is with my mother. They are not bonded by blood, only by love. I don't know if love is enough for the ancestors to make Losi become one with them. Perhaps she is with her own ancestors, and with her own mother. It is a thought that gives me some comfort.

When they call me *bibi*, I sometimes ask myself, is this you, Halima? Then I smile and tell myself, yes, Halima, it is you. And in my head, I talk to the departed spirit of my ancestors, and to my mother, Zafrene, to thank her for watching over me, for look at me now.

Who would ever have thought that a *mpambe* like me could ever own a house? Bwana Daudi's son, the one called Zouga because he was born by a river, although he went by the name of Oswell, well, he honoured his father's word.

Instead of taking me as his property, he gave me property of my own; he bought me this house and gave me the money for my magnificent door. And sometimes I remember how Amoda would insist that there was no such thing as a bondswoman with her own house. Poor Amoda. But it is best not to dwell on these things.

Mine is one of the old houses that has been built up like new. And it is not just any house. It is a house with a door the like of which has not been seen before. Those who have travelled in many lands say that the doors of Zanzibar are the most beautiful on Earth. There are doors that speak of destiny, doors that protect hard-won prosperity and that guard against evil. The more ornate doors do all three.

Mine is such a door. They say that mine is not an Arab door; they are entirely in accord that it is not an Indian door, and they also agree that it is not a Swahili door. It is like all these doors at once, they say, and yet like none of them individually.

'Look,' they exclaim. 'There is the chain around the edges to protect against evil and keep safe all who are within. And there is a row of lotus flowers to show that all is open within. And will you look at the big golden brass knobs with their outward spikes, it is as though the owner is carefully guarding the house from an elephant attack, for what elephant would break through such a door?'

Truly, there is no door like it, they agree.

My carpenter thought the same. He scratched his head in puzzlement when I described the door I wanted. He had never made such a door, he said, nor had any other carpenter in the whole of Zanzibar. Of course, it is nowhere near as grand as the door to the Liwali's old house, which is owned now by Ludda Dhamji, the customs master, along with half of Zanzibar, nor is it close to the grandeur of Tippoo Tip's door – how can it be when they have grown rich and fat from selling slaves when I am just a freedwoman – but my carpenter did himself proud, I will tell you that for nothing.

Sometimes, when it is not too hot, I sit outside on the long low *baraza* that runs the length of the house, enjoying the chatter. Those who know that this house is owned by the woman sitting on the *baraza* listening to them turn to me and exclaim, 'But this door, Bibi Halima, will you look at this door.' I laugh and tell them it is not a Swahili door nor an Arab nor an Indian door, it is a Halima door.

I am pleased more and more that I did not go with my very first thought, which was to buy the house on the street they now call Hurumzi. This house, with the special door, is just off that street, on a quiet corner in a little street called Kaonde, a street that no one knows. Or at least a street that no one knew before I came here, because it is getting more and more known, and that is all thanks to my door.

I wanted to buy a house on Hurumzi because it means 'Freedman'. That is the street where the Arabs with slaves took them when the slave market closed. Yes, indeed, the slave market has been closed. They say that the news that Bwana Daudi sent of the Manyuema massacre so outraged people that the English forced the Sultan to close the market. But that won't change anything for the poor souls who already lost their lives.

All the traders were in an uproar with all those slaves to sell and no buyers for them. So the English who had forced the market to close said, 'We will buy your slaves for you if you bring them to this street on this and that day.'

It was the best way, the only way really, for although the market had been closed, the trade was continuing underground in cellars and at night. So the traders brought their slaves to Hurumzi, and there they were manumitted, their freedom bought for them, and they were told, you are *wahadimu* now, you own yourselves now, you are your own masters.

But not every one of them is like Halima, poor things. Freedom is a bitter potion when you don't have the means to be free. It is a burden to be your own master when you have never been free. There are now simply hundreds upon hundreds of freed slaves roaming the streets with nothing to do because the Arabs won't employ them for pay.

They wait until all households are abed, then they cram themselves into doorways and onto *baraza*. I have found more than a few outside my own door sleeping on the *baraza*, and I feed them when I can. For without the grace of my mother, Zafrene, and my ancestors who watch over me, I might have been one of them.

Many more have begged to be enslaved again, or to work for food instead of wages, but for the rest, it is a life of banditry, ruffianry, or starvation. All of the rich householders in Zanzibar are in uproar against the English and want the market back.

In the evening, I set up a fire outside my house. People come from all over to buy food. They ask me if the fish is fresh, as if I need to keep fish. Almost all the food is gone in one day. And what remains, I give to the poor freed *wahadimu* sleeping out on Forodhani.

Now that I live in Zanzibar again, I am getting used to the narrow familiar streets with all their filth and the stench of dead cats. Bwana Daudi was right to call it Stinkibar. The only problem with my house is that it is too close to the fish market. When the wind is high and blows the smell of the fish market this way, I curse the location; but better dead fish than the smell of dead slaves, which you don't find so much now that the slave market has been closed. And, oh, the noise, always there is a fearful din. It is a wonder that anyone can hear the *muezzin* when he makes his calls to prayer.

There are new things to get used to as well, like the Hamamni on the way to Mkunazini that Sultan Bhargash built. It is a place of wonder, and when you leave it, you are cleaner than you thought possible, for in the baths inside is hot steam that reaches even the inside of the ears, and the nose too.

The Hamamni is close to Shangani Point. I could have bought a house there, but I cannot bear to be close to the sea. It is not the *chunusi* or *vembwigo* ghosts I dread, those fearsome creatures that Misozi talked of. I am afraid if I live that close to the sea I will always be at a window, looking at the sea and thinking of Susi.

On landing days, when the ships come into port, I go down with a dish of food, ready to sell. I go with a dish of food, and shout, chicken, chicken, good chicken, but all the while I am looking for him. I long to see him, and hide my longing in the shout of chicken, chicken, plenty good chicken. I am learning some English after all.

The ships from India and England brought newspapers that carried the story of Bwana Daudi's funeral. I did not understand all the words but I saw immediately the illustration of Jacob Wainwright carrying on his shoulder, together with Bwana Stanley and the Bwana's own sons, the coffin of Bwana Daudi to his final resting place. And I thought of Susi and Chuma, how it should have been them in that picture.

They did go to England, but not for the funeral. They arrived months after he had been buried, to help Bwana Daudi's friends and children to write a book about his last journey. I wish I could have gone with them, if only to see Bwana Daudi's favourite daughter, his Nannie, and tell her how much I tried to feed him up, even in his last days. And when they came back after a year, they brought me news of my good fortune.

Three days after they returned, I was called over from Bagamoyo, and all the others too, although many could not be found. We were to get medals, at least the men were to get medals, and they were to be presented in the garden of the consul. I also received a medal, but that was because they had made one too many and thought, well, there is Halima, she is there, the medal is here, and we may as well give it her. But best of all is that I received my house.

We all scattered after the awards were given out. Chowpereh and Laede are here in Zanzibar, with their children, and though Chowpereh still goes on expeditions, Laede has had enough of wandering. Majwara, Munyasere, and Saburi have joined Bwana Stanley's many expeditions, as have a great many of the other *pagazi*. Farjallah Christie is back in India, together with the other Nassickers, all but poor John Wainwright of course, and Jacob Wainwright, of whom there are many rumours.

It is said he offered himself up as a dragoman with Bwana Stanley but was refused. Another rumour said he went back to that school of his in India, to be a teacher, but they would not take him. Yet another said a pot of boiling water fell over him, and in that way he perished, but that cannot be, for I also heard that he was employed in Mombasa by one of those busybody missionaries who want to make every person a Kristuman, and this a year after he had supposedly died.

It was also said that he was here in Zanzibar, working as a door porter, and that makes me laugh, I tell you, for I cannot imagine Jacob, haughty as he is, opening and closing a door for anybody.

Munyasere, who travelled with Bwana Stanley close to the land of the Baganda, is the latest person to bring further news of Jacob. He met him, he says, on the way to the kingdom of the Baganda, where he is to be a scribe in the court of the Kabaka.

Much joy may that bring him, if that is true, for all I have heard about the Baganda is that they eat bananas like nothing on Earth. They stew them, and roast them in underground ovens, and make them into a mush that they drink with water. It will be bananas that he eats with bananas, and that every day too, if everything that they say about that land is true. Now, I am fond enough of a banana, I make very good fried bananas, they go wonderfully well with a bit of fish cooked in the juice of limes, but I could not bear a life of eating nothing but bananas, that I could not.

So I have not seen Jacob, but I have seen Ntaoéka. The first time, she was on her way from Zanzibar to Bombay, and the second time, she was on her way to the Cape. Her child, the one she caught on the horrible journey, was born here in Zanzibar. A babe in arms, he was, when they shipped off to India. Quite the madam, she has become, all starched skirts and shining shoes. And her hair is no longer in twisted twigs around her head, but smoothed back and tied to the nape of her neck.

'Ntaoéka,' I called out when I saw her.

She turned to me with a regal air, as if she did not know who it was. 'If it is not Halima,' she said, as though we had only met a few times. 'How pleasant it is to see you. But it is Maria now that you should call me. I am no longer called Ntaoéka.'

That business with Jacob Wainwright certainly stuck, the other business I mean, for she has remained a Kristuman. Married to Carus Farrar now, she said, and she even has a paper that says so, so she is not just his travelling woman. He came up at that point and was most cordial with me. They were on their way to Bombay, he said, where he was to be trained as a doctor.

I saw them again when they returned. It was six years later, it was, and they were now on their way to the new missionary establishment in Mombasa. Frere Town it was called; they were to build a new town out of nothing.

They had two children with them this time. The smallest was a little girl not far from Losi's age when she died. It hurt me to look at her. The wound, though healed, is still there. I focused on the boy. You could have knocked me down with a chick's feather when I beheld the older one, for it was as though it was Jacob Wainwright staring at me.

Ntaoéka was most keen to talk about all the work she and her husband would be doing in the Cape, all the healing of babies and converting heathens. The way Ntaoéka said 'heathens', you would not have believed that this was the same woman who had played the close buttock game with first one man, then another. As though a person can just shed who they have been, like taking off an old dress and putting on a fresh one. That person stays inside even under all the other new persons that you take on.

It was all the talk of the heathen this and the heathen that that did it for me. 'You sound just like Jacob Wainwright,' I said, 'and if I did

274

not know better, I would have said that boy of yours was his child, for he looks exactly like him.'

The child looked at me with Jacob's solemn eyes. His mother frowned as I spoke, but her husband gave an easy laugh and said, 'Now that you say so, it does appear so a little.'

What a fool that man is, doctor or no doctor! Even in the old days, he could barely see what was going on under his very eyes. Perhaps all doctors are like this, for Bwana Daudi was a fool too, in many ways. Perhaps it is all that learning that drives basic sense out of their brains.

But she is lucky to have Carus Farrar all the same. That is Ntaoéka all over. She will always come right, that she will. She will come out all right because she has her eye out for what is most important in the world, and that is the skin of Ntaoéka.

I would like to be married again, although the only two offers I have received have been from men so old you could make paper for all Bwana Daudi's maps and scribblings out of their skin. A woman expects a little more life in a man. And the burials would have cost me more than they were worth. No, better Susi or no man at all.

So I cook and wait, and cook and wait.

I do not know how long I will stay in this house. It won't be for much longer. If I am to tell the truth, I am growing weary of Zanzibar. It is too full of the *shetani* of all the dead slaves. Voices whisper in the night, and shadows appear out of nowhere. And they say that the spirit of Popo Bhawa, the evil *shetani* who was cast out to Pemba many years ago, is preparing to come back here and wreak further havoc. It is true that the last time he appeared, it was the men he was after, not women, but still. Who wants to live in a place where that sort of thing is going on? And even if he does not come back as they all say he is planning to, the truth is that the air here is foul with the smell of too many people.

But perhaps it is a longing to leave that makes me see these things. Perhaps it is not Zanzibar that does not fit, but me that is no longer fit for Zanzibar. I have thought until my head is almost cracked, but still, these many years later, I do not understand what is to be gained from leaving your home to go tramping and sleeping in the wild, all in search of the beginning of a river whose waters have flowed since the beginning of time.

Just as I said to Bwana Daudi at Nyangwe long ago, when he was in despair over all the people massacred, there is nothing you can do now to bring them back. You were given this life, and one day you will leave it, and even so, people will live and die and be massacred just like this, and the Nile will rise and flow and flow and rise whether you find its beginning or not. And I am told that many years later, they are still looking for this place where the Nile flows from, for no man has found it yet.

But even though I will not go traipsing and gallivanting round in search of the beginnings of rivers, I know a little now of what they meant, the men, when they spoke around the fire. I understand now what it means when the urge to travel bites you like a mosquito that gives you a fever that means your feet are never still and your mind is always wandering.

There were many things that happened on that journey with Bwana Daudi, part while he was living, part when he was dead, but one thing that it left with me is the feeling I get sometimes: as though I am hemmed in all round, and all I want is to go somewhere no one has ever been, and gaze at the sky and look for miles around to see nothing but trees and hear nothing but birds.

Sometimes I think I would like to travel again, but this time, if my mother, Zafrene, wills, it will be without any person's body. For it was, at bottom, a foolish business. I often think of Misozi's words when she heard what the men had decided. Whoever heard of a party of people marching across a strange land with a dead body?

I even think sometimes that I will sail on a dhow with Susi, though the thought of living on the ocean is enough to turn my stomach. Sick as anything I have been, every time I have crossed to Zanzibar, but for him I would brave it, I think.

Perhaps, instead of going to strange lands, or even to the sea, I will move across the water and live in Bagamoyo. It was a sorrowful period that I spent there, but I liked it well enough. The air is much cleaner there. I will get a big Swahili bed made, one with those carvings, just like the ones they all slept on at the Liwali's, the kind that is so big it has to be made right there in the room itself, the kind you use to sleep in and eat in and live in. Once you have a bed like that, you know you are not going to move.

I will sell this house, and buy a smaller house there. I will make sure it has a garden. But I will carry my door with me, it is too pretty to leave behind. They can admire it too in Bagamoyo, my door with all the symbols, though there won't be as many people there to admire it as there are here. And from my house with the magnificent door, from our house with the magnificent door, Susi can go travelling. And maybe I will go with him too. And we will come back to our house in Bagamoyo and go through that door and lie down on that bed.

And if he does not come back, well then. I had Amoda and I lost him. I had Losi, and I lost her too. But I am still here. I will still be here if Susi does not come to me. I have a house with a door that all wonder at, and soon I will have a bed that I will wonder at. With wealth like that, what more can any person ask for?

277

For now, I am content to live in my house, with my door and, soon, my bed with carvings all around it. The only thing I wish for is to hear news of Susi. In the meantime, I am content to walk to the dock and sell my food and listen out for news of him. Then I walk back home and admire my door, and enclose myself within my very own house. Every two weeks, I go to the public baths. I could afford to go once a week, but they might think that I have got above my station. And I make sure to walk at least once a day on Hurumzi, just to remind myself that I am free.

*An Entry from the Journal of Jacob Wainwright, written at the Court
of the Kabaka Mwanga, the Thirty-First King of Buganda; in which he
reflects on an Uncertain Present and a Disappointing Past, and contemplates the Doubtful Future.*

From this distance, the hills of the Kingdom are purple against the
sky. This is my favourite time of day here, when the mist is high
and the light is breaking with the promise of a new day. It is banana
season, the Kingdom's most productive time. In an hour, the landscape will be dotted with banana pickers who will work in groups
to slash and harvest the fruit. It is not the small yellow bananas that
the Baganda eat, but the large green bananas that they call *matoke*.
It is cheerful work; the pickers sing as they pick. From this harvest
will come the food that will sustain the Kabaka's Court and subjects
in the months to come.

When I first came to the Kingdom six years ago, it astonished me
to see how great was the variety of food that you could make out
of that humble fruit. The Baganda cook their *matoke* in a variety
of ways: boiled in water, fried with onions, and covered in peanut
sauce, or cooked in a pleasing mixture of fish or meat. They also
pound dried bananas to make a flour that is cooked with water to
make a stiff porridge. They even use banana leaves as a covering in
which they cook other things. When I find myself eating a particular delicacy, my mind immediately flies to Halima, for she would be
sure to delight in all this banana fare.

All of the Kabaka's subjects, from the highest to the lowest, from the aged to the young, are expected to join in the banana harvest. I am no subject here, I am a visitor merely, but even I have found myself drawn to the picking fields. It is not every day that I join them, but when I do, I work often enough and long enough that they can see that I am as capable of the labour involved as they are.

My six years in the Kingdom of Buganda have been years of great change. I first arrived in the Year of Our Lord 1878, sent by the Church Missionary Society to give support to the Reverend Alexander Mackay in his efforts to set up a mission in the Kingdom. The Reverend Mackay urgently needed an interpreter, they said, for the Kabaka would not give them permission to hire any of his people. It was welcome work.

Before the Lord opened up this path for me, He had cast me into the wilderness, and there tested me sorely. There was a most humiliating period when I was forced to work as a door porter in Zanzibar. I took to wearing Arab dress then, so that no one I knew would recognise me in the lowly station into which I had sunk. But a most kind gentleman from the Church Missionary Society recognised me, and, shocked to find me sunk so low, had arranged for me to accompany a new mission to the Kingdom of Buganda.

It seemed to me that my time had come. I opened up my heart in Thanksgiving because finally I could work as a missionary. But when I arrived in Buganda, it became clear that the Reverend Mackay, the mission leader, would not let me do any missionary work at all. I was supposed only to interpret and explain, and not do any preaching or converting. And what is more, the missionary expected me to serve him as his personal attendant, as though I were some low servant or base slave!

Even that work, which was like a yoke around my neck, was fruitless, for the people here spoke not Suaheli but Luganda, a language I was unfamiliar with. By the time a year had passed and I had gathered enough to be of use, Mackay himself had gained sufficient knowledge such that he no longer needed an interpreter. In the end, I became his household servant. Though I prayed the Reverend Bean's prayer against resentment, my heart burned with humiliation.

And so when I learned, through a servant of the Katikiro, one of the chief advisors to the Kabaka, that the Kabaka Mtesa needed a trustworthy man to write his letters and interpret for him, and that he had heard about me as one who knew the white man's knowledge, I seized my chance and offered myself up. I believe that Reverend Mackay was as glad to have me leave as I was glad to leave them.

It was a busy time in the Kingdom. There were missionaries from two countries here, France and England, petitioning the Kabaka to build churches. The Kabaka Mtesa was a wily man, adept at keeping them uncertain but expectant, always hopeful that tomorrow would bring the positive word they needed to build churches and schools.

But alas, within just months of my joining his Court, the Kabaka Mtesa began to ail, and in a matter of days, his life was extinguished. The sinful king had as many wives and concubines as King David and King Solomon, more than eighty, it is believed, and it was not immediately clear which of his sons was to succeed him. Great conflict was averted only when it was finally announced that he was to be succeeded by his young son Mwanga, a son of his tenth wife. I am afraid I cannot explain the convoluted manner in which the determination was made that this boy had the best right to the throne, but if I am to own the truth, the crown could not have covered a more unsuitable head.

Truly, when the old Kabaka died, with him went his wisdom. It is true that youth is not necessarily a bar to success, and that young monarchs have succeeded the world over, but it is clear to every person who meets him that, at the age of sixteen, Mwanga does not have the seriousness of mind and steadiness of heart necessary to make his reign a success.

The new Kabaka is rash and restless; he delights in japes and jests, and is unable to think seriously on matters of weight. Then there is the matter of the unspeakable acts that he is said to force on his pages. I will say no more about those acts other than to say they are strictly censured in the Book of Leviticus.

Nor does the Kabaka Mwanga have wise counsel about him, for the wisest of his counsellors, the Katikiro, through whose good word I was hired, has been banned from the Court. Now, although I am not of the Baganda nation, I had entertained a faint hope that I might become in time, if not Katikiro, then a counsellor and close advisor.

I had thought at first that the Kabaka's youthful age was a great blessing, and that my Lord had finally granted me favour, and given me the thing I longed for the most after my still-unfulfilled wish to be ordained and become a priest. Unfrocked as I was, I thought I could lead a mission of my own. I thought this was my chance to be close to a king or prince who had great influence over his people. But the Kabaka Mwanga has said many times that he keeps me only because not only do I have the white man's knowledge, but I also amuse him.

Chirango often talked of those who had swallowed the white man's knowledge. But thoughts of Chirango bring up other, darker thoughts, the darkest and most painful of which relate to Ntaoéka, and so when they come to my mind, I bid them go.

I am meant to work at the Kabaka's Court as a dragoman and scribe, writing the Kabaka's letters for him and reading those that he receives, and interpreting for him when visitors come to his Court who are unable to speak the language of the Baganda. But mostly, he treats me as a jester. He mocks my manner of speaking the Luganda language, for though I have become fluent after six years, it is only natural that I make the occasional slip in pronunciation. These small moments he treats as a great joke, however, and he calls attention to every mistake.

When he is bored with mocking me, he will ask that I read to him from my small stock of books. The Bible would be the best thing to read to him, but he refused to accept Christ and has no interest at all in the Holiest of Books. He demands that I read to him from my other books.

It is right, the Reverend Bean says, that we pray for even the most black-hearted of sinners, but I confess that I find it hard to pray for the heart of this man. My greatest moments of peace are when I find myself outside the Kabaka's Court in my small house at the foot of the Mengo Hill. Here I keep my own company, interrupted only by the presence of Nambi, the young handmaiden who has been given to keep my house. Since Mkasa Balikudembe, the Kabaka's majordomo, replaced the first servant assigned to me by the old Kabaka with this one, no hour has passed in which she has not giggled at something or other about my person or manner.

I will not complain, for the Mkasa Balikudembe is a good man, a Christian – though one who has most unfortunately chosen to be a Papist – and he has been most kind to me. And we should, says the Reverend Bean, stand prepared to meet with Christian Firmness that overbearing banter which attempts to put everything grave and serious out of consequence.

Though it has long been my desire that the distinction my education and status have given me be reflected in my physical person and attire, when I am not at the Kabaka's Court, I wear the colour-ful cloths of the Kingdom. The truth is that Nambi's housekeeping skills are lamentable; though I brought with me an iron and taught her how to use it, she is quite unable to iron straight the shirts and collars that I brought with me from England. When I reproach her, she only laughs behind her hand. This forced accommodation of dressing like a local is, I must confess, not too unpleasant, for the climate here is hot, although it means that from a distance, I must look like any other native.

While Nambi is most unsatisfactory, I am most pleased with Kizito, the page who brings me messages from the Kabaka's Court and calls for me when the Kabaka needs to see me. In person, he is very like Majwara, for they are of an age, though Kizito is much more amenable. I never could bring Majwara to Christ; he was too tied to the stories of his mother. Kizito is willing to learn, and he is already advancing well.

There is a small community of pages, among them Kizito's friends and brethren Yusufu, Mako, Nuwa, Kagwa, and Luanga; they are part of a small group that meet in secret. I have often hosted their prayer meetings in my house. But I fear I am losing them all to the lure of the Papists. Under Père Siméon Lourdel of the White Fathers, the Papists are fast gaining ground and attracting adher-ents. It has proved difficult for me to explain why the pages should be with my Church, and not that of the Papists, particularly when there is no identifiable Church to which I belong. Père Lourdel has made approaches to me on more than one occasion, encouraging me to convert to Papism, but when he said I could not be a priest, I told him that I did not see the point of it. Besides, I have always had a strong dislike of Papism.

I had thought that here, in the Kingdom, I might find the means and land to build a small parish church, nothing to equal the Abbey certainly; nothing even as grand as the smallest church in that green and pleasant land, merely a simple dwelling where His name would be sung by a small congregation of believers working in humbleness as they tended His vineyard. And from there, I had hoped, would be built a new Jerusalem, here on Africa's soil.

But the Kabaka refuses me permission to build a church. Even here, in my native land, I suffer under what the Reverend Waller called, in my hearing, 'the great and terrible disadvantage of being black'. It has been made clear by those of my own kind that the people would sooner listen to the white missionaries than to me.

And that has proved true. My experiences here have not been without bitterness. A few months ago, I interpreted for him when the Papists who call themselves the White Fathers asked to build a church. It was a bitter blow to convey to them the news that they could build a church, when the same Kabaka has refused me permission to start my own mission.

I try to be forbearing, to put all the bitterness aside. And I try to focus on the task that I have set for myself. In my small house is my humble library. I no longer possess only the prayers of the Reverend Bean, my *Pilgrim's Progress*, and my Bible. In addition to all of Doctor Livingstone's published journals, a gift to me from the Royal Geographical Society, I brought back with me a few more books from London. The Kabaka likes me to read to him from one called *The Water Babies*, written by a man of the cloth called Charles Kingsley. It reminds me of the stories that some of the companions told on our journey, stories of fantastical things that, while unreal, were nonetheless diverting.

I keep it not for its own sake, but as a keepsake of the affection shown to me by the Doctor's daughter Agnes, for she it was who gave it to me. It is the sole book that the Kabaka would have me read to him, even more so as I render the words in his tongue, the better for him to understand, and always he chuckles and wants it read again and again.

To own the truth, I spend more time in explaining than in telling, for the Kabaka wants explanations for everything: he wants to know what chimney sweeps are, steam engines, telegraphs, and so on. And though it is but a tale told to entertain children, I hope that its message of Christian charity and kindliness will get through to the man, and have him abandon his vicious ways. At the very least, if my words of Christ's love cannot do the trick, perhaps he can be turned by the homilies of Mrs Doasyouwouldbedoneby.

In my small house, I do my work, quietly and steadily. I have not told anyone yet of my great task. On the ship to England, when I was not struck ill, I finished my translation of the key passages: the Lord's Prayer, the Beatitudes, the Ten Commandments, a few prayers of my own, for times of heat and despondency. I had them bound in England. They cost me a small fortune, as well as many curious looks. I have now translated the Gospel of Luke, the Acts of the Apostles, and the Letter of the Apostle Paul to the Hebrews.

And when I need rest, I walk in the quiet of the forests. Here, where there is no single monument to His name, I feel Him in the movement of the stars and the laughter of the children. I feel Him too in the night, when the lights of fires have all been put out, and the dark is lit only with His heavenly stars.

In the unquiet company of my thoughts, I pray that the Lord may forgive Chirango all his sins, that the Lord have mercy on his soul, that the Lord truly have mercy on his soul, and that the Lord may have mercy on us all, that He may forgive us for all that we did to bring the Doctor home, and that He may bless us, in all the places we are scattered. And every evening, I say a special prayer for the soul of Abdullah Susi.

Only in rare moments do I look back at the past, because to do so simply brings me pain. For England was not the Celestial City after all, it was not the place of my ordaining, but a cold and unpleasant purgatory.

And yet my beginning promised much. My first days in England were such as to suggest that all that I longed and prayed for would come to pass. When Her Majesty's Ship *Malwa* docked in Southampton, the Reverend Horace Waller and others of the Doctor's friends met me most cordially. They gave me the news that I had been chosen to bear the Doctor's remains to his final resting place.

In the glorious magnificence of the Abbey of Westminster, I led the pallbearers, with Mr Stanley beside me on the left, and the Doctor's sons and friends behind me. Bearing the Doctor's body to its final resting place, I felt as one with them, an equal in their eyes and in the Lord's sight. Afterwards, I was presented to the Queen, who complimented me most kindly on the perfection of my English.

It was even more promising after that. The Church Missionary Society took me on a speaking tour all over England. On these occasions, I found myself addressing persons to whom the land of Africa was nothing more than a drawing on a map. There was lamentably little knowledge of the vast geography of the place.

I was at great pains to explain that drawings, always so beloved of geographers, give merely an approximation of distance. When they talked of establishing bases, they talked of establishing a base in the Seychelles, from which they would go on to Mombasa and the interior. And though I explained many times that the climate was hot, there was a strong fervour to knit socks in the thousands to send to the little slave children in Zanzibar. In the many instances that I made so bold as to correct them, I could tell that such corrections were not welcome.

But it was when I talked at length about my wish for a mission that things changed for me; it was when I talked about the hearts that I would turn to Christ, and about the ones I had already baptised, that the promising beginning came to nothing at all. In just a few months, I said, I had turned seventeen to God, more than the Doctor ever had in his entire lifetime. I told them I baptised them in a river, and gave them new names.

Instead of their receiving this news with joy, I was met with consternation. I had acted without the authority of a bishop or any Mission, they said. I was no missionary. Worse, they said I was boastful and arrogant, and my learning had gone to my head and driven out all humility. It was a pity, Mr Waller said, I had learned nothing from the Doctor I had had the good fortune to travel with.

In my anger I spoke unwisely. For it was then that I spoke of Bwana Daudi's association with the slave raiders Tippoo Tip and Kumba-kumba, and the ready assistance that they had rendered him in his time of need. The Society openly turned against me then. Not only was I boastful, arrogant, and disrespectful of authority, they said, I was also an ingrate who rained calumny on the Doctor's name.

That ended my speaking tour. From London I was taken to a great house called Newstead Abbey, a most magnificent place owned by a friend of Bwana Daudi's called Mr Webb. Here I met the Bwana's children, his son Oswell and daughter Agnes. But they were less concerned about my role in his salvation than in deciphering his writing and maps. In this I was of no help to them, for I could not explain those aspects of the Doctor's journal that remained obscure: I had not been there.

It was then that it was decided to send for Susi and Chuma. When the Doctor's last journals were finally published, they included a narration by Susi and Chuma, and not by me. In that narration, they contradicted everything that I had said about what happened on that journey. But perhaps theirs was the route of wise counsel, for who would believe we had endured all that we had suffered?

Then there was Susi, who had taken the life of Chirango. True, Chirango had killed Amoda, John Wainwright, Misozi, Kaniki, Losi, and the others, killed them too without mercy; but what did we know of white men's justice? No, it was better that they believed we were faithful attendants who had met much suffering on a journey to bring to the coast the body of our master.

A journey of two hundred and seventy-nine days can be told in few words. And that is the story that Chuma and Susi told. There was marching and sickness. There was strife, there was hunger, and there was death. Amoda and John Wainwright did not meet their deaths at Chirango's hand, but in the battle at Chawende's, along with Nchise and Ntaru. Losi died from a snake attack. In his malarial delirium, Dr Dillon shot himself with his own gun. And Chirango himself was among the first to die, along with Misozi, and with his woman Kaniki, for all three had died early in our journey before he could wreak his terrible vengeance.

Then we came to the sea and all was well, and we came to the church and that was our journey's end. That is how we brought Bwana Daudi from Chitambo to Bagamoio. And that is the story that has been told to the world.

And so my journey to England, a sojourn that began with such triumph and such high hopes, ended in a most ignominious manner. My diary remains unpublished. And I remain unordained. And so it is that I find myself here in Buganda, a priest without a collar, a servant of God without a church, all my hopes and ambitions dashed.

My only usefulness is to the Kabaka, though how long that will last, only Him Above can know. The news from Bagamoio is troubling, for it is said that the German nation is on the verge of invading Zanzibar and the whole east coast of Africa, if they can overcome the resistance of the Sultan.

The Kabaka Mwanga fears that the invading party will reach all the way to his kingdom, and that the white missionaries petitioning to build churches in his kingdom have been sent as forerunners to invasion. The news has reached the Court of a new party of English missionaries that are on the way to Buganda. They are led by Bishop Hannington. The news has convinced the Kabaka that these white men are the advance guard for the English, who have the kinds of designs on his land that the Germans have on Zanzibar.

Those of his advisors who have been particularly keen to rid the kingdom of all Christians are urging on him the bloodiest course possible.

This was confirmed to me by four of the Kabaka's pages. They are Kizito, Kagwa, Luanga, and Yusufu. They arrived at my house this morning with news of a most urgent nature. The Kabaka's counsellors have brought before the Court an *emandwa*, an oracle, who has prophesied that the ultimate conqueror of the Buganda Kingdom would come from the east. As Bishop Hannington's expedition has been sighted in Busoga, which is to the east of Buganda, the Kabaka Mwanga has been thrown into a most frightful panic.

He has given the order that Bishop Hannington is to be executed as soon as he sets foot in the Kabaka's kingdom. He has also ordered that all Christians are to be arrested and brought to him. In addition, the Kabaka's advisors are calling for all foreigners to leave on pain of death.

Though I have not been specifically mentioned, there is grave danger to me, Kizito says. They could turn against me at any minute. Kagwa, Luanga, and Yusufu have been ordered by Mkasa Balikudembe to help me to find a path by which I could get out of the Kingdom. I am to leave at once.

Kizito also brought with him a letter that was sent to me care of the Kabaka's Court. I blessed his good heart and placed on his head a benediction, asking that the Lord guide and protect him all the days of his life.

I packed up my few things. In the end, it was not hard to choose what to leave behind. I took only a few of the native clothes, my Bible, and the notebooks in which I did my great work, the translation of the Book of Books into Suaheli. The rest, though I regarded it with some longing, I did not regret leaving behind.

My packing was a matter of moments. All I had to do then was to await the return of the others. And to read my letter while I waited. It was from Carus Farrar. It brought news both bitter and balming. A stab hit my heart when he mentioned his wife. Maria, he said, whom you knew as Ntaoéka. And so she had still not told. The page misted before me. The Lord had blessed them with two children, he said. They had lived for some time in the Cape, where he had worked after he completed his training as a surgeon in Bombay.

They had then left the Cape, and had landed in Zanzibar on their way to Bombay. I must say that I felt some bitterness when I learned of his mission. He was to lead the relocation of the entire Nassick school from India, and oversee its establishment in a place they were calling Frere Town in Mombasa, on the east coast of Africa.

He had given the letter in hand to a Nassicker we had both known called William Jones, who was to travel with the incoming mission of Bishop Hannington to Buganda. By a stratagem that I may never discover, it had reached the Kabaka's Court and the Kabaka's major-domo, Mkasa Balikudembe, had intercepted it before the Kabaka could see it, and given it to Kizito to give to me.

I read on. He had news of even greater import. Abdullah Susi, he said, had died at peace in Halima's house in Bagamoio. Before the illness that finally took him, Carus Farrar said, Abdullah Susi had asked to be baptised. When I heard the name that he had chosen in Christ, I found myself weeping out loud in thanksgiving. I raised my face to the heavens and roared out an acclamation. From the rising of the sun, unto the going down of the same, the Lord's Name is to be praised. Praise ye the Lord! Praise Him, all ye Servants of the Lord. Praise the Name of the Lord. Blessed be the Name of the Lord, from this time Forth and for Evermore!

Kizito and his companions arrived at that moment. Finding me weeping, they rushed to me, their faces anxiously concerned. In that moment, all I could do, under their astonished gaze, was to sink to my knees in grateful supplication. The joy in my heart overflowed as I prayed that just as He had placed in the bosom of Abraham the soul of His faithful servant David Livingstone, the Lord, in His merciful goodness, would likewise receive the soul of His newest servant, David Susi.

EPILOGUE

Brought by faithful hands over land and sea here rests David Livingstone, missionary, traveller, philanthropist, born March 19, 1813, at Blantyre, Lanarkshire, died May 1, 1873, at Chitambo's Village, Ulala.

Plaque on the grave of Livingstone's bones,
Westminster Abbey, England

After 100 years, David Livingstone's spirit and the love of God so animated his friends of all races that they gathered here in thanksgiving on 1 May 1973, led by Dr Kenneth Kaunda, President of the Republic of Zambia.

Plaque on the grave of Livingstone's heart,
Chitambo, Zambia

We came to a grave in the forest . . . This is the sort of grave I should prefer: to lie in the still, still forest, and no hand ever disturb my bones.

David Livingstone, *The Last Journals
of David Livingstone*

END

ACKNOWLEDGEMENTS

I am notorious for my lengthy acknowledgements. As this book has been almost twenty years in the making, these acknowledgements could end up being longer than the novel itself. So I will only say a grateful thank-you to every single person whose ear I bent over the years and whom I bored incessantly about David Livingstone and his companions, all so very dear to me.

I am grateful to my agents, Eric Simonoff and Tracy Fisher, and to my publishers, Nan Graham and Stephen Page, for their confidence in me, and in this book. I am simply thrilled to have worked on this book with three redoubtable editors: Kathy Belden at Scribner, and Lee Brackstone and Ella Griffiths at Faber. I am also deeply grateful to Helen Moffet, my official first reader, and dear friend, for her patient generosity, and to Aja Pollock for her incredible copyediting and meticulous fact-checking. Thank you all for taming my excesses and disciplining my imagination.

This novel would not have been written without the generous support in 2017 of the Berliner Künstlerprogramm of the Deutscher Akademischer Austauschdienst, the DAAD. Their wonderful residency in Berlin proved to be the 'gift of time' that I needed to reflect, write, and bring together my many years of research on this book. *Ich bedanke mich ganz herzlich.*

I conducted more than ten years of historical research to produce this novel, but I am under no illusion that this work is in any way historically accurate. While rooted in historical fact, this novel is above all imaginative fiction.

I am nonetheless deeply indebted to the work of the historians Roy Bridges, Tim Jeal, Hubert Gerbeau, and above all Thomas Pakenham, whose first chapter of *The Scramble for Africa* sparked the idea for this book as long ago as 1999, and who was both generous and kind when I consulted him on this project.

In writing this novel, I had the privilege of consulting original letters, photographs, and other documents related to David Livingstone that are collected in the following institutions: the National Library of Scotland, Edinburgh; the Peace Memorial Museum, Zanzibar; the David Livingstone Centre in Blantyre, Scotland; and the National Archives of Zimbabwe, Harare. Thank you to all the Livingstone enthusiasts I met all over the world, from Blantyre in Scotland, where Livingstone was born, to Bagamoyo in Tanzania, where he spent his last night on African soil, and all the way to Zanzibar and Zimbabwe. I especially want to mention the youngest Livingstone enthusiast of them all, dear Tayani Mhizha, who wrote a brilliant International Baccalaureate analytical essay on him at the age of seventeen.

I also consulted letters and documents that are collected in different institutions around the world. That I did not have to visit every single place in which his letters are stored is due to the wonderful Livingstone Online, a project initiated by all the institutions that are the repositories for documents related to his life and travels. They have collaborated in placing online documents that are freely available to readers and researchers. Unfortunately, by the time they published extracts from the diary of the real Jacob Wainwright, I had already finished this book.

The following is a list of the main primary and secondary sources I consulted. I am grateful to all who continue to illumine the lives of David Livingstone and of his companions, and all the institutions and governments that keep their memories alive. The historians gave me facts, and my imagination supplied the rest. Thank you.

GLOSSARY OF ARABIC, SWAHILI, AND OTHER TERMS AND PHRASES

―――――――――

The Arabic words used in this text are filtered through the medium of Swahili by the narrator Halima, an uneducated and illiterate woman, and thus may occasionally represent her imperfect understanding.

The Swahili terms used by Jacob Wainwright are in keeping with conventions of written Swahili in the eighteenth century, where it was commonly written as 'Suaheli'. While Halima uses the spellings as they sound to the ear – for instance, 'Bagamoyo', 'Swahili', 'Zambezi', 'shenzi', etc. – Jacob uses the words as they were spelled at that time, that is, 'Bagamoio', 'Suaheli', 'Zambesi', 'shensi', etc.

Alḥamdulillāh	Arabic for 'All praise to God' or 'Thank God'.
Allāhu akbar	The Islamic Takbir, a chant that translates as 'Allah is great'.
askari	A soldier, part of the informal army of an expedition (plural *askari*).
baga	Onomatopoeic word indicating falling or breaking.
bahari	A large body of water that can be a sea, the ocean, or a large lake.
baraza	A long, low stone bench outside most Zanzibari houses. The word also means a public meeting place.

bibi	Mistress.
bwana	Master.
Chemchemi ya Herodotus	'The fountains of Herodotus'.
chunusi	A sea ghost.
dhow	A long, low wooden boat with a lateen sail, common to the Indian Ocean countries. See also '*jahazi*'.
djinn	From the Arabic word '*jinn*', this is a term for a supernatural creature, both malign and benign, in early pre-Islamic Arabian and later Islamic mythology and theology. It is also called a 'genie' in Western culture.
dragoman	Combination of an interpreter, translator, and guide who worked mainly in the countries and polities of the Middle East. A dragoman usually had knowledge of Arabic, Persian, Turkish, and European languages, and sometimes conducted mediation and other diplomatic duties.
emandwa	Luganda word for 'oracle'.
hadimu	A freed slave, plural *wahadimu*.
hadith	Teachings or actions of the Prophet Muhammad that are not officially recorded in the Quran but were passed down through oral history.
Hamamni	Public baths in Zanzibar constructed on the Persian model between 1876 and 1888 by order of Sultan Said Bhargash bin Said (from the Arabic '*hammam*').

haram	An Arabic term meaning anything that is forbidden under Islam. This can be anything that is sacred and to which access by certain people is forbidden, or an evil or sinful action that is forbidden.
Hindoo	Hindu.
hongoro	An intoxicating beverage. See also '*pombe*'.
horme	A wife of equal birth or an official wife.
imam	The leader of worship in a mosque.
jahazi	The Swahili word for 'dhow', i.e., the long wooden boat with a lateen sail that is common to the Indian Ocean African countries.
Kabaka	The title given to the king of the Baganda, monarch of the kingdom of Buganda.
kirangozi	The standard-bearer in a travelling party.
Liwali	Title given to the representative in Zanzibar of the Sultan of Oman and Zanzibar during the period when the capital of the sultanate was in Muscat, and before the sultanate was split into two.
madrassa	Islamic school.
makesi	River oysters from the Lualaba River. (This is a Manyuema, not a Swahili, word.)
matoke	Bananas. (This is a Luganda word.)
maẓālim	Islamic judicial courts that were presided over by the *qadi*.
mganga	Traditional healer, the closest approximation at this time to a medical doctor.

miraa	A chewable leaf of the genus *Catha edulis* that has stimulating effects for the chewer. Similar to betel nut in use and effect. Also called *quat*, now known more commonly under the spelling '*khat*'.
mjakazi	One of many terms for a female slave.
Mohammedan	Muslim.
moyo	Heart.
mpambe	A captured or enslaved person, and therefore one of many terms for 'slave'. (Plural *wapambe*.)
mpundu	A southern African tree of the genus *Parinari curatellifolia*; also known as the *myomba* tree and *mobola* plum tree.
mtoto	A child (plural *watoto*).
muezzin	The man who calls Muslims to prayer, usually from a minaret.
mzungu	White person (plural *wazungu*).
mvula	See '*mpundu*' above.
Mwili wa Daudi	'The body of David'.
njari	An idiophonic musical instrument made from a wooden board to which resonating metal keys are attached. Originally from the area now called Mozambique, it is related to the *mbira* of Zimbabwe or *kalimba* of the Democratic Republic of the Congo.
pagazi	Porters or load bearers in an expedition.
pombe	A thick, traditional beer brewed from millet.
qadi	Judicial officer presiding over the *maẓālim* (see above).

quat	See '*miraa*'.
safire	The flag bearer marching at the head of an expedition.
salat	Muslim prayer, one of the five pillars of Islam, along with *shahada*, faith; *zakāt*, charity; *sawm*, fasting; and the Hajj, the pilgrimage to Mecca.
sefra	A long, low table from which food is served in a Zanzibari household.
sepoy	The lowest designation given to Indian soldiers recruited by the British East India Company. In colonial travel, they were slightly better paid than the *askari* (see above).
shensi/shenzi	A pejorative term used by Arab slavers to describe East African slaves: closest meaning is 'savages' or 'barbarians'. The modern spelling of the word is *shenzi*.
shetani	An evil spirit.
sola fide, sola gratia, sola scriptura	Latin for 'by faith alone, by grace alone, and by scripture alone'. These are three of the five sola principles underlying the doctrine of salvation as espoused by the Reformed Protestant churches, marking a key departure from the teachings of the Catholic Church.
suria	A slave woman who is also a concubine (plural *sariri*).
taabibu	An approximation of the Arab word for 'doctor'.
ugali	An East African staple food made from white maize meal and water, cooked over heat.

umm al-walad	A slave woman who bears children for her master, and consequently cannot be sold.
vembwigo	A sea ghost.
zakāt	See '*salat*', above.

BIBLIOGRAPHY

Primary Sources

Authorised Report of the Church Congress Held at Plymouth: October 3, 4, 5, & 6, 1876. London: W. Wells Gardner, 1877.

Brode, Heinrich. *Tippoo Tib, His Career in Central Africa, Narrated from His Own Accounts.* Translated by H. Havelock. London: Edward Arnold, 1907.

Burton, R. F. *The Book of the Thousand Nights and a Night: A Plain and Literal Translation of the Arabian Nights Entertainments.* London: The Burton Club, 1885–90.

———. *First Footsteps in East Africa.* London: Tyston and Edwards, 1894.

Cameron, Verney Lovett. *Across Africa.* New York: Harper and Brothers, 1877.

Gray, Sir John Milner. 'Correspondence relating to the death of Bishop Hannington.' *Uganda Journal* 13, no. 1 (March 1949).

Livingstone, David. *Missionary Travels and Researches in Southern Africa.* London: John Murray, 1861.

———. *The Last Journals of David Livingstone.* Vols. 1 and 2. Chicago: Jansen McClurg, 1874.

———. *Narrative of an Expedition to the Zambesi and Its Tributaries.* London: John Murray, 1865.

Ruete, Emily, Princess of Zanzibar and Oman. *Memoirs of an Arabian Princess from Zanzibar.* Zanzibar: Galley Publications, 1998.

Stanley, H. M. *How I Found Livingstone in Central Africa.* London: Sampson Low, 1882.

———. *My Dark Companions and Their Strange Stories.* London: Sampson Low, 1882.

———. *Through the Dark Continent.* London: G. Newnes, 1899.

Thomas, H. B. *The Death of Doctor Livingstone: Carus Farrar's Account. Uganda Journal* 14, no. 2 (September 1950).

Secondary Sources

Baxter, T. W., and E. E. Burke. *Guide to the Historical Manuscripts in the National Archives of Rhodesia.* Salisbury: National Archives of Rhodesia, 1970.

Beals, Herbert K., R. J. Campbell, Ann Savours, Anita McConnell, and Roy Bridges, eds. *Four Travel Journals: The Americas, Antarctica and Africa, 1775–1874.* London: The Hakluyt Society, 2007.

Bromber, Katerin. 'Mjakazi, Mpambe, Mjoli, Suria: Female Slaves in Swahili Sources.' In *Africa, the Indian Ocean World, and the Medieval North Atlantic,* edited by Campbell Gwyn et al. Vol. 1 of *Women and Slavery.* Athens: Ohio University Press, 2007.

Coupland, R. *Livingstone's Last Journey.* London: Readers Union Collins, 1947.

Dugard, M. *Into Africa: The Dramatic Retelling of the Stanley Livingstone Story.* London: Bantam, 2003.

Gates, H. L. 'Ending the Slavery Blame Game.' *New York Times*, April 22, 2010.

Gerbeau, H. 'L'Océan Indien n'est pas l'Atlantique. La traite illégale à Bourbon au XIXe siècle.' *Outre-Mers* 89 (2002) 336–37.

Hazell, A. *The Last Slave Market.* London: Constable, 2011.

Jeal, T. *Livingstone.* London: William Heineman, 1973.

———. *Stanley: The Impossible Life of Africa's Greatest Explorer.* London: Faber and Faber, 2007.

———. *Explorers of the Nile: The Triumph and Tragedy of a Great Victorian Adventure.* London: Faber and Faber, 2011.

Jeal, T., et al. *David Livingstone and the Victorian Encounter with Africa.* London: National Portrait Gallery, 1996.

Miers, Suzanne, and Richard Roberts. *The End of Slavery in Africa.* Madison and London: University of Wisconsin Press, 1988.

Mirza, F., and M. Strobel, eds. *Three Swahili Women: Life Histories from Mombasa, Kenya.* Bloomington: Indiana University Press, 1989.

Pakenham, Thomas. *The Scramble for Africa.* London: Weidenfeld and Nicholson, 1991.

Sherif, A., and F. D. Ferguson, eds. *Zanzibar Under Colonial Rule.* Oxford: James Currey, 1991.

Simpson, D. *Dark Companions: The African Contribution to the European Exploration of East Africa.* London: Paul Elek, 1975.

Thomas, H. B. *Jacob Wainwright in Uganda. Uganda Journal* 15, no. 2 (September 1951).

Wahab, Saada Omar. 'Suria: Its Relevance to Slavery in Zanzibar in the Nineteenth Century.' In *Transition from Slavery in Zanzibar and Mauritius*, edited by Abdul Sheriff, Vijayalakshmi Teelock, Saada Omar Wahab, and S. Peerthum. Oxford: African Books Collective, Project MUSE, 2016.

Other Sources

Bunyan, J. *The Pilgrim's Progress: From This World, to That Which Is to Come.* London: Penguin Classics, 2008.

Thucydides. *History of the Peloponnesian War.* Translated by Rex Warner. London: Penguin Classics, 2000.